MW00849330

EASY
PREY

Other books by Douglas Watkinson

~ THE NATHAN HAWK MURDER MYSTERIES ~

Haggard Hawk

Scattered Remains

Evil Turn

Jericho Road

White Crane

~ OTHER BOOKS BY THE SAME AUTHOR ~

The Occasional Jonas Kemble

EASY PREY

DOUGLAS WATKINSON

QUARTERMAIN
PRESS

Published in the UK in 2022 by Quartermain Press

Copyright © Douglas Watkinson 2022

Douglas Watkinson has asserted his right under the
Copyright, Designs and Patents Act, 1988, to be identified
as the author of this work.

All rights reserved. No part of this book may be reproduced, stored
in a retrieved system or transmitted, in any form or by any means,
electronic, mechanical, scanning, photocopying, recording or
otherwise, without the prior permission of the author and publisher.

This book is a work of fiction, and except in the case of historical or
geographical fact, any resemblance to names, place and characters,
living or dead, is purely coincidental.

Paperback ISBN: 978-1-915497-04-8

eBook ISBN: 978-1-915497-05-5

Cover design and typeset by SpiffingCovers

Dear Reader,

When you lose your car keys, or something equally daft, they always seem to turn up in their own good time. It's the same with missing people. Nine times out of ten they aren't missing at all, they're just… out of sight. Okay, so in the tenth case it isn't quite so simple.

When John Stillman asked me to find his daughter, I told him I couldn't help. It was the kindest way of saying she didn't want to be found. Or she was dead. Then my own daughter went missing for just a few hours and I jumped on the same nightmare bandwagon John had been riding. My own panic lasted just five or six hours. Ellie had stayed over somewhere and I'd missed her text message informing me. John Stillman's agony had lasted for months. I decided to try and give her father some closure and find out what had happened to his beloved daughter.

At the time, of course, I'd no way of knowing just who I'd be dealing with, but it wasn't a simple matter of tracking down a well-known barrister's only child, dead or alive.

Hawk

Before

It had been one of those changeable days you sometimes get in late spring. A sharp wind first thing had made it feel like winter again yet by lunchtime it was almost too hot to move. An hour later the rain clouds moved in, tipped it down with a vengeance, making way for a perfect blue sky by five o'clock. At each change The County Landscapes workforce had complained, albeit in a very English way, as a matter of course and not conviction.

Teresa Stillman hadn't complained. Teresa knew how lucky she had been.

Her good fortune began when, just before Christmas, her tutor at Greenwich called her to his office for a chat about her dissertation on Japanese gardens. He'd been impressed with it and, the verdict delivered, he shrugged off his tutorial guise and informed her that he was about to make her day. He began to ebb and flow a tide of paperwork across his desk until a handwritten letter rose to the surface. It was from an old friend, he told Teresa, and when he said old he wasn't kidding. The lady in question was 89, a landscape gardener working near Oxford and a week ago she had been asked to create a Japanese garden. The trouble was that neither she nor any of the odd-balls who worked for her had ever set foot in a Japanese garden. Did he perhaps know of someone who had?

Teresa phoned Mary Harper that evening and they met at the latter's cottage the following Saturday. Mary had half expected to find in her visitor a typical student with silly ideas and a lifestyle neither of them could afford. Teresa had feared that with a 60-year age gap between them, Mary might be set in her ways and mildly terrifying. Both women were pleasantly surprised and three months later here was Teresa with her first professional design brought to life. The inspiration for it had come from the lady of the house, Yoshie Carter, who had wanted a living reminder of her birthplace created right here on the outskirts of Oxford. She had made outlandish suggestions, Teresa had turned them into a set of practical plans and then she and Mary's team had transformed Caversham Heights on the Woodstock Road from a wasteland of dying trees, rampaging creepers and half a century's worth of domestic junk into a perfect Japanese retreat.

There was just one problem. Now that the garden was finished Teresa was reluctant to abandon it, which explained why, at the end of each day when her workmates packed up and went home, Teresa stayed on in the asumaya. The long, oak-framed shelter with its bamboo walls and thatched roof was the first thing Tom Gibson had built and ran the length of the koi pool. It was here that the usual tea-breaks Mary Harper allowed her workers had become a civilising ritual. In true Japanese style, Yoshie served them tea three times a day and spoke of her idyllic childhood in Hokkaido, the northernmost island of her homeland. It was a place she clearly longed to return to. A place, Teresa felt increasingly, that she wished she had never left…

At the other side of the pool lay the first of three arboreta planted with maple, juniper and escalonia specially imported from Hakodate under the watchful eye of Yoshie's father, Mr Ueda. Between the slender branches of the trees, now heavy with opening leaves, the eye would glide, just as Teresa had intended, towards a jasmine-clad moongate, the second of Tom Gibson's creations. From there the onlooker's gaze would be drawn into the Zen garden where limestone shingle bore the weight of massive granite boulders, the whole area lit in the evenings by stone lanterns, again courtesy of Mr Ueda.

Beyond that was Oxford, five miles away. Not a bad place, Teresa thought, for the eye to finally come to rest.

Yoshie came bustling out of the house and called to her in her squeaky Eastern way, "Teresa, I go to pick up the girls from their dance class. Half hour. Will you still be here, or will I lock up?"

She wanted an immediate answer. As ever she was running late.

"I'll be here," said Teresa.

Yoshie hurried to the side gate and out towards her car, calling as she went, "Why don't you stay, have tea? You know how the children love you so. Please stay."

Teresa rolled a cigarette, lit it and watched the smoke gather like frayed ribbons around her. In the spurious calm brought on by nicotine and pride in a job well done, it would be a good time to play tag, she thought. Not the chase me, you're it kids' game, but the Stillman family's version of it. The Appraisal Game. It had been devised by her mother as a confidence booster and players were called upon to summarise their lives in a sentence of no more than eight words. The eight-word rule was her father's idea. John Stillman had always been finicky and precise when it came to language. Eight words.

"My life is beginning to go in the direction I want it to."

Thirteen words. She could hear her father tutting. She tried again.

"My life is at last going the way I intended."

Ten words. She heard her father whimper encouragingly. She held out both hands and curled each finger as she spoke.

"Life is finally going the way I planned."

It left her with two thumbs up. She'd got there.

Then she heard her father again, forever wanting to know what lay behind a simple answer. There were several things, Teresa acknowledged, not least of them Tom Gibson.

She'd been present when Mary had interviewed him, if you could call it an interview. He needed the work but he'd been in prison, he said. Mary had asked him what for. He'd rung cars in Bristol, he told her. If she had a problem with that she could stick her job. If not, when did she want him to start? Neither Mary nor Teresa were entirely sure what a 'rung' car was but guessed that it had nothing to do with telephones. Mary hadn't wanted to appear naïve by asking and, given that the only things he could steal from her were gardening tools, she'd taken him on. Gradually he'd revealed a gentle, romantic core beneath the shaven head, the violent tattoos and rough good looks and, in the excitement which comes from doing exactly the wrong thing, Teresa had fallen in love with him...

A voice behind her suddenly said, "Penny for them, Teresa."

She turned with a start to see Michael Carter the other side of the stone wall, leaning back on the driver's door of the car he'd just driven up in. She wasn't sure how long he'd been gazing at her.

"Hi!" she said. "Didn't hear the car..."

He gave her his scythe-like smile and reached across to the passenger seat for his jacket. He slung it over one shoulder and entered the garden through the iron gate – a wedding anniversary gift from Mr Ueda – and came down the steps towards her. She stood up, brushing non-existent dirt from the seat of her jeans, determined to exude confidence.

Carter stopped by the koi pool and looked round at the garden without betraying emotion.

"I see you're almost finished," he said.

"Yes, yes, what do you think of it?"

He shrugged. "If Yoshie's happy with it then so am I. Where's Mary?"

"She left early today. She's visiting an old friend in Hastings this weekend."

He seemed slightly offended. "She said yesterday that

she wanted paying. I'm away myself tomorrow, to France for a fortnight. I take it you know where she lives?"

"Yes."

"Then follow me."

He turned to lead the way up to the house, then paused and stabbed the air between them with his forefinger. "I know I keep on about this, Teresa, but I'm sure we've met before." He had said as much, five maybe six times during the past three months. "It bothers me, not being able to pin it down."

They went up to the house and Teresa removed her boots before entering through the French windows. The room she found herself in was a kind of study and Carter immediately poured vodka into a glass already prepared. What servile, unseen hand had set that down, Teresa wondered: vodka, glass, tonic, a slice of lemon, ice, all ready for the master's homecoming? What might happen if one day it wasn't there or was late in arriving? Would his quiet indifference suddenly explode into anger, the kind she felt lurking just beneath his surface, and God help those who got in its way?

He nodded at the far side of the partners' desk, indicating that she should sit in a hard-backed chair that would guarantee her continued uneasiness. She watched as he flicked through a small sheaf of paperwork in a wire tray and came to the cream-coloured letter headed 'County Landscapes'. He studied the itemised quotation for a moment, then folded it in half and gently fanned himself. He wasn't smiling anymore.

"If you go into business yourself one day, do make sure you stick to the original estimate." He took a swig of his drink, clinking perfect teeth on the rim of the glass as if he would bite a chunk out of it. "Mary's seen fit to spend, spend, spend. There's an extra bill here for 140,000 yen, plants and stone artefacts. Another here for koi carp, 90,000 yen." The curved smile was back, the thin lips skewing towards his left ear. "Yet I'm reliably informed that the Japanese economy is in difficulty."

Teresa shifted forward in her seat. "These things weren't in the original design, no," she said. "Your wife wanted them, she told Mary there'd be no problem, that we should go ahead and…"

He raised a hand to silence her. "…and turn my house into the Emperor's Palace? I specifically asked Mary to discuss any change of plan with me. He who pays the piper, Teresa…"

"She's an old lady," said Teresa. "She forgot."

She had interrupted him. He wasn't used to women doing that and there must have been defiance in her voice, though she hadn't meant there to be. He rose from his chair and, without taking his eyes off her, drifted round the desk until he stood over her, forcing her to look up at him.

After a few moments studying her face he said again, "Are you sure we haven't met before? I mean it isn't just some line I'm spinning, believe me, I really do think we have. Either that or you've got a double."

"We might've bumped into each other, though I can't imagine where."

He chuckled. "When you put it that way, I can't either. Cash. Mary prefers cash. Where does she keep it, I wonder? In a mattress, like old ladies are supposed to? If I give it to you now will you take it straight round to her?"

"Of course," she half protested.

He left the room and she sat waiting, feeling incredibly young, silly and exposed, as if cameras were watching her from every angle, recording her every discomfort. Although she dearly would have loved to cast an eye over the letters and hand-written notes on the desk, she rose from it and feigned interest in less telling things: a map of Oxford in the seventeenth century, for example, a couple of family portraits and a poster of her host – a full-length photo taken in his mid-twenties. No wonder Yoshie had fallen in love with him. He was then, and still was, a curiously handsome man with a face of many contrasts, captured by the photographer. Long black hair fell either side of his face, making his already pale skin seem even paler. Blue eyes peered out from beneath an intellectual forehead yet the scar on his left temple spoke of belligerence not bookishness. The looks had been his passport to the Far East, Tom Gibson had said with a touch of envy. Carter had been to Japan, taken his pick of the trophies, married one and brought her home. And then stopped talking to her. He was a man, Tom believed, who would die before he reached 40, at which point he, Tom, would move in with the lovely Yoshie and her even lovelier money.

"A lifetime ago," Carter said of the poster as he came back into the room.

Again he'd caught her unaware and she turned with an apology, perhaps for the thoughts she'd just had. He sat at the desk again and with practised fingers began to count out the sum of £7160. He clearly didn't expect his tally to be double-checked and sealed the wad of notes in a polythene wallet.

"I'd like a receipt," he said.

"Certainly, yes, yes."

He scribbled the details of the transaction on a blank sheet of paper and handed her a pen, tapping the place where he needed her signature. She wrote it in her best hand and gave it back to him. He examined it and just as Teresa began to think that he'd found some fault with it, he looked up at her.

"Stillman? I told you we'd met before. Well, not you and me, exactly, but… It must be the eyes. Look at me. Yes. John Stillman, the barrister. Are you his daughter?"

She had been brought up not to speak freely of her father or his work. You never knew who was listening, he said. Carter mistook her hesitation for embarrassment.

"Don't look so worried, Teresa. We all have a mother and father and, by and large, inherit their characteristics. Is he well?"

"Last time I saw him, yes he was. How do you know him?"

Carter smiled, the lop-sided smile. "Professionally. Be sure to give him my regards when you see him."

"Will he remember you?"

"Oh, yes."

"Just in case, though," Teresa persisted.

He looked at her. "Harrow Crown Court, June '97. He got me sent down. For eight years."

***

Teresa drove straight to Stanton St John and knocked on Mary's door five, maybe six times before accepting that her boss had probably already left for the coast. She tried phoning her, but as usual Mary's phone was switched off...

What was to be done, then, with the £7000 Teresa had come to deliver? Should she drop it in through the letterbox, let it lie there all weekend? Hide it somewhere in the garden? Keep it in the boot of her car? Or, perhaps, take it back to Michael Carter? None of those ideas really appealed to her, especially the last. What she needed was a safe, like the one her father had built into the wall under the stairs at Mayfield House.

She decided to call him. As usual he'd forgotten her birthday last week, but then he always did. She wouldn't bother reminding him because three months from now he'd remember that he'd forgotten and buy her something fabulous to make up for it.

John Stillman answered the phone in his quiet, off-handed way. "Hallo."

"Dad? It's me."

"Oh, hi, Teresa," he said. "How are things?"

"Things are fine," she said. "I was thinking of driving over to see you."

"Tonight?"

"Well, yes, tonight if that's okay..."

"Of course. Er, when do you think you'll be here?"

"I don't know, Dad. Soon as I can."

"Will you have eaten?" He was finally beginning to sound pleased. "Only I can always ask Mrs Jenkins to…"

"Dad, don't make a production of it, just break out a bottle of something special."

***

When she drove up to Mayfield House at around seven o'clock he was waiting for her outside, seated on the bench beneath the big copper beech, the eternal cigarette smouldering away between his lips. He removed it as she came towards him. They gazed at each other for a moment. For John to see that she was fit and well and as beautiful as ever was greeting enough. Not so for Teresa. She suddenly threw her arms around him and held him in the embrace until gradually he responded in kind. A second or so later he patted her shoulder, like a referee calling break to two boxers, and they stood back from each other.

"Well, there's a greeting!" he said, drawing on his cigarette. "Nothing wrong, I hope?"

She laughed. "No, Dad, nothing wrong, though I would like to lock something in the safe overnight."

"Yes, yes, of course."

She explained briefly how she came to have £7000 in cash on her. Then she slipped an arm though his and they sauntered across the shadows cast by the group of ancient cedars and in through the front door.

The house was Victorian, a nouveau riche country getaway with a mere ten bedrooms and everything else that such an excess of sleeping quarters implied. There were too many rooms downstairs, most of them with high ceilings and low chandeliers, fireplaces that were never warmed, curtains that were never drawn, clocks that never chimed. Most curious of all, though, were the oil paintings of men and women who might easily have been Teresa's ancestors, but weren't.

As a child she had always felt that these people didn't belong here, that given the right prompting and a taxi waiting at the door, they would step from their canvasses and go in search of their identities, calling in at the nearest doctor for a tonic to put the colour back in their cheeks. Four years ago, just before Teresa went off to Greenwich to do her design course, John admitted that he didn't know who these intruders were. He had bought the paintings as one job lot from a dealer in Norwich in the vain hope that they would obscure his council house origins and replace them with some gentrified illusion. It had been foolish and pretentious, he owned, not to say cruel beyond words to his parents. Yet somehow these people, with their backs so firmly to the wall, had become his family or at least his familiars. He had given them a home when their own relatives had turfed them out of theirs.

Nevertheless, John himself was still known, and in some circles revered, as the council house boy who had made it to the very top of his profession.

For all the rooms they might have repaired to, for all the sofas, couches and chaises longues they might have sat on, John led the way to the kitchen where at the table he opened a bottle of some ancient red wine and poured them each a glass. He coughed profoundly, as if a sack of gravel were being hurled around inside him, then asked, "So how's life been treating you? Very well, would be my guess. Then again, children only contact their parents when they're in trouble. When did we last … meet up?"

"Christmas, Dad."

She reminded him of how she'd spent the intervening months, told him about Yoshie's garden, how it was almost finished and that some day she'd like to drive him over to see it. He nodded enthusiastically. When she was a child, she recalled, he had never said yes, thereby making a promise he'd no intention of keeping. But he had nodded a great deal.

She smiled at him and asked, mischievously, "When shall I pick you up, then?"

He reached across the table and patted her hand. "Are you sure there's nothing wrong?" he said.

"Dad, if you mean why have I suddenly come to see you, then…" She looked away from the benign gaze. "It just seems so odd that since Mum died we haven't seen much of each other."

"You mean since the one person who came between us isn't there anymore?"

"Well, I wouldn't have put it quite…"

"I would." He smiled. "I just did."

It was the first time in her life that he'd levelled a criticism at her mother, at least within her hearing.

"Anyway," she said. "I thought of you because the client, who's been saying for weeks that he thought he recognised me, finally learned my surname today and the penny dropped. We evidently have similar eyes, you and I…"

"Not just the eyes, Teresa. Character, temperament, drive. What's this man's name?"

"Michael Carter. He said you'd remember him."

The goodness went out of the gaze. "I do. Eight years. I suppose he only served half of it."

"What was it for?"

She could see him wondering whether to tell her the truth or wrap it up in euphemisms, just as he'd done when she was a child. "Well, he had an argument by the roadside with some chap. More than an argument, really, I mean Carter lashed out at him…"

"Killed him?"

Stillman rocked his head a little, trying to make Carter's crime seem trivial.

"Yes, yes, the chap did die."

"What was the charge?"

He paused again and then remembered that she was 22 years old. "Manslaughter," he said, then smiled. "Maybe I won't go over to see his new garden after all."

They chatted on right through the evening, demolishing more wine as they went, until at midnight, and still in the kitchen, they decided to call it a day. Teresa made them a cup of tea for bed. Tea and a book, it was a habit of his that she had acquired. Reading helped him sleep, he said, the tea kept him awake long enough to be able to do so.

As she set his cup and saucer down in front of him he took her hand and said, "What I said about other things we have in common, Teresa, I meant it. I've always known that you would do well…" He shrugged and let go of her hand. She was pleased. She'd felt it begin to tremble. He gazed up at her, benign but intense. "…not just because of your beauty or even your brains but because people think of you as… more than they are. They look to you for ideas, inspiration and luck. They want some of you to rub off on them. No wonder you're making a success of your life, my darling. I'm so proud of you."

***

Unable to sleep, Teresa sat up in bed with the light on, looking round at the familiar shapes that had once terrified her. Chief among them was the giant wardrobe whose door would suddenly creak open in the dead of night and waken her, its oval mirror reflecting such light as there was, chasing it across the walls. That would be her cue to close her eyes and slide quickly beneath the covers. Had she been able to hold her nerve and stay watching, she would have seen the monstrous form that doubtless emerged from the hanging space to stalk the room. Under the bedclothes she would wriggle to the edge and peek out towards the window where the shadow of the nearest cedar would advance and retreat in the breeze. At times it came so close that surely the most handsome of princes, straight from the stories she used to read, would slip down one of the branches, step into the room and whisk her away.

She giggled. Was the monster called Michael Carter, the prince Tom Gibson?

She got out of bed, went over to the window and drew back the dusty curtains. There before her, softened by the swaying branches of the trees, was the picture she would take with her to the end of her days, the setting of her childhood. A flagstone path led down to the stone bridge, past the tennis court and the walled kitchen garden. The other side of the river, rising to Copeland Hill and ringed by woodland to keep the rest of the world at bay, lay the grazing for the horses her mother had loved so much. Far more than her only child.

She flopped into the wicker chair, more wide awake now than ever. She reached for a book, then let it fall to the floor knowing that she wouldn't be able to read it. Her mind was beginning to race again, filling up with the compliments she'd never expected to hear from her father. "I've always known that you would do well, not just because of your beauty or even your brains… I'm so proud of you."

There had been no mawkish, fatherly conceit in his voice, no sentimental tears welling up in his eyes, courtesy of the wine he'd drunk. He'd just said it dead straight. And he'd meant every word.

***

When Teresa walked into the kitchen, John was already there, smoking and sipping coffee at the kitchen table, The Times spread out before him, centrepiece of his morning ritual.

"Plans for today?" he asked, taking off his reading glasses.

"I thought we'd do more of the same, maybe. Talk?"

He smiled. "I'd like that. Out in the garden." He tapped the newspaper. "Forecast is for a sunny day, 17 degrees. That's the thing about reaching my age, Teresa, you know useless things like how hot it was on Wednesday, how much rain fell in April…" He rose and poured her some coffee and pushed the milk across the table towards her. He lifted a rack of cold toast. "I can warm this for you. There's a setting on the toaster, re-heat, not that I've ever had occasion to use it. It does this thing whereby…"

"I'll eat it cold, Dad."

He nodded and after a further moment said quietly, "I don't want us to lose each other, Teresa. You read of these people who just drift apart, parents and children, don't see each other for 20 years. And when they collide again after so much time they're strangers…" He stopped himself, then tried to dismiss what he'd said. "I'm being silly… forget it."

And for all her father's power to put away the likes of Michael Carter, Teresa saw for the first time a man growing old, a man she didn't quite recognise. Her phone rang and she ignored it.

"Better see who it is," said John, when the caller tried again. "I mean could be another commission."

"At eight in the morning?" she said, reaching down into her bag.

She answered the call in the same way that her father would have done, quietly, anonymously.

"Hallo?"

The voice at the other end of the line was quiet too but purposeful. "Miss Stillman? My name is Richard Crane. I hope this isn't too early in the day for you?"

"Not at all. I've been up for some time."

She exchanged a smile with John, who went back to his paper.

"On the recommendation of a friend I went yesterday to see the Japanese Garden you designed at Mike and Yoshie Carter's. It's nothing short of magic, Miss Stillman."

"That's very kind of you. Your friend, who is he?"

Crane chuckled. "Did I say it was a he? Listen, I've just bought a house in the area. What it really needs to make it heaven on earth is a garden. I wonder if we could meet?"

"Well, yes. Where are you calling from?"

"I'm in Oxford today. Is that near to you?"

"As a matter of fact, yes. I'm staying with my father, near Thame."

"Excellent! I've nothing pencilled in for lunch. Shall we say Giacometto's in Jericho, 12.30? Do you know it?"

"I do."

"Look forward to meeting you."

She ran the conversation back through her mind for more information about the man she'd been speaking to. Thirty-something and efficient. Not used to being argued with or found wanting. Not as posh as he thought he was, either, but courteous. That always did it for Teresa. Men with good manners went straight to the top of her tree.

"Was it business?" John asked, lighting a fresh cigarette.

"It was."

"Didn't I tell you!"

She smiled. "You told me, Dad. He wants a garden like Yoshie's. Richard Crane. Mean anything to you?"

John shook his head. "Never heard of him."

***

The clock in the hall was chiming eleven when Teresa said goodbye to her father. She was dressed in a smart jacket and trousers, with slight frills at the neck and wrists, and shoes that made her taller than John. He had come from the library to wish her good luck and that done he looked her over for a moment and nodded approvingly.

"You'll be coming back?" he asked.

"Yes, tonight. We've more catching up to do, remember?"

He watched her drive away. It took a good half-minute for her to reach the end of the winding drive but when she finally disappeared from view, behind the sentinel chestnut trees, so memory pitched the news of his wife's death at him again. It had come from a young policeman, three years ago, right here beneath the beech tree. The poor lad was too young to know the full vocabulary of compassion. He'd hardly been able to look John in the eye. He'd informed him with just a few textbook words of condolence thrown in to the silence that followed, that there'd been a car crash, his wife had been...

John shook the memory from his head. This was not a day for re-hashing grief, this was a day for rejoicing, for considering the future. He and his daughter had taken a fresh look at each other and had liked what they'd seen. For his part, having briefly acknowledged his wife's shortcomings, if not his own, he had regained Teresa's confidence with long-overdue praise.

It was a timely reparation, for within a matter of hours his beloved daughter would have disappeared from the face of the earth.

-1-

It had been a fabulous holiday, four weeks in Los Angeles with all my children and I hadn't lost my temper once. With anyone. Mind you, we'd been living in luxury and that does help to ease the tensions. My youngest son, Jaikie, had put us all up in the Wilshire Plaza and from day one it had been: "Who is the woman (or man) over there, I've seen her in something, she was married to so-and-so who played in that what-was-it-called?" A pointless rally of questions as far as my companion on the trip, Laura Peterson, was concerned since she's never owned a television. She's not much help when it comes to film stars, either. The last thing she saw in the cinema was Indiana Jones and the Temple of Doom and she fell asleep 20 minutes into it. From utter exhaustion not boredom, I hasten to add. But I digress.

Four weeks of self-indulgence, then, in the City of Angels and now I was on a plane bound for Heathrow with something making me feel… uneasy. I'd kept it to myself for a good three hours but now felt the urge to share it. I laid a hand on Laura's arm and she surfaced from sleep.

"Hallo," she said. "Where are we?"

"Well, I'm not actually flying the plane today but…"

I nodded to a small screen where a flashing dot on a fuzzy line suggested we were two thirds of the way home. Laura went into a Deep Vein Thrombosis routine.

"And you woke me why?"

"Something's niggling me," I said with a suitable frown. "I think it's Fanny Fernackerpan back there."

"Ellie? How can you feel uneasy about your own daughter?"

"By definition," I said.

I turned to Ellie for the umpteenth time. She was sitting eight or nine rows farther back, chatting to her good-looking neighbour, an all-American boy who'd made a bee-line for her in the departure lounge at LA International. I'd never had that kind of luck at his age. If I took a fancy to a girl on a trip abroad you could bet your life my seat was at the front of the plane, hers was at the back. This bloke's was right across the aisle.

This wasn't their first meeting either. We'd bumped into him before, in a Beverley Hills travel agent's two days previously. We'd gone there to book Ellie a connecting onward flight to Paris. The all-American boy was ticket-hunting too and I saw them connect, smile and move on.

Ellie caught my eye and waved with the tips of her fingers. I waved back, allowing my smile to fade as it slid sideways to the all-American boy. That's my daughter, the fade said. Tread carefully.

I turned back to Laura. "That's the trouble with long journeys," I said. "They give you time to invent a dozen scenarios and, in my experience, the worst one usually comes true."

"Well, this journey's nearly over," she said.

She took my hand, closed her eyes and dozed off again.

Ellie has always worried me. Of my four children, she does have the most baggage in every sense of the word. At the flight check-in, for example, on the outward journey, I'd had to transfer some of her stuff to my suitcase. God knows what she'd packed but it can't have been clothes. She wore the same pair of jeans and trainers for almost four weeks running, admittedly with laundry breaks in between.

As for her other baggage, the emotional kind, it came packed in a series of three-act dramas and most of the villains in them were men. Men? I glanced back at the all-

American boy. Wasn't she still just a child? My youngest, the one I'm supposed to have spoiled without knowing it so that she wouldn't grow up and leave me? What were men doing in her life? Truth be told she was 19, nearly 20, with a rangy kind of beauty that fathers aren't supposed to notice and certainly aren't meant to comment upon.

Eventually I must've nodded off but dozed fitfully. Plates of airport egg and bacon kept sliding into my mind on slicks of their own grease. I woke up at Heathrow feeling decidedly queasy.

Hacking our way through Terminal 5, and fearful that if separated from each other, never mind our luggage, we might never see either again, Ellie stopped and pointed up to a restaurant on the second floor.

"How about some breakfast, Dad?"

I glanced up at a clock. "Have you got time, love? When's your flight to Paris?"

"Don't worry about that," she said. "Change of plan. I'm not going today. Three weeks' time. Where's the ticket desk?"

I could sense the curtain rising on one of my dozen scenarios.

"And between now and then…?" I asked, feebly.

"I'm coming home to stay with you," she replied. "Give us a twenty. That's what they charge to change the booking. Mean bastards."

I watched my hand dig into my wallet, take out the twenty pound note and give it to her. I opened my mouth to protest but she was gone.

I turned to Laura, my case against Ellie proven. "You see what I mean about something bothering me? She's coming home with me!"

"Well you're her father, Beech Tree Cottage is her home, it makes perfect sense."

"Is there nothing that child can do that'll make you suspicious?"

She smiled. "Not a lot, actually. In many ways she's the girl I never was."

Ellie returned twenty minutes later, with a smile from ear to ear, fanning herself with a voucher for a ticket.

"Done!" she said.

The word 'done' has too many connotations for comfort. She led the way up to the restaurant and we ordered breakfast. Laura and Ellie had bacon and eggs, I had a black coffee that kept me awake for the next three days.

***

Funny how when you go away, even for just a few weeks, you come back and the house is never quite the same as you remember it. With Beech Tree Cottage the thatched roof always has a steeper pitch than I recall, the chimneys are taller and the whole place is in need of a lick of paint. The last is true, of course, but expensive, so I try to get used to the flaky walls as soon as possible. It usually takes me about half a day.

Ellie came down from the spare room where she'd dumped her stuff. She was rubbing her hands like someone who'd, well… just moved in.

"Right," she said. "Where's Dogge?"

I was going through a month's post in kangaroo court fashion. Anything that looked like a mail shot went straight into the bin, the rest was given a stay of execution in the jaws of the big clip on the notice board.

"Dogge's at Jean Langan's. We'll have a cup of tea then pop round and fetch her. Long-life milk in the utility room, top shelf."

She fetched a carton and tore it open with her teeth. Like her mother used to. Then she reached up to the rail above the window and took down a couple of mugs. She looked in each, turned up her nose and rinsed them under the tap.

"Dad…" she said after an ominous pause, "don't think I'm prying into your personal life but does Laura live here?"

"Yes, you are, and no she doesn't."

"Only I thought she might've moved in by now. I didn't like to ask her in the bogs at Heathrow and the opportunity didn't arise in LA so…"

She cocked her head as if that might prompt a fuller explanation. It didn't.

"But do you?" she said, smiling.

"Do I what?"

"You and Laura?"

I pretended that I'd gone deaf. I'd reached one of those letters, which, before opening it, you torture yourself with speculation as to who it's from. It was personal, with a handwritten address in real ink, but I didn't recognise the writing. Once upon a time all letters came addressed like that. Nowadays when they do I feel slightly paranoid. Nathan Hawk, Esq., it said so formally, Beech Tree Cottage, Morton Lane, Winchendon. The postmark was Thame.

"Who do I know in Thame, Ellie?"

"Quite a few people, I expect," she said, unhelpfully.

She had found the tea-bags and dropped one into each mug. She was turning packets over in the cupboard.

"You still take sugar…?"

"Not since meeting Laura."

"…only you don't appear to have any."

"That's because I don't take it anymore."

I held the envelope up to the light at the window and squeezed it in several places trying to make out the signature. Ellie strode the distance between us, whipped the envelope out of my hands and before I could object slit it with the bread knife. She handed it back to me.

The letter was from John Stillman, a man who had come to see me the very morning we'd flown out. A month in LA and I'd forgotten all about him, not to mention his problem.

Dear Mr Hawk,

First of all I trust that you and your good
lady enjoyed your holiday and have returned
to England much refreshed.
    You were kind enough to say, on the last
occasion that we met, that I should get in
touch with you on your return. You may
remember that I asked if you would be
kind enough to look into the matter of my
daughter's disappearance.
    I would be grateful, therefore, if you
would ring me at Mayfield House so that we
can arrange to meet and discuss the matter
further.

Yours most sincerely,
John Stillman.

I looked at Ellie who had set down a mug of tea on the table
in front of me.
    "What?" she asked in response to my gazing at her.
    "Just wondering how I'd feel if you'd been missing for
three months. I mean I think I know but that's not quite the
same thing, is it…"
    "Devastated, I hope. Is that what the letter's about?"
    I pushed it across the table for her to read.
    "You're not even a policeman anymore," she said when
she'd finished. "Why's he asking you to find her?"
    Feeling only marginally crushed I said, "He thinks I'd
be good at it. I used to be."

-2-

I arranged to meet John Stillman for lunch a week later in Giacometto's and since I knew that Ellie had 'one or two things she wanted to do in Oxford' that day I offered her a lift. I had an ulterior motive, of course.

I'd been a policeman for thirty years, twenty of them as a detective. I was involved in twenty-eight murder cases and must have interviewed thousands of witnesses. If I couldn't extract from my own daughter what her plans for the next few months were, what could I do?

We started off chatting about trivial things. They were erecting marquees for Thame Fair as we drove through and that opened up the subject of tents, camping and a memorable occasion when all six of us had gone to The Lakes in a caravan for two weeks. According to Ellie I'd been 'grouchy' on that holiday, as I'd been on most others, which made my equanimity in Los Angeles such a treat. Then, as we lingered in the Summertown traffic, I threw in as randomly as possible, "Looking forward to going back to Paris?".

"No."

"Oh."

I could've left it there but I would only have worried about the implications of her answer.

"No?"

"No."

The conversation was developing a certain déjà-vu quality but I ploughed on.

"Why not, love?"

She turned and gazed at me with the pale grey eyes.

"Dad, do we have to do this now?"

"Sorry, love, what are we doing?"

"Giving Eleanor the third degree? What are your plans, Miss Hawk, for the rest of your Life?"

"No, really, I'm just interested in, well… things. I mean there's a travel agent up at Carfax, why don't you pop in…"

"I might."

She was still gazing at me but giving nothing away. "Is there anything else I can help you with?"

Yes, I thought, you can tell me what you're up to because sure as hell there's another agenda taking shape here. Then tell me who taught you to play your cards so close to your chest. Your mother, siblings, hormones, friends… me?

"Well, is there?" she asked.

I shrugged. "No, no, that's fine."

The woman behind me hooted. The traffic ahead had cleared.

I parked the Land Rover up at St Giles in the angled spaces beneath the lime trees. Ellie said she'd get the bus home and touched me for fifty quid. I didn't realise the buses out of Oxford were so expensive.

"Thanks, Dad," she said, as I handed over the money. "You're a star. Most of the time."

I watched her stride off towards the centre of town, hair piled up beneath Jaikie's old baseball cap, a pair of her sister's jeans trailing frayed ends on the pavement, a shirt of Con's billowing away from her body at every point. I knew for a fact she was wearing socks of mine, she'd asked for a pair before we left. No wonder the kid was having trouble finding her own identity.

Clarendon Street was unusually busy and at the point where it dog-legs down to Jericho a crowd had gathered around a single being up on a stone bench. I couldn't hear what the man's beef was but the spectators, mostly foreign tourists, were fascinated. They didn't understand what the guy was saying but they held their cameras aloft to snap the way he was saying it. This, they would tell their friends and relatives back home, was an English eccentric, dressed as you might expect one from Oxford to be. Tweed jacket with a scarf wound around his neck. Corduroy trousers. Leather lace-up boots.

He had his back to me so I couldn't really get a measure of his age but from the stoop, if not the bald head, I put him at mid-sixties. When he turned, I recognised the man who had come to see me at Beech Tree the morning we flew out to Los Angeles. It was John Stillman.

"Ah, Mr Hawk," he called out. "Just let me hand these round to my good friends here and I'll be with you."

All eyes and cameras turned to me. Was this another eccentric come to join the party? If so, this one was more casually dressed than his friend. Leather jacket and jeans, grey T-shirt underneath it, Skechers on the feet. Dark hair, greying at the sides and cut short in a Number Two, the internationally accepted way of going bald without admitting it.

Stillman gave me one of the hand-bills as he swept round the circle of onlookers. Dead centre of the half-page was a picture of his beautiful daughter, smiling out at us just below the word 'Missing' in red. Beneath her were the details of her disappearance. Teresa Marie Stillman, it said, 22 years old, last seen in Oxford at Giacometto's on Monday, April 22nd this year. Were you in the city that day? Did you see her by any chance? Have you seen her since? If you have any information about her disappearance please contact Detective Sergeant Jim Kelloway at Thame Police Station, or Mr John Stillman. The two phone numbers were also in red.

As even those without an English phrasebook began to realise when they studied the leaflet, there was something more to the tweedy eccentric than mere entertainment value. The red urgency of the word 'Missing' and the large print phone numbers, the intensity of the hand offering the leaflet spoke of a tragedy unresolved. And now that his audience looked again they saw in John Stillman's posture the utter weariness of a long and fruitless haul. In the pallid skin and watery eyes lay proof of self-detriment, too many skipped meals, too much alcohol, too much coffee and fronting it all the thin, quick smile was not one of pleasure but of desperation. Sensing the force of it, the spectators moved away in search of less troubling diversions.

"I do it whenever I can," said Stillman, brightly. "Hand out a few leaflets. I'm becoming quite a fixture."

He lit a cigarette and pointed across the street at Giacometto's. He laid a hand on my arm and gently pushed me towards it as if launching a boat into a stream.

"I'll join you in a second," he said.

He broke away towards a young man sitting cross-legged on the pavement, a blanket over his lower half, an upturned cap in front of him. He looked up at Stillman with a face so thin and sharp you could've cut your hand on it.

"Morning, Danny," said Stillman. "How are things?"

The boy nodded, unable to break through whatever substance was shielding him from the rest of us. Stillman dug into his pockets and fished out some coins. He stooped and placed them in the cap.

"Take care now, you hear me?"

As we turned away from the boy, upended by my generation and seemingly thrown against this Oxford wall, we heard him reprise his whispered mantra for spare change. Nobody was really listening.

We sat at one of the pavement tables set in the shade of Giacometto's several awnings. Out here in the fresh air, Stillman said, he could indulge his chain-smoking habit. The front windows of the place were open and inside it was jam-packed with noisy, lively students from one of the greatest universities in the world – educated, confident and privileged. I'd have bet money that one of them was called

Danny too and almost certainly an aspiring parasite, be that lawyer, accountant or broker…

And I'm beginning to sound like my father.

John Stillman was known here at Giacometto's, in fact he was downright fawned upon. The manager was an old-before-his-time sort of bloke, overweight but able to carry it on account of being tall. His hair stood up like black flames, fuelled by half a pot of gel. He emerged through the front door and descended on us rubbing his hands in a mixture of deference and delight.

"Heh, Mr Stillman, good to see you, man!" The accent was an uncanny mixture of Romford and Rome. "How you keeping? In good shape, huh?"

He looked at me, extended one of the wrung hands and tried to break my fingers in a display of trustworthiness.

"This is Mr Hawk, Roberto."

"Let me get you a drink both." He called through the window. "Heh, Sally, you get these guys what they want to drink, then you feed 'em!"

He took a napkin from his jacket pocket, flicked away all trace of the previous customers, then pushed the ashtray towards Stillman.

"No news, I take it?" Stillman asked, quietly.

"No, sir, not this week." Roberto leaned down towards him, lowering his voice. "You know the guy I told you about, the friend of one of the customers? It came to nothing but… we press on, yeah?"

Stillman clasped Roberto by the hand and nodded, his mouth twisting in a perfect display of acceptance.

When Roberto returned to his managerial duties Stillman explained, "This is where she was last seen. I come here every week to find out if there's been any news but so far…" He shrugged. "I'm being unmannerly. It's good of you to come, Mr Hawk."

"You're welcome."

He leaned towards me, elbows on the table, fired up

again in the manner of his soap-box oration. "The police have done their best, Mr Hawk, but you know their problems better than I do. Three month's have gone by, no progress, so they pare down the inquiry. Can I blame them for that? I cannot."

And then, to the fleeting concern of several passers-by, and me, he coughed. I once owned a car that coughed like John Stillman. I used to go out to it of a winter morning, turn over the engine while whispering sweet nothings in its ear. All I got in return were the heaving lurches of its imminent demise. It didn't go red, like Stillman did. It didn't splutter, either. It just died. It certainly didn't apologise.

"Sorry," he said. "Bit of a chest."

I glanced down at the hand-bill he'd given me. "For some reason you think I can find her?"

"I'm sure you can! You have that about you, Mr Hawk, that says nothing is beyond you. You take a job, you see it through…"

I corrected him swiftly. "I haven't taken any job yet, Mr Stillman."

He closed his eyes, nodding in agreement then turned to the skinny waitress who had come out to take our order. "Sally, this is my friend Mr Hawk."

When I'd sat down at the table I was plain Mr Hawk. Five minutes later I was his friend. Where would it end, I wondered. A proposal of marriage? The waitress smiled at me, pencil poised.

"What can I get you to drink, sir?"

"I'll have a whisky," I said. "Fill the glass with ice, right to the brim."

Stillman ordered a Bloody Mary and beckoned the waitress closer. "The boy over there, by the wall. Danny. Hamburger and chips."

She smiled. "I'll see to it. And you'll have the usual, I expect?"

He nodded and gestured to me. I ordered a chicken salad with no dressing.

When the waitress departed, Stillman lit a fresh cigarette from the butt of the previous one and leaned in towards me again with a nervous glance around to check our privacy.

"Listen," he said. "Money. Please don't think I'm being vulgar but… you name a price for finding her, I'll pay it."

I nodded.

"Is that yes?" he asked.

"No! That's I hear you."

When the drinks came he seemed to relax a little, something to do with both of his hands being occupied, his left with a cigarette, his right with a glass. He leaned away from me and glanced inside at the mainly young, jabbering faces.

"I love this place, Mr Hawk. Mainly because Teresa was here, I suppose. Just inside. The window seat." He smiled. "I can feel her presence sometimes. You have children?"

"Four."

He laughed. "That is a tribe, Mr Hawk, which makes you a lucky man! And one who will appreciate what I'm about to say." He tapped the pile of leaflets on the table beside him. "Things like this, they change you. Death, well, lose a relative you can bury them now, grieve later. That isn't the case if someone you love goes missing. What you get instead of a resolution is… altered vision. You see things, people, events differently. That boy over there, Danny? Two years ago he was in my way, he spoiled my view when I walked down the street, he embarrassed me by asking if I had any change I could spare. Now I look at him and all I see is somebody's son, right at the bottom of the human pile and I don't ask anymore what's happened to his dignity that he begs in the street. I say where is his father?" He turned back and looked at me with a steady, benign gaze. "What do you say?"

"I say maybe his father's got problems of his own."

He nodded. "There is that, of course. So where is his father's father? You see, I've come to realise how badly we've treated our children. People say there's a cult of the young, they're sick of it, we should put them back in their place." He shook his head in an exaggerated fashion. "If there is a cult it's of our generation's making. We've flattered their youthfulness in order to sell them grown up things. What we haven't done is give them the wisdom to distinguish between what they need and what they want. So they buy everything and come to us when they run out of money. In stealing from them we've stolen from ourselves." He paused and took a long drag of his latest cigarette. "Forgive me. Hobby horse."

I said that he shouldn't mind me. He took me at my word.

"I caused a bit of a stir here once, a lunchtime rather like this. I was inside with a friend, trying to prove my point. I stood up, tapped my glass for silence and told the assembled company that I had a proposition. A job to offer. I could guarantee that its intellectual demands would bring them fulfilment. I threw in travel, adventure, a touch of fame, a hint of sexual encounter. I had them in the palm of my hand, just like in the old days at The Bailey. And then I told them that it paid just £25,000 a year and the laughter was deafening." He paused. "It's more than money we lost when we started exploiting them. We took away their ability to value anything that doesn't have a bar code on it. Where were we before you allowed me to ramble on?"

"Teresa and what you think I can do."

"Yes, well, first things first. None of this would make any sense, of course – the leaflets, coming here every week, getting in touch with you – but for one crucial thing."

"What's that?"

"I know she's alive, Mr Hawk!"

It was time to tread warily, to step around his hopes without raising the dirt of near certainty that his daughter was dead. I could have quoted statistics to prove it. He wouldn't have believed them.

"How do you know?" I asked.

"I've seen her."

It wasn't a retired copper he needed but a working shrink. He must've picked up on my inner flinch.

"When I say I've seen her, I don't mean actually seen. I mean I walk round a corner at home, say, and there she is for a split second. I look up from the book I'm reading, in the drawing room, and there she is again. Fleeting moments, Mr Hawk, and yes they are mental projections, the stuff of wishful thinking, but there she is."

"And because of that you think she's alive?"

"I told you that I see things differently now. Two years ago I wouldn't have believed in presentiment. I'm a lawyer. Habeas Corpus and all that."

"Tell me what happened the day she went missing."

As I picked at the big salad, batting away the occasional friendly wasp, and Stillman dallied with a plate of chips, a cigarette on the go and a constant Bloody Mary to hand, he told me how Teresa had returned to the family home, Mayfield House, on Friday April the 21st, the day she finished a garden design job on the outskirts of Oxford. The husband there, Michael Carter, had a record and both Stillman and the police thought that might have a bearing, but Carter had been interviewed and cleared. On Saturday the 22nd Teresa had received a call on her mobile from a man called Richard Crane. He'd seen Carter's garden and was most impressed. Wanted one for himself. Teresa left Mayfield House to meet him, right here, in Giacometto's.

"And Roberto was working here then? Remembered them?"

"Oh, yes. He's been most helpful."

Roberto was at the doorway, gushing farewell to three middle-aged women who were just leaving. He thanked them for the umpteenth time and they went on their way. I beckoned him and he came over, hands wringing.

"Gentlemen, what can I do for you?"

I pushed out a chair for him. "You can give us a minute of your time."

"Sure thing. Heh, Sally, drinks again for Mr Stillman and Mr…?"

He looked at me.

"Hawk."

He raised a forefinger of salute as if to say that he'd filed the name away. Picking my words carefully, to avoid raising Stillman's hopes that I was going to look into the matter, I said, "I'm interested in Mr Stillman's problem. Teresa, she came here to meet a man on…"

"She did," said Roberto, interrupting me, keenly. "Richard Crane."

"What did he look like?"

Roberto glanced away at Stillman for permission to speak. The latter quickly blew a cloud of cigarette smoke skywards, then nodded.

"Tall, fair hair, long, in a ponytail. Dressed very smart. Big guy, dark suit, shirt like snow and the tie, blue. Real class."

"How old?"

"Thirty, thirty-two."

"Did he arrive before or after Teresa?"

"About half an hour before. I sat him down there in the window. He asked me for that."

"What did he order?"

"You mean for lunch? Well…"

"I mean when he first got here. Drink maybe?"

Roberto shrugged, high shoulders and hands like dinner plates. "I don't remember."

"You remember the colour of his tie. You don't remember what he ordered?"

He shifted slightly. "Gin and tonic, maybe."

"And when Teresa got here, what happened?"

He pulled a face as if there wasn't really much to tell. "She walks in, I say Hi, you here for lunch? She says I'm meeting someone and she looks round. This Richard Crane is on his feet, coming over to her. She smiles, the hand out for shaking. He says, Miss Stillman? I'm Richard Crane." Roberto shrugged. "That's about it."

"What did they eat?"

He smiled. "The police ask me this. Why's it matter so much?"

"Well, if he'd asked for pastrami on rye, say, wouldn't it tell you something?"

"Sure! That he couldn't read. It isn't on the menu."

"Okay then, it'd tell you two things. He couldn't read and he was a Yank maybe. What did they eat?"

"She had smoked salmon. We do this thing in a bagel with cream cheese. He had chicken salad, like you."

"Were they friendly? Did you hear them laugh?"

"Oh, yeah. She laughed at him quite a few times. He laughed back, very friendly."

"And when they left, how did he pay? Cash?"

"Sure."

"Can you remember what he gave you?"

"Jesus, man…"

"Listen, he gives you a £50 note, chances are the man's well-heeled. If he scrapes through his pockets to dig out pound coins it tells another story. So how did he pay?"

"You want me to make something up? I don't remember. And then they left."

"Together?"

"Out the door, back up to St Giles."

He spread the dinner-plate hands. End of his story. I thanked him for his time and he went back into the restaurant but I saw him drift towards the open window occasionally, no doubt checking to see how badly he'd pissed me off. He knew he had even though I'd tried not to let it show.

I waited for Stillman to finish a coughing fit and then light another cigarette to settle his chest, as he so quaintly put it. Then I said as gently as I could, "Mr Stillman, I don't know if I can help you…"

He weighed in immediately, trying to make a virtue of my reluctance. "Of course you don't! I don't expect written guarantees, Mr Hawk! But you're in the help business. You bring things to the surface, you dig things up."

I wanted to tell him that that's exactly what I'd be doing if I ever found his daughter. I said instead, "The only thing I know is that she isn't coming back, Mr Stillman."

He smiled. "You see, you can't bring yourself to use the D word, can you. Why is that? To spare my feelings? Jesus, you must have used it hundreds of times, right in the faces of people whose loved ones had been killed. But the difference there, I venture, was that you had a body. In Teresa's case we haven't and not for want of looking. You ask Sergeant Kelloway because he's as puzzled as I am." He paused, as if recalling with affection the copper who'd handled the case. "And you know, I believe part of him thinks that one day soon she'll walk into Thame police station and give a reasonable account of the past three months. What a day that will be!"

In pure delight at the prospect, he slapped the table. A few heads turned in response to the dull, metallic ring, to see what had happened, and quickly judged it unimportant. I could feel Roberto looming. I held up a hand to keep him at bay.

"You're right," I said, quietly. "I don't know anything for sure. But experience, mood, copper's nose, call it what you will, they all tell me that Teresa is dead."

He just kept looking at me, shocked that I'd failed to meet his expectations of me. Then, when he'd found the strength, he asked, "So why did you come?"

"I thought you were going to ask me to find her body. So that you could lay her to rest."

He looked down at the table, shaking his head. "No, no… I want you to find her. We have so much to talk about, so much catching up to do. Years that were lost in a fog created by a mother who didn't like her very much and a father too self-interested to realise what he was missing…" He looked across at me. "Please. Money is no object."

"I can't help you," I said.

He seemed to consider one last ditch attempt on my sympathies but knew there'd be no point. He closed his eyes as if to blink away his anguish. When he opened them again he said simply, "I hope you never have to go through this, Mr Hawk. I'm not playing for sympathy or trying to change your mind, believe me, and I admire your frankness. But I wouldn't wish this on my worst enemy."

***

We said goodbye in the street, shaking hands rather formally, with Stillman asking how much he owed me for my time. I told him he owed me nothing and he spared me further feelings of guilt by not pursuing the matter. He thanked me, I thanked him for lunch, then he turned and made his way up towards St Giles, handing out leaflets to passers-by. I saw him home in on a bunch of tourists identified by their cameras and cagoules. A fresh audience. A reason for going on, for getting up the following day, people to tell about his beloved daughter.

I crossed the street to an Indian gift shop. Inside, a couple I'd noticed in Giacometto's were examining the thrown together pots and badly made furniture. The lady who ran the place, herself an Indian and dressed in a full and colourful sari, was watching them. The look on her face was of weary recognition. They would browse for half an hour, untidy her stock and leave without buying so much as a joss stick.

I made my way to the front window, batting aside the child-woven rugs and flimsy shawls that hung like cobwebs from a series of washing lines strung out across the space. Perhaps it was the clingy nature of one particular garment that set me off, heartbeat soaring in strength and tempo, the back of my neck going ice cold, hands curling into a clench with a will of their own.

The owner had followed me to the window and now asked if she could help. I muttered that she couldn't. No one could. It was a small matter of a Map, I added. In the spirit of enterprise she gestured to a rack of them, street maps of Oxford, but I shook my head. Mine was a Map of the World but I'd left it at home, mainly because of the physical state of it. She nodded wisely, pending more explanation of what the hell I was talking about. In its present state, I rattled on, I couldn't carry The Map around with me and I was feeling the absence of it profoundly. But not as profoundly as Roberto from Giacometto's might in a few minutes' time.

In mentioning Roberto I had struck common ground. She asked how he and a Map of the World were connected. I told her that, in spite of it being imaginary, without its distracting properties I was liable to go back into Giacometto's and break open his head. She smiled. Perhaps her dull day was about to be enlivened.

"Roberto," said the lady, "he is a thief of his customers, a fat slimy git!"

I turned to her. The Indian accent had given the words a comic touch, but the passion behind them was all too heartfelt.

"He steals from grannies," she went on. "They go there for coffee in the morning. I see him butter them up. I see him smarm and flatter and then what does he do? He double-charges. He is so big, so much a bull, they are frightened to go back and complain."

It was vindicating news.

"Right," I said eventually, "on behalf of all those ladies, not to mention a certain friend of mine..."

I had referred to Stillman as a friend. I hadn't meant to. The Indian lady nodded.

"Be careful," she advised.

I looked at her. Didn't I seem capable of rendering down an overweight thief?

"Not for what he does to you," she explained. "But what you do to him."

Out in the street there was no sign of John Stillman. The only evidence that he'd ever been here, in all his well-mannered despair, was a puzzled man and his wife strolling down the pavement, exchanging words about a Missing leaflet. Respectfully, the woman folded it and put it in her handbag.

In Giacometto's the lunchtime crowd was still there, spinning out its cappuccinos. Roberto came towards me, hands not wringing this time but clasped. In a form of prayer, I chose to think, that my return was purely social.

"Heh, Mr Hawk! You forget something?"

I gave him a middle-aged smile, the self-deprecating one that goes with a slipping memory. He released his hands and lowered his voice, reached out and touched me on the shoulder.

"You leave something? I find it for you."

"It's not a thing. It's something I forgot to do."

The dinner-plate hands came right at me again, telling me that I should go ahead and do whatever it was. I picked up an empty glass from the bar and started to toss it gently in the air and catch it. That was the point at which his table-side manners visibly deserted him, replaced by real concern.

"I don't understand," he said, after three or four spins of the glass.

"I tell you, Roberto, as a young copper I trashed places like this just because somebody looked at me the wrong way. It would just hit me... wham."

I clicked my fingers and missed my catch. The glass fell to the floor and smashed. The place went quiet. Such is the power of oncoming violence that his customers knew something was brewing and it wasn't just the coffee. Roberto turned to appeal to the onlookers. None of them really wanted to help. None of them really wanted to be there anymore.

"Okay, Mister, what's your problem? What you want that I should do about it?"

"Empty your top pocket onto the counter."

He found his balls at last, somewhere in the back of his throat if the croaky voice was anything to go by.

"Fuck you!" he said.

I kicked him in the knee, he bent forward to clutch it, I took hold of the gelled head and brought it down on the counter with a crack. A gallant regular scraped back his chair and I turned to face a boy no older than my own sons.

"Stay where you are!" I yelled at him. "This bastard isn't worth it."

On a level rugby field the boy would have left me for dead but right now he was up against 30 years of facing down everything from joy-riders to serial killers. Experience won the day and he re-took his seat, but as he did so it occurred to me that one day soon experience wouldn't be enough. I needed to steer clear of situations like this.

I reached into the top pocket of Roberto's jacket, took out the pressed handkerchief, a clip of business cards and a cigarette lighter and laid them on the counter. I reached in again and this time came up with a £50 note. I pushed him away. He staggered into the nearest clutch of stools, grabbing at them to stop himself falling.

"Does he give you one of these every week?"

"Who?"

"John Stillman. I saw him press it into your hand when you came to our table. How does it work? Does he ask you every time if there's news of his daughter? Do you say yes, a guy was here the other day, hopeful, then next week sorry, it was all came to nothing Is that how it goes?"

"What you talking about?"

I thumped the bar and the tray of glasses trembled in sympathy with their fallen comrade.

"Is that how it goes?!"

There was a pause before he glared at me and said quietly, "I do him a service. He pays me. Since when is that a crime?"

"Since right now," I said, wiping my gel-covered hands on the handkerchief. "Did Richard Crane really come in here?"

"Sure."

"And Teresa?"

"What, you think I lie?"

"I think you turned his personal tragedy into a profitable side-line. Stop taking his money, Roberto, or I will be back in an even worse frame of mind than I'm in now and it won't be a glass I toss in the air, it will be your head."

I picked up the £50 note and left.

Out in the street I could feel the eyes watching me from the restaurant as I crossed over to Danny, still there, still asking the passing legs for spare change. I stooped down and handed him the fifty. His eyes came to rest somewhere between me and him, not on my face, not even on the money.

"It's from John Stillman," I told him.

He winced, trying to recall the name unaided, then said, "Who?"

I straightened up, gave a discreet wave to the owner of the Indian gift shop and walked back to the Land Rover.

***

When I got back to Beech Tree Cottage I went straight up to the cabin and contemplated failure, not just in a general sense but my own particular example of it earlier that day.

I had been to Oxford on a mission to help John Stillman but it wasn't his distress that marked the day, as should have been the case. It wasn't even his agonising attempt to persuade me against the cruel inevitability that his daughter was dead. I will remember our meeting for the red mist that slowly descended when a two-bit Italian waiter exploited Stillman's anguish right in front of my eyes.

I was lucky, though. A shopkeeper had given me good advice. Be careful, she had said, and I'd heeded her words. Even so, it was something of a miracle that I hadn't ripped Roberto's head off and punted it across the Jericho rooftops. Instead, I had settled for kicking him and cracking his head on a handy surface. If I'd had The Map with me things would have been different. I thought I no longer needed it. I thought I'd taken to heart the words of Laura Peterson who had said that such outbursts, such displays of aggression, were bad enough in a man half my age. At fifty-two and rising they were at best undignified, at worst harmful.

Recalling her diagnosis lightened the mood I was in. I remembered the straight face I'd put so much effort into keeping when she told me of her own way of controlling her temper. Amused though I was at the idea of her ever flying off the handle, she assured me that as a young doctor she had been driven to fury on many occasions. Her way of dealing with it involved snatches of her favourite poetry. If she felt anger coming on she would recite chunks of it until calm had been restored.

"Out loud?" I asked.

"Of course not. In my head. You know the sort of thing. All that stuff we learned at school."

"You might have learned it at your school…"

"Or heard along the way. Radio Three, the World Service. Keats, Shelley, Byron, Browning. You can't really go ballistic if your mind is reeling with 'Season of mists and mellow fruitfulness! Close bosom-friend of the maturing sun; Conspiring with him how to load and bless…'" She paused. "Well, at least I can't."

"I can see how it would be difficult," I muttered.

She'd made me promise I would try it sometime. I said I would. Meantime, I reached into the bottom drawer of my filing cabinet and took out a walnut jewellery box and set it down on my desk.

The box was a simple and beautiful object, an apprentice piece from the 19th century, given to Maggie by her father when he bought her her first necklace. She was seventeen. Thereafter all manner of valuables had been placed in it for safe keeping, not just by Maggie as a girl, but later on as a wife and mother. Such things as the kids' first drawings, her engagement ring, spare sets of keys, a few milk teeth, pin numbers, locks of hair, passports, a blown bird's egg. Since her death the only thing I'd placed in it for safe keeping was The Map.

I really should explain about The Map. An old villain by the name of Roy Arthur Pullman introduced me to the power of it when I was a young Detective Sergeant in the Met. My temper was as fiery and violent as his and our interviews formed the basis of many a book. The betting kind. Which of us would reach across the table to grab the other first, who would strike the first blow, deliver the first head butt. I sound proud of this. I'm not. And to do him justice, Roy Pullman wasn't proud of it either, which explained the change I noticed in him on one particular occasion.

I was questioning him about fencing some stolen fridges and expected to meet the full force of his rage. I could see it in his eyes, the desire to rise from the table, turn it over, storm round the room threatening seven kinds of damnation; but instead he simply reached into an inside pocket for an imaginary Map of the World. He mimed, with great attention to detail, the process of unfolding it and smoothing it out on the table. Then he reached again for a pair of imaginary spectacles and put them on. He closed his eyes, held a forefinger in the air, brought it down on The Map in what he described as 'a far more agreeable place'.

I don't know what connection he had with some of the countries his finger landed on. Maybe he'd fought there in some twentieth century war, perhaps he'd holidayed or gone to ground there after a robbery. Maybe, like mine, his kids had gone to live in some of these unpronounceable places. What I knew for sure was that two, three minutes of contemplation of this 'far more agreeable place' took the heat out of everything.

A year or so later I arrested Roy Pullman again. I forget what for. He sat opposite me in the interview room and it was all too apparent that his inner fire had gone out. He was dying, he told me, of some fancily named disease. He reached into his pocket and took out The Map. He didn't unfold it. He didn't need it. He handed it to me across the table.

"You'd better have this now," he said. "Might keep you out of trouble. Go on, take it."

The odd thing is, I did. The insupportable logic of The Map, starting with the fact that it didn't exist yet had to be kept in a safe place and cherished by its owner, didn't bother me then and hasn't bothered me since. I knew why I took it. He was right, I needed it and it has saved my skin on many occasions down the years.

I removed it from the walnut jewellery box and laid it out on my desk, having due regard for the fragile state it was in. The colours were fading. It was frayed along its edges, worn through at some of the folds. Pieces of it had worked loose and become detached, but it was all there. I closed my eyes, raised my hand and brought my forefinger down on Canada – Vancouver, to be precise.

That morning I'd had an email from my eldest son, Con. His message was typically brief but uncharacteristically there was no sub-text of him being strapped for cash, asking for money without actually asking.

It said, "Vancouver, Dad. Thinking of settling here, making a go of it. Con."

Who with? I thought. Kirstie, The Nightmare Redhead? Doing what?

About an hour later an email from my other daughter Fee answered none of those questions but unsettled me further.

"Dad, Con's thinking of emigrating! To Canada! Do something!"

Well, okay, no sooner the word… but any suggestions as to what? Fee had none but the rest of her email went on to say that, yes, they'd all flipped off round the world to see what it was like but none of them had ever agreed that home was anywhere but England. Okay, not Winchendon, but one of the big cities. Easy reach of one another. So why had Con decided to put two fingers up at the agreement? And again the command: do something.

About ten minutes later Jaikie emailed from Los Angeles, part concern, part ego-trip.

"Dad, mate, what's this about Con emigrating to Canada? And while I've got your attention there's a rather good still of me in Film Weekly next month, taken from a scene between me and Josh Hartnett in All Good Men and True. J."

I was losing them. They were losing each other.

I folded The Map with extra care and placed it inside an envelope – not one from the stationary drawer but from a side drawer of my mind. I put it in the inside pocket of my leather jacket.

-3-

With John Stillman's plea for help still ringing in my ears, I met up with Ellie that evening and we wandered round to Plum Tree Cottage to do battle with one of Laura's vegetarian lasagnes. I would have cheerfully given it a miss but Ellie's never been known to pass on halfway decent grub. We went armed with a couple of bottles of Fitou, survivors of a holiday in the South of France four or five years previously from which I'd returned with about three hundred bottles strapped to the roof rack.

The initial small talk, as we watched Laura prepare supper, was promising and lifted my spirits a little. How does it feel to be back? we asked each other. Okay, said Laura. But only okay. Surprising how you slip back into routines. Here we were, after three weeks in Los Angeles, and what had she found? Mrs Johnson's psoriasis hadn't cleared up, Annie MacKinnon was still pregnant, Mr Butterworth was still complaining about... She stopped herself. She wasn't supposed to disclose the intimate details of her panel's problems. We threatened to shop her. We demanded money to keep our mouths shut. She said she was a doctor, she could kill us both without leaving a trace.

All easygoing stuff then, and just as I was building up an appetite for the lasagne, Ellie went and spoiled it.

"Dad, how did you get on with John Stillman today?"

"Not too well," I said. "Man's in a bad way."

Laura joined in. "Hardly surprising, I suppose, if his daughter's still missing."

"She's worse than missing, Laura, she's dead."

"How do you know?" she asked. "Have they found her body?"

"No, and Stillman doesn't want them to."

"Sounds like you'll have to tread carefully."

Ellie mumbled her agreement and it may have been my imagination but I thought I sensed conspiracy in the air.

"I won't be treading any way at all," I said. "I'm not going to look for her."

I glanced from one to the other, defying any possible objection.

"Well, if that's your decision," said Laura, "fair enough."

Ellie seemed to agree with that. "No, you can't be at everyone's beck and call. He should go to the real police."

"He has been. They can't find her either."

Laura turned away to grate cheese, Ellie stayed to grate on my nerves.

"And even if you found her, Dad, where would it leave you? Or the real cops, come to that? You'd be taking away his hope and that's what he's living on."

"Ellie, could we just define a few terms here? 'Real cops', for example. Real as opposed to what?"

"You know what I mean."

I suppose I did but the implication still bothered me. Since retiring I was no longer real but a figment of the onlooker's imagination. I changed the subject as sharply as I could.

"Laura, how long is dinner? I'm starving."

"Twenty minutes," she said. "Ellie, there's a bag of nuts in the cupboard by your head. Reach it down for your father, will you. Bowl in the dishwasher."

I wound some salt into the nuts and drew a disapproving glance from Laura MD but she forbore to lecture me on blood pressure. Instead, she left the lasagne to its own devices and joined me at the table, reaching for the wine bottle.

"Do you mind if I voice an observation?" she asked, gently. I minded but said that I didn't. "Stillman would most certainly like you to find her, alive and kicking, but what he really wants is – dreadful word – closure."

"And until that happens," added Ellie, slipping down onto the bench beside Laura, "he can't move on. It must be dreadful to put your life on hold over something so uncertain."

I slapped the table between us.

"Uncertain be damned! She's dead. How many more times do I have to say it?"

"Until I believe it, I suppose. It's the optimist in me, Dad. Blame Mum…"

She always mentioned her mother when she wanted to bring me back down to earth.

I took a swig of the wine and in doing so recalled the trip to France that had brought it to this very table. The return journey from Languedoc had been marred by Maggie's map-reading and, while I should have headed for Rouen, she'd missed the turning and we found ourselves on the road to Dieppe. It didn't matter. It brought out the best in us. Sure, we blamed each other for half an hour then took our them-and-us-against-the-world stance. We needed it. The ferry was crowded and expensive, it was two hours late in departing and we got back to Winchendon thoroughly shattered and a day behind schedule. But not one of us has logged it away as a bad day in our lives. Quite the opposite. And was this just a random memory or was it taking me somewhere? Ah, yes. Wine, France, Dieppe, Paris… the Sorbonne. If I picked the moment I could ditch the chat about John Stillman in favour of what Ellie would be doing for the rest of her life, or more specifically the next semester, already paid for, rent and all. But Ellie was rattling on.

"…you see, what's going on here is this. You're feeling pissed off because you can't help the poor old git. Bloody frustrating, I agree, but like Laura says, maybe there's another way of looking at it."

"Ellie, I was a copper for 30 years, I know a lost cause when I see one."

She pushed away the remark, hands out in front of her, just like her mother used to do. The voice was Maggie's too, thoroughly sensible and irritating because of it.

"If it were me out there, Dad, you'd be singing a different song. My daughter wouldn't just disappear off the face of the earth, you'd say, without so much as a whimper. Then you'd come looking for me."

"Yes, because I know you! I know that you're the most unpredictable of all my children, the most unpredictable creature I've ever met. Teresa is, was, the exact opposite."

"How do you know that?" asked Laura, rising in response to a timer going off.

"And what difference does it make?" Ellie tossed in.

"That girl has toed every line in front of her, just to please her parents. Why? Because her old man neglected her. Her mother didn't like her very much. Two selfish people, charged with bringing up a third, a task they made a complete pig's ear of. That's why he's feeling so damned guilty. He watched his daughter fight, fight, fight to gain their attention… and lose. None of my children ever had that problem."

Laura donned a pair of oven gloves, opened the Aga door and turned the lasagne, leaving the questions to Ellie.

"So what's your point? Her predictability is… some kind of proof?"

Sight and smell of the meal to come had calmed me a little.

"I'm saying if she weren't dead, she'd be back trying to please her father, not putting him through the agony he's in."

They both acknowledged the point and John Stillman took second, third, even fourth place in the conversation. The Sorbonne, however, began to move up a notch or two and I seized the opportunity presented when the small talk hared off in a culinary direction. Laura had begun to wax lyrical about the cheese she'd been using. It was a new one from Waitrose's repertoire, Saint Julien d'Albas, a powerful French cheddar. My mind took the obvious route from Waitrose to cheese, France, Paris and wound up at the Sorbonne and all of a sudden I heard myself ask,

"Listen, Ellie, speaking of French cheese, are you going back to the Sorbonne this year or what?"

I'd said it with as much positive bounce as I could manage but she stared across the table at me, judging where to pitch the level of her resentment at being challenged. She settled for haughty self-defence.

"Dad, no way am I going to discuss this right now!"

"In front of Laura, you mean? Maybe she could act as referee."

I turned to see if that was a working proposition.

"Keep me out of it," said the ref.

Ellie was back looking at me, the pale grey eyes seeming to harden into stones.

"How could you do that? Put Laura on the spot?"

"Answer the question and it's all over, we can tuck in to the lasagne."

She rose from the bench and looked down at me.

"I've just said in damn near perfect English that I've no intention of discussing my future here and now!"

"I hear the words but I honestly don't see what…"

"It's my Life we'd be talking about, not my plans for the next twenty-four hours."

"Well, sure…"

I was struggling and no one was helping me. I stood up, went towards her and she backed away.

"…so let's talk about your Life. How do you propose to earn your living?"

"There, you see! Two seconds and it's all about money. Is that what's bugging you? The room already paid for, the fees, your investment to date, all going down the pan?"

"I'd be a fool not to care."

"But whether I'm happy there would be another matter!"

"Let me tell you something about happiness, Eleanor. Your generation seems to believe…"

It had taken less than a minute but there we were, edging our way round Laura's table, me advancing, Ellie retreating. I was about to insult her generation as well, not the smartest verbal move I've ever made. I reached out to grab her by the shoulder but it wasn't Ellie I made contact with, it was Laura, hand raised, forbidding me to go any farther. I stopped dead when I realised what was going through her mind and there followed what, in polite circles, would be called a hiatus. In truth my actions had… unnerved all three of us.

"Don't be absurd," I said with as much quiet dignity as I could muster. "You think I was going to hit her?!"

"No, just hold me still," squawked Ellie, the big guns now on her side. "The better to shout at!"

"When did I ever hit you? Any of you?" I had to qualify that before she did. "Con, just the once. And God knows he deserved that! But if you think that makes me an abuser…"

"You said it, Dad."

Laura glared at each of us in equal measure.

"I think you should both sit down, opposite ends of the table."

Neither of us moved. Eventually, Ellie shook her head and reached out for her jacket.

"I'm sorry Laura. I can't. I have to go."

"No!" was all I could manage.

"I understand," said Laura, reaching out to help Ellie into the jacket. Ellie shrugged her off.

"I'm sorry about dinner, letting you down like this, but…"

"I can give you some to take with you," said Laura. "I've some foil containers in the pantry."

"That's kind of you but I'll pass."

And with that she fled the room and a moment later

we heard her stomping down the path and the front gate slamming behind her. I went to the window and just caught sight of her as she stepped beyond the glow of the security light. The hands were deep in her jacket pockets, head down, shoulders hunched – an almost classic gait with which to disappear into the night.

The ensuing silence was broken by the glug and swish of Laura pouring more wine into my glass.

"I wish I'd been able to do that at her age," she said eventually.

I turned to her. "Do what?"

"Stand up for myself. Handle my father so effectively. I can barely do it now but at nineteen what a difference it would have made to my life!"

"She's a wayward, reckless, mouthy little bitch," I muttered, reaching for the glass. "Self-willed, arrogant, irresponsible, disorganised, unmotivated…"

"She is magnificent!"

"You think so? Well, let me tell you what her magnificence did today in Oxford. She took me for fifty quid as we parked the car. Bus fare home, she said."

Laura shrugged. "So she had things to buy. Personal stuff she didn't want to discuss with her father."

"Stuff she'll be smoking with some old schoolmate down in Thame, half an hour from now."

She looked like she was trying not to be shocked. "You mean… marijuana?"

She pronounced all five syllables of the word. I looked at her for a moment, then smiled.

"What's funny?" she asked.

"You said it just like Maggie used to. As if reading a new word from a blackboard."

The argument, not that it had ever really taken off, crash-landed at our feet. But the fact that it had threatened us in the first place with all its destructive power was down to John Stillman. And me. I had wanted to help him but knew there was no point. Ellie was right. The frustration of that, with guilt to match, had put me in a bad mood. And with Jericho being the last place Teresa had been seen in, and it now being the focal point of all her father's hope, fear and obsession, it must have felt to him as though I'd simply passed by on the other side.

***

I got back to Beech Tree Cottage at about one in the morning, slightly the worse for Fitou. There must have been a worm of doubt in one of the bottles and I'd unwittingly swallowed it. The effect it had was to replace my concern about John Stillman with genuine concern about Eleanor Hawk. I went up to the log cabin for a family conference. Why deal with this on my own, I thought. She has siblings. Two brothers and a big sister. It seemed perfectly right and proper that we should all worry about the baby of the family.

I fired up the computer and as it whirred into life I started composing an e-mail in my head. "Hi, Fee! Great holiday, yeah? Don't know about you but I think we should do it at least once a year. New Paragraph. Listen, need your advice. It's Ellie, she's not going back to The Sorbonne and well, frankly, I don't know why…"

I didn't need to write it, let alone send it. I knew what Fee's answer would be. Try asking her, Dad. Try talking to her calmly, no hidden agendas, just unadulterated concern. I'd probably get the same advice from the boys. That's what I would do, then. I would ask her in the calm, post-argument light of reason just what she intended to do. I'd shrug a lot, to prove that none of it really mattered anyway. I'd cook her something nice to eat. Maggie used to do that if there was ever a post mortem to be held after a family punch-up. She'd set the table heaving with all sorts of goodies and we'd dive in like dogs. For years I thought she was just pampering us. She told me the Christmas before she died that it was to get our blood sugar levels up and thereby make us nicer people. Easier to control.

I'd bake a cake. I'd go in the house and do it right now. Chocolate fudge brownie. And as Ellie and I sat gorging ourselves on it, sometime tomorrow morning, I would Listen. With a capital L. The trick would be to make her believe that I didn't give a toss about her education. Or the prestigious scholarship she was about to throw away. All I'd ever wanted was her happiness so there'd be no bleating from me about the rent I'd surely lose on the Paris flat. That was just money. If she didn't fancy going back to The Sorbonne then so be it. Never mind its place in the world as one of the finest stepping stones a young woman could ask for. And when it came, specifically, to the modern languages course, well, why would a woman of nineteen want to study German and French when everyone in the world speaks English? Especially the Germans and the French. It makes you realise what a sad, redundant little place The Sorbonne is becoming. What an ordinary little city Paris really is…

It was half two in the morning by the time I finished baking the fudge brownie. I lifted it out of the tray and set it down on a rack to cool and placed a muslin hood over it. Ellie still wasn't home. I settled Dogge and went up to bed, intending to lie awake pending Ellie's arrival. I knew how it would go. She'd tiptoe up the stairs, push the door ajar and whisper:

"You still awake, Dad?"

"Sure. You okay?"

"Yeah! You?"

"Fine. G'night, sweetheart."

"Night, Dad. Love yer."

"Love yer back."

There'd be no grudge. No face-pulling. No sulk. She didn't go in for that. None of them did, which made it virtually impossible for me to.

I must have dozed off, however, and woke to sunlight hacking its way into the bedroom through the badly drawn curtains. There was a smell of baking in the air. The fudge brownie. And floating alongside it, in case I'd forgotten, was a brief history of last night's events.

I struggled out of bed and into some clothes. Five minutes later Dogge and I were heading across the field at the back of Beech Tree Cottage towards The Biggin Pond, where several anglers had been camped out all night. They seemed to take a dim view of our intrusion. It meant that the party was over, I suppose. Time to go home to their wives and families and face the reality of Wednesday morning.

Back in the kitchen I dusted the fudge brownie with icing sugar and replaced the muslin hood. Then I made breakfast, just toast and cereal, against the background hum of Radio Four. On offer there was Thought for the Day, a slot whose homespun self-righteousness would normally see me lunging for the off button but this morning, for some reason, I was more kindly disposed towards it.

A Rabbi was telling us of a woman who'd approached Mahatma Gandhi in the streets of Delhi one day. Her son, she told him, was a diabetic with a passion for sugar, which she had begged him, without success, to forego. However, if Gandhi were to ask the boy to give up sweets he would almost certainly do so. Gandhi thought for a moment, then told the woman to come back and see him in a week's time. When she returned, Gandhi spoke to her son and asked him to stop eating sweets as a personal favour to him. The boy, as you might imagine, did as he was asked and is alive and well to this day.

But what difference had waiting a week made? the mother wanted to know. Gandhi explained that he too had a sweet tooth and would not ask anyone, especially a child, to give up something that he himself had not. Don't ask me why the story stuck. I guess it has something to do with putting yourself in the other man's position, heart and mind, before you offer advice, let alone make any suggestions. And yes, I did think of John Stillman and his missing daughter, in fact hardly ten minutes went by without me recalling that riven look on his face when I'd turned him down. I doubt if Gandhi would have had one of his children go missing in order to understand Stillman's agony but I don't suppose he would have left him to get on with it either.

Breakfast came and went and Ellie slept through it. By nine o'clock I was getting restless. At ten I turned the radio up louder than necessary. By eleven I was getting annoyed that Ellie wasn't responding to it. The only thing that kept me in check was a sense of history repeating itself. My mother hated me sleeping late, no matter what time I'd fallen into bed the previous night. She would tap on the ceiling with a wooden spoon and threaten to send my father up to rouse me from slumber. He never came, of course. I'd hear them arguing about it, heated whispers presumably so as not to wake me. He'd tell her off for using him as a threat. She'd come back at him with how stupid it was for me to sleep my life away. He'd put an end to the discussion by going to the pub for a lunchtime drink.

Truth was, they didn't fancy a confrontation with the hormonal teenager above their heads, recovering from a boozy night out. Anymore than I did, thirty-odd years later. On top of everything else the fudge brownie had started to dry out. I cut a slice off to go with an early lunch and, as I raised it to my mouth, I realised what it had been trying to tell me all morning. Ellie wasn't here. If she had been, no matter what time she'd come home last night, she'd have hacked off a slice and eaten it.

It was 12.15, I noticed, as I climbed the stairs, calling as I went. "Ellie? You there?"

I knocked on her bedroom door. No answer. I opened it carefully, watching the hand that turned the doorknob. I had so gripped it that my fingernails had gone red, the flesh around them bloodless white. I took a deep breath and entered.

She wasn't there. The bed hadn't been slept in. I stood back and took another deep breath. Then another and another. I was being stupid, I told myself. Ellie had lived in Paris on her own for a whole year. Did I believe that every single night she'd gone back to the flat in Saint Germain? Had I really wanted her to be street-stupid and dumb innocent, tucked up with a mug of cocoa by ten-thirty? Well, yes but no, if you see what I mean. She'd stayed out in Paris. She'd stayed out here, in Winchendon. Go downstairs, I told myself. Make a cup of tea. Eat that chunk of brownie.

By two o'clock I needed some serious help. I phoned Laura to ask if she'd found my binoculars in her suitcase.

"Why would I have taken them?" she said.

"I didn't say you'd taken them, I asked if you'd found them."

"To have found them I would have had to take them in the first place."

"Okay, then, have it your way. Why did you take them?"

There was a pause before Laura fell back on an old favourite.

"What are you drinking?"

"Tea."

There was a grunt of disbelief at the other end and we were all at sea in one of our typical phone conversations, suspicion on her part, defensiveness on mine and the whole thing shot through with power pauses.

"There's something wrong. I'm coming over."

The phone went dead and I set the binoculars in question down on the kitchen table.

Ten minutes later Laura propped her bike against the kitchen wall and entered through the back door. She looked round, presumably checking for whisky bottles, and I raised the mug I was drinking tea from. Only then did she come close and kiss me on the cheek.

"I see you found them then," she said, her eyes coming to rest on the binoculars.

"They were in Ellie's room."

She nodded and filled the kettle.

"How is she?"

"She isn't here. She hasn't come home yet."

Laura glanced at her watch. "Then she certainly is annoyed with you…"

She'd done exactly what I knew she would. She had cycled over at a leisurely pace, heard that Ellie wasn't home yet and, like the good doctor she was, had seen off my worst fears. Ellie was probably with an old friend in Thame, probably stoned out her mind, yes, but alive and well nonetheless. The imagined pile-up on the M40 that had flickered through my mind an hour ago, leaving seven people under the age of twenty dead, had been just that – a flicker.

I was about to confess my slight embarrassment at having thought otherwise when the tables began to turn. I hadn't reckoned on the infectious nature of worry where teenagers are concerned.

"All the same," Laura began, pensively, "I never thought of Ellie as one for revenge."

"She isn't," I assured her. "None of them…"

"Then why stay out and get you in a lather?"

"You just said there was nothing to worry about."

"I don't think I used those words, though of course there isn't anything to worry about, but…" She glanced at her watch. "It's 2.30. That makes it sixteen hours since she walked out of Plum Tree. That's a hell of a long time to go AWOL. My father would have killed me."

"I like the sound of him."

"Have you rung any of her friends?"

"No. Why would I have…?"

She was frowning now. Anxiety had taken hold. "Do you know if she has an address book, or something on her computer? Of course she does. Where is it?"

"Upstairs in her room," I said. "So you are concerned, only you gave the impression that…"

"Go and get it."

When I returned from Ellie's bedroom with a print-out of her address file, Laura dug into her shoulder bag for reading glasses, perched them on the end of her nose and went over to the phone. She turned and gestured that I should make the tea which either of us really wanted.. It was the doctor keeping the patient occupied in the face of alarming news.

The first three numbers she rang were old friends of Ellie certainly, but they hadn't heard from her in months. How was she doing? Would Laura get Ellie to ring them? The fourth number had seen Ellie the last time she came home, at Christmas, but as far as he knew she was back in Paris now. Did Laura want her email address? The fifth number, another bloke, had seen Ellie just the other day in Thame, but he couldn't suggest where Laura might find her now…

Eleanor Margaret Hawk, nineteen and tall. That would be the first line of any description. Blond hair down to her waist, grey eyes, good skin, good figure, wears lots of costume jewellery. Rings, bracelets, stuff round her neck. Dressed a bit classily today. Black and white top, black trousers, smart boots. The usual leather jacket, though…

The sixth number didn't know where Ellie was either. The seventh and eighth on the list hadn't seen her since before the trip to LA.

How do people do it? How do you walk into a mortuary and while those around you, coppers included, observe the courtesies of bereavement, how do you look down at your daughter's face and say yes, that's her?

The ninth number hadn't even heard that Ellie was back in England. Nor had the tenth. The eleventh couldn't have cared less…

Laura screwed up the printout angrily.

"This is lunacy!" she barked. "When I walked in here the worst I expected to see was you, pissed! Twenty minutes later I'm halfway to believing Ellie's dead! I'm not playing anymore."

She batted the ball of paper across the kitchen.

"So now you think she's okay?"

"Of course she's okay! She's one of the most sensible women of her age I've ever met!"

"Ah, of her age… that makes a difference?"

Her anger released its grip as quickly as it had taken hold.

"Maybe that's what all this is about, Nathan. You still think of her as a child."

She reached out and straightened the neck of my T shirt and just as I was about to argue the point she'd made, we heard a car draw up on the gravel at the end of Morton Lane.

We hurried to the window and looked out in time to see Ellie get out of a battered Fiat Punto. She thanked the driver and watched him execute a five-point turn before juddering off the way he'd come.

I paused for a moment, then turned to Laura and said, "Best not say anything, eh?"

"What a good idea," she said, with only a hint of irony. "Let's pretend that you haven't just spent three hours up on the ceiling."

And with that agreed upon, Ellie entered to find Laura washing up two mugs and me examining the leg of the kitchen table. She paused at the door to gauge the temperature.

"Hi, Ellie," I said, glancing up.

"Hi! What's wrong?"

"Laura thinks it might be… woodworm. Still…"

I brushed the leg with my hand as if that would cure it. Ellie's face lit up.

"Ah, brownie! Thanks, Laura."

"No, no, I made that," I said, feebly.

She chuckled as she reached for a slice. "Sure, Dad, like you baked a cake!"

She jerked her head at Laura, inviting girlie agreement that fudge brownie was beyond my powers. She sat down at the table.

"You got my message, then?"

You could've cut the air between me and Laura with a cake slice.

"Message?" I asked, eventually. "What message?"

"Call-minder, Dad? You know, messages on the phone?"

I looked at her for a moment, rose to my feet and went to the phone. I dialled 1571. "Welcome to BT Answer," the voice told me. "You have one new message. Message received today at 7.30 a.m…"

I'd been down at The Biggin.

"Dad, it's okay," said Ellie's voice on the tape. "I forgive you. Listen, just to let you know, I ended up at Clare Parker's house. I'm going into Oxford with her this morning. Thought I might as well, seeing as how I'm all tarted up. See you this afternoon. Love yer."

I put the phone down and looked at her.

"What?" she asked, in her usual combative way.

I went over and gestured for her to stand up.

"You didn't get it, did you? You thought I was dog meat somewhere? Dad, for God's sake!"

I threw my arms round her and held her.

"No, no, I wasn't worried, or anything, just…"

Laura was heading towards the back door. She paused to take a slice of brownie with her.

"Don't go Laura," said Ellie. "Things to tell. Don't fancy him pulling the heavy father again."

It's an ill wind that blows nobody any good. Above all else I shall remember the day of Ellie's non-disappearance as the moment when Laura was officially welcomed into our family, at least by one of my children. Ellie asked her to stay. She needed her help.

Over the next half hour Ellie laid her soul bare and we listened, occasionally asking a question and nodding in wise agreement at the answer. Ellie had had enough of being a student and had decided to quit. She knew I wouldn't be pleased, she knew I'd paid good money for the course at the

Sorbonne, the room in Paris and the peace of mind that comes from giving your daughter a good start in life. However…

Yesterday she hadn't been into Oxford to buy dope, she had gone to meet Clare Parker who was working on The Oxford Gazette. They'd been emailing each other for the past three months and the possibility of Ellie working at The Gazette had been mooted. She'd written to the editor, sent him articles about being a student in Paris. He'd liked them. Today she'd been to meet him and he'd offered her a job, right down on the bottom rung for two pence a week, starting Monday week. She'd taken it.

What she didn't say, of course, was that for the foreseeable future she'd be living with me, here in Beech Tree. But that was okay. The fifty quid she'd skanked off me wasn't explained either. But even that was okay. I didn't give in to my worst fears or suspicions. I just carried on listening to her, glad to be hearing the voice, to be held by the wonderful grey eyes. An hour ago it had been a different story. In my mind at least, I'd been hovering near that state of dread brought on by the death of a child. Ellie had gone missing, never to be seen, heard or argued with again.

And what I had felt for that brief period of time, John Stillman had been feeling for three solid months.

***

The Rottweiler in female form who answered the door at Mayfield House was six foot tall and it suited her down to the ground. She gazed at me from over the top of lowered spectacles for just long enough to let me know that she didn't like the look of me.

"Can I help you?" she asked.

"I'd like a word with Mr Stillman."

"He's not back yet, I'm afraid. And since you've made no appointment…"

The steady gaze, the arm on the door barring my entrance said: go away. A slight twist of the thin lips seemed to add: and don't come back again.

"I'll wait then," I said.

"He may be some time."

"All the better. You and I can get to know each other, Mrs...?"

"Jenkins. Mr Stillman's housekeeper."

I was still on the doorstep and, short of using a blunt instrument on her, that's where I was going to remain.

"Then give him a message for me, will you?" I said. "Tell him I've changed my mind."

"Will he know what that refers to?"

"He will if you tell him my name. Nathan Hawk."

She clearly knew where I fitted in and what I was talking about. Her attitude changed almost immediately, not to anything soft and approachable, but formally polite.

"You'd better come in, Mr Hawk," she said. "If you'd care to go through to the library, I'll bring you some tea."

-4-

Detective Sergeant Jim Kelloway, the copper who'd investigated Teresa's disappearance, looked exactly like he sounded on the phone. He was just shy of six foot tall with thick, white hair that seemed to melt over the crown of an unusually large head. The quick, blue eyes bespoke intelligence and, I guessed correctly, a range of other interests outside the job. He was dressed in cotton slacks and a lightweight jacket, shirt and tie, all good quality. However, he told the time from a bog standard watch with a leather strap and wore no gold at his cuffs or round his neck. His brand of aftershave was the same as mine. He was a man who lived on his salary and nothing more.

He stretched an arm across the counter at Thame nick and shook my hand. "Guvnor, nice to meet you!"

There was a trace of Irish in the accent but nothing to write home about. Originally from County Cork, the family had settled here after the war. Fifteen years in the Met, then another four in the Thames Valley backwoods, had knocked most of Kelloway's native lilt out of him.

"I thought we'd go to The Swan," he went on. "Maiden Lane. Do you know it?"

I nodded. "Didn't know it was a coppers' pub, though."

"It isn't. That's the beauty."

With it being market day, Maiden Lane was bollarded off and jam-packed with stalls whose owners had wound down for the lunchtime break. On the edge of proceedings, in nervous permanence, stood a row of shops whose owners struggled to make a living the rest of the week. And no wonder. The Cake Shop, for example, hired baking trays to young women whose nagging children had imminent birthdays. A novelty shop sold adult car stickers and double entendre T-shirts. Above Giovanni's Deli you could buy or rent second-hand curtains from Giovanni's mother, so long as you were quick about it. She was having a closing down sale.

The Swan was a sixteenth century pub, tall and crooked with timber-framed rooms upstairs that overhung the cobbled walkway below and seemed to be pulling the building forwards into impending collapse. We ducked beneath a sign warning us to mind our heads and stepped down into the main bar. The reason for it not being a police pub was immediately obvious. You couldn't have swung a baton in the place, let alone settled a squad of coppers down for the night. Despite the fact that the floor level had been lowered – in 1873, Kelloway told me, he was Chair of the local history society – it was still a dangerous place to stand up suddenly in. To make things worse it was badly lit by a low-voltage strip-light in the centre of the room, beneath which half a dozen flies were dive-bombing the market traders who'd come in for lunch.

"So, you're going to show us how it's done, Guvnor?" said Kelloway as I set a Belgian beer down on the table in front of him.

"If I thought I was smarter than you, Jim, I wouldn't be here picking your brains."

He'd asked for his beer in a bottle and when I raised my own whisky I realised why. An inch of scum, courtesy of the previous users, was welded to the rim of the glass. I turned and signalled to the barman, who chose to ignore me.

"I've known John Stillman for twenty years," said Kelloway. "From way back in the Met. He can be very persuasive. I mean when he rang to report her missing he asked for me by name, so I was obliged. Regional Crime

Squad had a full book at the time – a Securicor hi-jacking at Wheatley, a bombing in Oxford – so I knew I'd be dealing with it on my own."

"Christ, at least Morse had Lewis."

"Oh, I had a couple of DCs on call, much good they did me. There are no artisans left in our job, Guvnor. It's all BAs in Criminology, computer printouts, lazy bastards who'd rather nick an old lady for three motoring offences than a villain for something decent…" He paused and smiled at himself. "Sorry."

He took a swig from his bottle then placed a thumb over the rim to stop the contents foaming over.

"Anyway, Teresa Marie Stillman," he went on. "With no body and no weapon it was a case of a grown woman not turning up when she said she would. Officially, she's just another Missing Person." He bit his lip for a moment or two. "Missing, with over seven thousand quid unaccounted for, though. Cash."

"Where from?"

"Michael Carter, the man they were working for. He asked Teresa to take the money round to the County Landscapes boss."

"And she didn't?"

"She tried, we reckon, but Mary Harper, the said boss, was at the doctor's." He took another swig at the now becalmed beer. "It's tempting to follow the money, but poor old Mary fell off her perch about a month ago. Coronary. Closed a few doors on us."

"That doesn't stop seven grand being a fair old sum to kill for. Not life-changing to most, I grant you…"

He began drumming his long, bony fingers on the table, watching them intently, as if one might suddenly make a dash for it. I reckoned he was deciding just how much more to tell me. The drumming stopped.

"Listen, I'll help you all I can. Out of respect. For you and John. But I'd like your assurance. Anything you turn up, bring it to me."

I nodded. "You can have the kudos, Jim, I'll take the money."

He smiled. "We boiled it down to three names, none of them much to write home about. Michael Carter was front-runner. Forty years old, successful, beautiful wife – Japanese, which explains the garden. However, just as they were finishing the job, Carter found out that Teresa was the daughter of the man who'd put him away for eight years. John Stillman."

"I like that. What did he go down for?"

"Manslaughter. Thing is, Carter's rich now, respectable, his star's in the ascendant. Why mess all that up just to get even?" It was a naïve remark for someone in our trade, but I let it go. "Besides, to take it any further we'd have needed a body, not just Stillman nagging away at us."

"Who was your second name?"

He drew in his lips then let them go with a smack. "A bloke called Thomas Gibson, thirty years old. He was taken on to do the hard graft. Carpenter by trade, but handy at most things." He smiled. "You know how it goes, Guv. Good-looking bloke works with beautiful woman, 24/7, the rest is natural history."

"Till something goes wrong."

"He has form, true enough. For car theft. Long way from murder."

"Your third?"

"A woman called Joanna Bailey. She hit the radar because she's known to us as well. Credit card stuff six years ago. Suspended sentence." He shook his head. "Jesus Christ, talking to that woman was a right bloody chore." I was beginning to feel that quite a few things were a right bloody chore to Jim Kelloway, in spite of his rant about lazy coppers. "Butterfly mind. Flits from bloom to bloom, you follow and just as you get there she moves on. She couldn't focus long enough to murder someone."

It was another strange belief for a copper of his rank and this time I couldn't let it pass.

"How long does it take to kill someone? A minute to boil over, two seconds to pick up a knife, another two to stab someone. I might just prove it if that bastard carries on ignoring me."

I was referring to the barman who was still refusing to catch my eye, being more interested in one of the market traders. Young and female.

"What about this Richard Crane?" I asked.

"Well, I'm not sure he even exists. True, somebody phoned Teresa, the day she went missing. Call came from The Travel Lodge in Botley. Payphone."

"Same guy she met at Giacometto's?"

He turned to me with a smile that showed absurdly small teeth but no doubt they did the job. "Yes, I hear you've taken to eating in Giacometto's, Guvnor."

"That bloody waiter reported me?"

"Must've done. It came down to me as a memo from Kidlington."

There was a time when slamming someone's head down on a bar was enough to guarantee their silence. Not anymore, it seemed. They complained.

"I was told to have a few words with you," Kelloway went on. "These are they. Go easy."

I was about to protest when I realised I'd be getting hot under the collar about someone who wasn't even in the room. It wasn't Map stuff but a fair testing ground for poetry, maybe.

"Let me try something on you," I said. "What men or gods are these? What maidens… something or other. What mad pursuit? Loth! Maidens loth! What struggle to escape? What pipes and… oh, fuck it, I get more wound up not remembering."

"Timbrels," he said. "Ode to a Grecian Urn."

He explained quickly that Mrs Kelloway was a big wheel in the local poetry society, but I reckon he was covering up his own love of the stuff. That would certainly explain him not asking why John Keats had suddenly hi-jacked the conversation.

Back on an even keel I said, "Listen, Jim, any chance of you pulling down Teresa Stillman's file one dark night, copying it, fetching it over to me?"

He nodded as he thought about it. "I'll see what I can do."

We shook hands on it. He finished the rest of his beer and began drumming his fingers again. Another debate with himself, it seemed, maybe he was wondering whether to confide in me again. He came down in favour.

"You know, this'll sound weird, coming from a hard-bitten old sod like me." He'd said it without a trace of self-mockery. "By rights Teresa Stillman's dead, agreed?"

"The only thing I expect to find is her body."

"Well, that's still on the cards, of course, but…"

The drumming stopped, he flattened out his hand and confessed. "…somewhere not too deep down I think she could still be alive."

I started to laugh but turned it into a cough. "You know what I think, Jim? I think you've bought into Stillman's wishful thinking. You said it yourself, he can be persuasive."

He nodded and looked down at my glass, my fingers now scratching at the muck on the rim.

"Guvnor, why don't you get yourself a fresh glass?"

"Good idea. You want another beer?"

"No, I'm fine," he said, then added with a smile, "Remember, go easy."

I rose and stooped my way across to the bar where the traders were downing their drinks ready for the two o'clock start. The Thame housewives would soon be pouring out of the farmhouse cafés ready to spend their money again.

The barman turned, raised an eyebrow for my order. I leaned in towards him and said quietly, "Beauty is truth, truth beauty, that is all ye know on earth and all ye need to know."

I won't say it changed his attitude towards me or that it put me in a better frame of mind, but at least he was now giving me his full attention.

"It's John Keats," I said. "You must know him, surely."

He delved into his memory but nothing surfaced.

"Does he come in here?"

"Not any more and I think I know the reason." I tapped the rim of the glass. "I didn't specifically ask for a clean glass but that's what I wanted. Can I have one?"

He glanced at Kelloway who endorsed my request with a long, slow blink. The barman filled a clean glass to the brim with ice, then poured a double measure of scotch over it and raised a hand to assure me that it was on the house. No hassle, no threats from me, no raised voice. Witness the power of romantic poetry.

***

The following day, while I was out shopping, Jim Kelloway delivered a CD of the Teresa Stillman case notes to Beech Tree Cottage. According to Ellie he was a bag of nerves. She invited him in for a coffee but he declined, preferring to stand on the doorstep glancing round all the time, presumably for fear of being spotted by colleagues. He needn't have bothered. Morton Lane hadn't seen a beat copper for over seven years. Eventually, he drew the disc from an inside pocket, slid it towards Ellie on the palm of his hand and went.

When I arrived home from Waitrose she dived into one of the shopping bags before I'd even set it down and took out a packet of cheese and onion crisps.

"I'll put that stuff away," she said.

"No, it's okay, love, you finish your crisps…"

"Dad, just dump it."

I did as she asked, but with a fair degree of apprehension. It wasn't simply that Ellie was tidy beyond human endurance it was more that her sense of where things go follows a logic all of its own. We noticed it when she was about twelve. Her homework lived in the shoe cupboard, that being somewhere she would have to visit before leaving for school. Her ballet stuff lived in the boot of my car because I was the one who drove her to the class on Saturday morning. She kept her pocket money on the top shelf in the attic. The effort involved in retrieving it meant she only spent what she absolutely needed to. There wasn't much danger to the food I'd just bought but I feared for the batteries, the shoe-polish and the new dog brush.

I printed off the case notes and sat down in Maggie's dad's rocker to read them while Ellie bustled back and forth to the fridge and the utility room.

"Coffee?" she said when she'd finished.

"That'd be nice."

I laid the notes aside. "Teresa Stillman. Who would you think had the key to it, Ellie? Apart from her father. Not that parents seem to know too much about their kids these days."

The remark wasn't lost on her. She smiled. "What are the options?"

"The man she worked for, a female employee and a sort of boyfriend."

"What do you mean 'sort of'?"

"Thomas Gibson. Criminal record, prison, nothing really drastic. Father was a brickie, did his back in, mother served school dinners to make up for it."

She nodded. "Sounds like he was Teresa's bit of rough. Some women are like that. It's either low self-esteem or, more usually, rebellion against their parents' aspirations."

"I hope that isn't the voice of experience talking."

"No, Dad. A-level Psychology."

"Doesn't chance play a part in it all?"

"Dad, chance doesn't play a part in everything. A-level Religious Studies. Old chestnut of an essay question. There's your coffee. GCSE Domestic Science."

"Right, boyfriend first, then. Where's Dogge?"

Dogge answered by rising from beneath the table and shaking out her coat, head to tail.

"Where does he live, this Gibson?" asked Ellie.

I went back to the case notes. "Chapel Farm, Tiddington."

"On the way to Oxford," she said, brightly. "You can give me a ride."

"Wherefore Oxford?"

"I was thinking of getting myself a couple of tops for next week, The Gazette. And I've got some money left over from the holiday."

Really, I thought. Then why did you touch me for fifty quid the other day?

"Trouble is," she went on, "I kind of know what I want and, well…"

"How much?"

"Fifty should do it. I'll pay you back when I start work."

The magic number fifty again. What the hell was she up to? And why, with all the questions I wanted to ask her, did my hand go to my wallet and draw out two twenties and a ten? She pecked me on the cheek as I handed her the money.

"Thanks, Dad, you're a star."

She grabbed her jacket from its new home on top of the fridge and hurried to the door.

"I thought you wanted a lift…"

"There's a bus in ten minutes from the church. See yer."

The back door was opening, she was walking through it, and I was fighting for words.

"Dinner, Ellie, what about…?"

"Count me out, Dad," she yelled from the garden. "I'll get something in Oxford."

She was gone. I've wanted Maggie back on many occasions since she died. Less as time's gone by. But I wanted her then. I wanted the niggling doubts about our youngest daughter, which were costing me fifty quid every time she saw me, nipped in the bud.

-5-

When I was a kid, ten years old, I used to dream of becoming a farmer. It was more than a dream, now I come to think of it, it was a deep-seated yearning.

It all began when my grandfather bought me this set of encyclopaedias one Christmas. Volume 11 was entitled Farming in Britain and was the only book in the set I ever read and I read it from cover to cover, over and over again. There wasn't a photograph or diagram I can't recall to this day, not a page in it I didn't virtually know by heart. From the tables of pig breeds, to the 30 pages on dairy farming via the section on hill farming in Wales, I kept the text in my head as if one day I might be called upon to hand it down to ensuing generations. It was like poetry to me. On those harsh winter nights – they were much colder then, much darker, longer, quieter – I would read under the bed-clothes by the light of a torch and be pitched into an exquisite dilemma.

The book straddled two worlds and I felt obliged to know them both and choose between them. The one was a gentle, seductive place where men tilled the land, tended stock, gathered the harvest with bare hands and crude implements. The other was a place where tractors were the new factotums, reluctantly admired for their versatility, grudgingly praised for their speed and economy. I knew where my loyalties lay, however. In the hands-on world of hayricks and working horses. The horses were kings. I could hear their hooves on the cobbles, I could feel the power they exuded, smell the sweat on their bodies – I could name them, harness them, groom them, work them, feed them in days of sunshine and gentle showers.

As with most fantasies, it was hollow at the core for not once did I consider – the book didn't allow the reader to – the prospect of icy winds or acid rains. Undisclosed were the ethics of the abattoir, the veal calf, the battery hen – the knacker's yard for my beloved horses. And, strangely, even at ten years old, I knew I was turning a blind eye to the downside of my romance. I knew, for some reason, that it was all too good to be true.

And as I drove down the track to Chapel Farm I felt as if fate had rescued me from a dream that was a mere slip of a cog away from being a nightmare, for there in front of me, up on the high field that overlooked the farmhouse, was the solitary tractor, spraying poison on the ripening maize. The lone farmer seated in the cab was chained for yet another long day to the far away company of Radio Four. At the mercy of his own thoughts. He saw the Land Rover on the track beside the field, raised the arms of the sprayer and drove down between the lines of sweetcorn towards me. He switched off the engine and climbed stiffly out of the cab, removing the protective mask from his nose and mouth.

He was a man probably in his late 50s but looking ten years older, with a thick red skin, bluing at the surface, and crooked teeth I tried not to look at.

"You shouldn't be here," he said, severely. "This stuff is dangerous."

"What is it?" I asked.

"Well, that ain't hardly the point. I mean I tell you it's dangerous and you… It's okay after a couple of days, but not right after you…"

This was a man who didn't finish his sentences, presumably because most of the time there was no one around to listen to them.

"You from DEFRA?"

I laughed. "I'm not the man from the ministry, no."

He looked at the Land Rover, battered and bruised in all its glory. "Come to think of it, they'd give you a better deal to ride round in."

"I'm looking for Tom Gibson. I've got his address as Chapel Farm, Tiddington."

He looked past me while he thought how best to answer.

"This is Chapel Farm alright and I'm Brian Chapel but… Well, it isn't strictly true that he lives here. Nor is it not. What you want him for?"

"I need his help."

That seemed to reassure him. "You want him to work for you? Bloke sure knows how to work. He helps me occasionally and him and me, well… you can imagine…"

I couldn't but it didn't really matter. "So where is he? Up at the house?"

He chuckled again, as briefly as before. "Oh, no, no. My old girl and him, they don't see eye to eye on much at all. He's down by the river."

He turned and nodded eastwards, down the dip in the landscape to where a small woodland of beech trees seemed to float on a sea of flowering rape.

"Other side of them trees. Follow this track down, then drive across the field. You'll see a meadow, few sheep, goes down to the Thame and well…"

"Is he fishing there?" I asked.

"Could be. You'll see his tent." He nodded into the Land Rover at Dogge. "Don't want her chasing the stock. You keep hold of her."

"She'll be okay." I sniffed the air before getting back behind the wheel. "I see what you mean about the spray. Gets to the back of your throat."

He took it as a criticism and justified the use of it. "Yeah, but it means you get to eat the sweetcorn and the bugs don't."

As far as I was concerned, the bugs could have it. I hate the stuff. I fired the engine and left him to his poison.

The furrowed slope of the hill rocked and tossed the Land Rover on its way down to the woodland. As I neared it a gang of rooks, having left it as long as they could, suddenly rose from the tops of the trees they were conferring in. They circled the newcomer, waiting for me to pass and when I was safely out of the way the first of them descended again.

Ahead of me now was an ancient meadow, dusted yellow with buttercups, scuffed white with sheep. But for its proximity to the crop sprayer it might have been out of my childhood fantasy, apart from the metal gate to it, chained and padlocked against the twenty-first century.

I parked the Land Rover and climbed over the gate, reaching back to give Dogge a hand and together we walked down towards the river. The water was low and slow moving and dying grasses hung long and tangled down the steep banks. In the distance, on the other side, I could see a small, green ridge-tent, large enough for two. Close to it, on a bend, a man was crouched over a small wood fire, raking the embers. I couldn't make out details of him or his encampment, but he spotted me and began to tidy his kingdom.

When I reached the river bend, I stopped at a long wooden stave, stuck loosely into the ground. Some device for measuring the water's depth, I imagined.

I called out across the river, "Tom Gibson?"

He was preparing a fish for cooking over the fire, running a wooden skewer through it, nose to tail. A trout, I guessed. He scrutinised me for a moment before owning his name.

"Yeah?"

"I'd like to talk to you. About Teresa Stillman."

He looked as fit as a flea and with living down here, three miles away from the nearest community, my guess was that he'd gone slightly feral. I wasn't too keen on the knife in his hand, either. He'd been working on the fish with it.

"You a copper?"

"Was a copper. How do I get over there? Is there a bridge?"

He smiled. "There's a bridge alright. Two mile down. Otherwise, do what I do."

He lifted a ten-foot pole, similar to the one planted in the ground beside me.

"You pole vault it?" I said, unable to hide my admiration.

"Take a good run, dig it in firm and over you come."

"Next time." I sat down and took off my boots and socks. "How deep is it?"

"About a foot today."

I hand-sledged down to the water's edge, stepped in and set off through the curling weeds and over a bed of sharp gravel, working to keep my balance.

The water was cold, colder than I'd expected, and I guess it was the feel and sound of it rushing past my ankles that shrank my fear to almost nothing. Maybe Ellie hadn't acquired a taste for skunk after all. Maybe she wasn't scrounging off me in order to get as baked as a cake…

Tom leaned down and stretched out a hand. I took it and in three ascending steps I was up on the bank beside him. Dogge was already shaking the water from her coat, prior to a nose job on the surroundings.

"Nice place you've got here," I said.

It was too. It was like a homestead without the house. Clearly an able man with his hands, Gibson had made a 15-yard fence out of wood from the nearby willows and set it against the prevailing wind. This side of it he was growing cabbages and beans in an immaculate plot. At one end of it there were flowers. Maggie's favourites, sweet peas.

"Just temporary," he said of the camp, as if trying to excuse it.

He must've seen me eyeing the tattoo on his chest, or as much of it as was visible. A bird of prey appeared to have him at its mercy, the hooked bill either side of his throat. Not a hawk. Something far bigger. He undid the shirt.

"Golden eagle," he said. "Aquila Chrysaetos. Or was it the gold chain you had your eye on? Teresa gave it to me."

The voice was quiet and clipped and somewhere along the line Tom Gibson had been educated, I reckoned.

"You and her were friendly, I gather?"

His whole head seemed to smile at that. His eyes screwed up, the beaky nose buckled and the furrows on his forehead rippled all the way to the crown of his shaven head. He said nothing so I carried on.

"Let me tell you something you won't like," I said. "I think she's dead and if I'm right the most likely person to have killed her is you. See, most people are killed by someone they know, usually husband, wife or lover."

That wiped the smiled off his head. "Who sent you?"

"I'm working for her father. You know him?"

"Not really. When I met him he seemed friendly enough, given his trade and my past history."

He stooped and laid the skewered fish across the glowing embers of the fire.

"How long have you been here, Tom?"

"Couple of months. Came just after Teresa went missing, to help Brian out. His regular man had just left."

"Will you make it through the winter out here?"

"Can't see why not. If it gets too cold I'll go sleep in one of the barns."

In her sweep of the area Dogge had arrived at the tent and now barked to attract my attention, feinting at the zipped opening.

"What's her problem?" Gibson asked.

"Cannabis, at a rough guess. Or any one of fifty other substances."

"So you are a cop."

"No, we're both retired, but for different reasons. Me on account of... a spot of bother, her because she was useless at the job. Though clearly not as useless as they thought."

He smiled and called Dogge to his side. He fussed her gently and she looked up at him.

"Cannabis," he told her. "Personal use."

He gave her a couple of fish heads and their friendship was sealed.

"That spot of bother sounds interesting."

"Quite the opposite. I smacked a fellow officer, broke his jaw."

I went over to the fire and looked down at the fish.

"You want one?" he asked

"Wouldn't say no."

He went to a keep net, took out a trout and minutes later had cleaned it, boned it and run it through with a wooden skewer. He set it down above the embers next to his own.

As we sat eating the fish with rock hard bread and a salad of nearby leaves that he assured me were safe, I tried again.

"What happened that Friday, the weekend she disappeared?"

He thought back to it with a familiarity that comes from regular visits. "Funny day, weather kept changing and we were… crabby. Tired, I suppose. End of jobbish."

"Teresa was crabby too?"

"More on edge, I'd say. She didn't want to leave the garden to the Carters."

"Didn't trust 'em to look after it, eh?"

"Something like that."

"You ever heard of a man called Richard Crane?"

"Yeah. From Kelloway."

"You didn't know him before?"

"No." He addressed his further thoughts on Crane to the fire in front of us. "I know he's the big unanswered question in all this but I reckon he was a genuine punter. Kelloway was so short of suspects he blew him out of all proportion."

"Genuine punter? Why?"

"Why would you buy lunch for a woman you're going to kill?"

"Crane's never come forward to clear that one up," I pointed out.

He shrugged and said there could have been a dozen innocent reasons for that. I agreed.

"When did you first learn that Teresa was missing?"

He moved a fish bone forward in his mouth and spat it onto the fire.

"Tuesday, when I turned up at the new job. Jo – Joanna Bailey – was already there, along with a couple of students who did the fetch and carry stuff. Teresa wasn't. I waited most of the day then phoned her father."

"You didn't try her own phone?"

"Switched off. That bothered me."

"Well, whoever turned it off, he's the guy I'm after. If you know anything else, Tom, something you couldn't tell Jim Kelloway…"

He turned and looked at me coldly. "Just one thing. You may not like this but there are people on the edge of this business with reasons for being there… other than just… finding out what happened."

He had put the sentence together haltingly and stripped it of any compelling sense.

"What the hell does that mean?" I asked. "You'd like it to be more complicated than it is? It's dead simple. You were keener on her than she was on you."

He laughed sourly. "You couldn't be more wrong."

"So why didn't the pair of you have a date that Friday evening? Or the Saturday, Sunday, Monday?"

There was a weary self-righteousness in his voice as he proffered his alibi.

"Because I went home to see Mum and Dad for the weekend. Manningtree, Essex. I borrowed the County Landscapes pickup to drive down there."

"It gets more straightforward by the minute," I said. "You went home because that's where people go when they screw up, when they're in deep shit. D'you know, I reckon there's a lovers' quarrel in here somewhere."

"Jesus, you coppers are all the bloody same!"

"It's the main reason people kill each other. Things got out of hand, you thumped her and down she went. And, covered in confusion, you fucked off to Essex." I glanced round his territory. "Is that where you've dumped her? Not here."

He sprang to his feet and looked down at me. There was plenty he wanted to say, if the screwed up face and limbs were anything to go by, but the words wouldn't come.

"Well if that isn't how it was," I said, "why didn't you phone her over the weekend?"

"I did, I just told you!" he yelled. "Her phone was switched off. The whole time."

"Which points to her copping it on the Friday."

And as if in response to a cue, the relative calm of the place was suddenly broken by a mobile phone pumping out a grotesque version of Greensleeves. Gibson turned and reached into the tent for the phone.

"Hi, what can I do for you?" he said, tersely. He knew the person calling him. "No, no, right now I'm not."

Not what? Not alone? Not at ease? Not telling the truth about Teresa Stillman?

He ended the call and turned to me, all set to apologise for the intrusion, but Dogge and I were making our way to the water's edge. One of us galloped, the other waded back across the river. Tom watched and as I reached the far bank and yanked on socks over wet feet, he tried to regain some of the nice guy image he thought he'd lost.

"Listen, sorry I lost my rag a bit," he said. I waved away the apology and pulled on my boots. "No, really. Teresa was the best thing that ever happened to me." I nodded. He still wasn't sure. "If you need my help again, call me?"

"I will."

I stood up and turned to walk back across the meadow. Gibson called after me with a final request.

"Whatever happens, let me know how things go, will you?"

I made a brief calculation. Of the twenty odd killers I'd known, at least half had said roughly the same thing when first interviewed. Keep in touch. Meaning, of course, let me know how close you are to nailing me.

-6-

Searching your daughter's room is a terrible thing to do. It smacks of all things controlling and abusive. So why am I doing it? I asked myself as I stood in the middle of Ellie's room later that evening. Why not just ask her if she'd be kind enough to dispel the nagging doubts that were picking away at me? Doubts made worse by her scrounging two lots of fifty quid in three days.

I ran a possible conversation through my head.

"Straight answers, Ellie. Why are you quitting The Sorbonne?"

She turns to me. Shutters come down. Her voice loses its laugh.

"Being a student isn't for me, Dad."

"Well, I don't believe you. Maybe it's years of listening to people who lied to me when their chips were down. It's made me so that I can't hear the truth even if it comes with a cast-iron alibi."

"That's your problem, not mine."

"Why so touchy now, Ellie? Why happy at night, slow in the morning? Why the two bowls of cornflakes when you come in late? Why the mood swings?"

"Because I'm your daughter."

And I'm not sure whether I say this, or just wish I had the nerve to, but Ellie where has all that promise gone? You were the kid everyone couldn't get enough of. You were bright as a star, smarter than Jaikie, Fee or even Con. You made us all laugh, you made us all gasp at your perceptions, you made us all steady our gaze on your beautiful face...

I sat down on the edge of the bed and looked round. She hadn't really had time to personalise the space yet, but there were still definite footprints that only Ellie could have left. The notes and photos pinned to the wall, the soft toys arranged in comic groups. A teddy bear was reading a book of Greek plays to a racoon. He was leaning back against her rubbish bin. I stooped down and carefully removed its contents.

I was looking for signs of disenchantment, reasons why she'd decided to change the whole course of her life. A name, an address, details of a meeting, notes to self that might have held the key. All I found were spent tissues, empty fag packets and a couple of used plasters. Not even the end of a spliff and I knew she smoked weed. I didn't know many kids who didn't. I knew dozens whose parents thought they didn't.

And as I reached the bottom of the bin so a flush of relief overtook me. There was nothing here to say that Ellie was in trouble. Not one single thing. Except, perhaps, the fact that there was nothing…

I took a deep breath right there. I felt bad enough, having ploughed through her rubbish, without making things worse by denying the evidence in front of me. Why didn't I go downstairs, make myself a cup of tea and see if there was any more fudge brownie left in the tin?

As I reached the kitchen I saw Laura through the long window, cycling down Morton Lane, majestically weaving around the pot-holes. She entered with a smile, which a moment later changed to a comical frown.

"What have you been up to?" she said.

I wouldn't have described my face as a readable one but, given what I'd been doing for the last twenty minutes, it must have had guilt written all over it. I drew her towards me, arm around her waist, and kissed her on the cheek.

"Nothing. How are you? And what's in the carrier bag?"

I could see that it contained books, mostly. The Thame Book House logo rather gave it away. She took out a small, fat anthology of poems and handed it to me.

"All sorts, modern, ancient and in-between. Great thing is it'll fit in your jacket pocket."

"I see, so I'm just about to bring Roberto's head down on the counter and I turn to page forty-seven and there she is, Miss J Hunter Dunn, Miss J Hunter Dunn, furnished and burnished by Aldershot sun."

That delighted her. "You see, you know more than you think you do!"

"There was a documentary about him the other night." I leaned in and kissed her again.

"Now tell me what you were up to."

"Worrying about Ellie. She's gone into Oxford. To buy clothes for The Gazette. She said."

"And you don't believe her?"

I smiled. "No, but since there's no evidence to prove otherwise would you mind if I changed the subject? Teresa Stillman. You've got the brains and I've got the questions to pick them with."

I explained that I'd been to Chapel Farm to see Tom Gibson and found him camped out beside the river. While I was telling her the story, Laura took a packet of Bakewell Tarts from the carrier and tried to free them from their packaging, finally using her teeth as scissors.

"Teresa was the best thing that ever happened to Tom Gibson, he said. So why has he done bugger all about finding her? In six months he hasn't turned over a single stone."

She pushed the packet across the table to me. "Maybe, like you, he feels there's no point?"

"But wouldn't he want to know what had happened to her?"

"Well, I would, certainly."

"Unless…?"

I gestured for her to complete the thought and she did so with appropriate gravitas.

"Unless I already knew."

"Right. So, I love you. We have a fight. I kill you. Accident. Problem? I have to get rid of your body. I know this farmer with land, down by the river."

I explained that Tom Gibson's encampment was definitely a place you could bury a body in and be very unlucky to have it discovered.

"On the other hand," she said, "having disposed of his victim, would he then stand guard over her grave?"

"Good point," I said. "Apart from which, Dogge would have found her. She quartered the whole site and all she found was a bit of weed. Something else bothers me. The phone. Why does a man who shies away from the rest of the world have a mobile phone? Whose beck and call is he at?"

"He has a mobile phone because the whole world has one," she said.

"You mean he doesn't have hot water, heating or sanitation, he lives in a tent, eats plants that he picks from nearby, fish he gets from the river and cooks over a wood fire… but he does have a smartphone?"

"What an advert that would make!" She ran a descriptive hand through the air between us. "The only thing in life you need!"

She then shook her head in despair, went over to the kettle and emptied out the chalky dregs. I went to the fridge to check that any milk we had was drinkable.

"As for Teresa's body," I said, "and what Tom should do with it, how about a long weekend in Essex with Mum and Dad? Bury it there?"

"Assuming she is dead."

"Tom and I both agree that she is." The milk was fine. I set it down on the table. "I was searching her room."

I don't know what made me say it. Apart from guilt. Laura looked at me and frowned her frown.

"Whose?"

"You asked me what I'd been up to. I was searching Ellie's room."

The kettle overflowed in her hand. She turned off the tap and set it down on the draining board. "That is a dreadful thing to do." She was deadly serious. "What did you find?"

"Nothing."

"Which makes it even worse."

"That's nonsense," I pointed out. "If I'd found something, fair enough, but because I didn't...?"

"It's a matter of degree, yes, but at all levels it's unforgivable."

"Okay, then, you tell me why she's thrown her Life up in the air and, in passing, why she's taken me for fifty quid, twice in three days."

She poured away the excess water and plugged in the kettle.

"Far be it from me to poke my nose into family matters," she said, "but you do know why you're doing this, I hope?"

I had a feeling that Ellie wasn't the only one who'd taken A level psychology. I raised an eyebrow, inviting her to tell me more.

"According to you, John Stillman's daughter is dead and his neglect of her will figure somewhere. So, as an antidote, in The Great Scheme of Things, you've decided to swamp Ellie with attention even though she spent last year in a foreign city all on her own and lived to tell the tale."

I waited a few moments in case there was more.

"Two birds with one stone, Nathan. Find Teresa Stillman, dead or alive, and you can get off both their cases." She paused before asking, "So what next?"

"A trip to Bath. It was going to be Michael Carter, him being the favourite on paper, but he's in France, buying wine."

"So who's in Bath?"

"A woman called Joanna Bailey who has a police record and used to work for County Landscapes. Mary Harper, the old dear whose business it was, had quite a soft spot for losers."

-7-

My trip to Bath began with an early phone call to what I hoped was still Joanna Bailey's house. A young male voice, half asleep, answered with a grunt.

"I'm sorry to call so early," I said, "but is Joanna there?"

"No."

The helpful sort, one of two sons, I imagined, whom Kelloway had diagnosed as being averse to leaving home.

"So can I reach her today?"

"She's working." My reasonable request seemed to panic him. "What time is it?"

"Eight-thirty."

"Jesus…!"

The phone went dead. But at least I'd found Joanna Bailey. Almost.

***

It was one of those freakish, blistering days that fool everyone into believing that summer has well and truly arrived. By eleven o'clock, both temperature and humidity had soared way beyond the point where tempers fray at overlong stares or imagined driving insults. We were all in the same boat, drifting down the M4 equatorial river, with some of us feeling that our own carbon emissions were partly to blame for our discomfort. And as green guilt, for having boiled too full a kettle that morning, was about to sting me, I noticed a silver grey Freelander, just after the Membury turn-off. I fancied I'd seen it way back at an Oxford filling station and I don't suppose I would've cared much but for the vehicle's tinted windows, a blue mist obscuring the driver. I put my foot down, went up to eighty and so did the Freelander. Then I dropped down to fifty and the other driver overtook me, persuading me that I'd misread the situation.

I reached the outskirts of Bath at about two o'clock and entered that contradictory world where cars, vans and juggernauts crawl bumper to bumper through the most beautiful architecture imaginable. In one reverie, however, allowed by an overlong traffic light, the gridlock dissolved and the horse-drawn carts and carriages of a former age took to the streets. From the cream stone tenements stepped maids and their mistresses, bankers and their clerks, to sing and dance in some horrendous musical. Then someone behind me hooted. The lights had changed. I checked that I'd remembered to bring The Map and moved off.

On the other side of Bath the traffic gained momentum along the Lower Bristol Road. Joanna Bailey lived on a street of small terraced houses that ran down to it, Carmody Place, built in the local stone at the turn of the century.

The front garden of number 23 was neat but not showy. A few tubs and a hanging basket drooped a profusion of winter pansies. A dividing box hedge on one side had been clipped with finicky precision. A small laburnum tree on the other side was pinched between two uprights of an iron railing.

I knocked on the front door and got that hollow sound that tells you nobody's in. You never quite believe it so you knock again, just as I did. I peered in through the bulbous square of glass above the knocker and made out the doors off the hall, all of them closed. I was considering the possibility of breaking in, perhaps from the back of the house, when a voice the other side of the hedge stated the obvious.

"They're not in."

I turned to an elderly man in a collarless shirt and baggy old trousers. He had a rough and reddish face with a host of veins near the surface, all colours of the rainbow. Red blooded, though. He'd cut himself shaving to prove it and a piece of kitchen towel marked the spot. He had a dog with him, a whippet lying flat out in the shade. They must've been ninety years old, man and dog.

"What about this weather then?" he said.

"Amazing." That could have meant I loved it or hated it, but either way we agreed. "Do you know where she's gone?"

"University. There's a do on." He smiled, a naughty boy smile. "Jo and the boys are cooking for it. That's why I'm staying home today. She brings back the leftovers."

"And where will I find the university?"

"Bottom of the road, turn left, follow the signs."

"Thank you, Mr…?"

"Conroy. Archie Conroy."

***

I turned into the campus near Newton St Loe and followed the narrow road through two miles of working farmland. It rose either side of me, in small vistas, changing as the road twisted but always declaring that this wasn't a farm struggling to survive like most I knew. This was rich man's land and plenty of money had been spent on wrought iron fencing, freshly planted woodland and brand new cattle grids.

Rounding one of the bends, I slowed to a halt and looked down on the collection of buildings, half a mile ahead of me. Central to them was the main house, four square Georgian in the local stone. Once an extravagant reminder of its owner's wealth, now it was the hub of the academic village that had grown up around it, some of the buildings in keeping with the original, other more recent ones reflecting the age they'd been built in. The very latest was more glass than stone, more steel than timber, more offensive than pleasing to the eye.

Just as I was about to drive on, I glanced in the side mirror to see a vehicle come round the bend behind me and brake hard enough to raise smoke from its back tyres. It was the silver grey Freelander. I waited a full minute to see what the driver would do next but he expected me to make the first move. I got out and walked back to him. He chose to stay put behind the obscurity of tinted windows, his engine still running. I pulled at his door. It was locked.

"At least roll down the window," I said.

There was a pause before the window slid down and John Stillman looked out at me through a haze of cigarette smoke.

"Mr Hawk," he said with forced casualness. "What a pleasant surprise."

"Not for me, I'm afraid. What are you doing here?"

He fixed me with a courtroom stare and a voice to match. "I should have thought that was obvious. Value for money." He turned to light a fresh cigarette from the lighter on the dash, then stepped down onto the tarmac. "How much did we eventually settle on?"

"Fifty quid an hour."

He shrugged. "Well, there you are, you see. I need to know that I'm not wasting it."

"My expenses were on top of that."

"All mounts up…"

"And there was a bonus for if and when I find her."

It was the wrong thing to have said. He threw down his cigarette and turned to me, eyes darting all over my face.

"So now you think you will?!"

"You're editing. You know what I meant."

But the pistol had been fired and John Stillman was off down the track, hurdling over logic, chasing the unlikely possibility that Teresa was still alive.

"Correct me if I'm mistaken," he said, "but I detect a sea-change here. I'm a lawyer, we home in on slips of the tongue. People have been hung on the strength of them and you said… you said 'when' I find her. You can't unsay a thing like that!"

"John…"

He held out his hand and slowly screwed it into a fist, his finger joints cracking.

"That bonus. How much was it? I'll double it!" I must've smiled, though I certainly hadn't meant to. "What's funny?"

"There was no bonus, Mr Stillman. We didn't even discuss an hourly rate. I threw them in to prove that you're not here to keep track of your money."

He raised his hands in capitulation, then slapped his pockets for his cigarettes but they were in the car. He followed the smoke from the long butt he'd thrown down, picked it up and drew on it.

"So why are you here?" I asked.

He took his time answering.

"When you find her…" He waved away any possible dissent. "When you find her I want to be there. I don't care what she's done, where she's been or who with or why or… I don't care. You've a daughter, man, you must know what I'm talking about!"

"Of course I do, but if I'm to find her you must let me do it in my own way. That doesn't involve you being two paces behind me, cheering me on."

He eventually nodded, in something close to agreement, then said quietly, "It's over four months since I last saw her, you know. Usually it seems like only yesterday. Today it seems a hundred years ago. Why is that?"

"That's the kind of trick your mind plays when you give it nothing else to think about. Look, why don't we go get ourselves a drink, a bite to eat. The grub's good here today, I'm told."

He shook his head. "No, you're right, I shouldn't be traipsing round after you. I'll head home and leave you to it." He smiled and climbed back into the Freelander, yelling one final inducement to me through the open window. "On the subject of bonuses, though, when you find her you can have everything I've got!"

He bumped a perfect U-turn on the grass verge and sped away.

***

I parked the Land Rover in a field of small salary cars, the kind that researchers, teachers and lecturers buy. The odd Jag and Bentley must've belonged to the top brass or visiting dignitaries. Near to the gate, a black limo, older than me but just as serviceable, sported a City Corporation badge on the bonnet. A sign pointed the way to a marquee pitched behind the main building, which itself stood beside a long, narrow lake, fashioned a century ago by damning the stream that once flowed there. Beyond the lake a beech woodland rose, then fell, towards Bath itself.

I entered the marquee, drawn by the chatter and laughter of a lunch party in full swing. At fifty-odd white-clothed tables, guests were being served dessert by young waiters and waitresses. Sixth-formers making extra pocket money, I guessed.

At the first table I passed, a life-and-soul type was telling a risqué joke that sent the hands of his well-oiled female companions up to their mouths in mock outrage. They'd been drinking since eleven that morning, I heard someone at the next table say. And why not, a female friend added, if the university was paying. She half nodded to the other end of the marquee, presumably to where those picking up the tab were seated. I headed towards them.

At their end of the marquee, faculty members and their guests were eating off superior china to the workers down wind. The wine was better too, by a good ten quid a bottle, and was flowing just as freely.

A girl with a serried row of desserts along one arm entered the marquee from the powerhouse of these very

English festivities, a field kitchen in a canvas annexe. Through the flap I could see a young chef, in whites over scruffy jeans, stirring a pan of chocolate sauce. He dipped a finger in and tasted it.

"Where will I find Mrs Bailey?" I asked the girl.

She jerked her head back to where she'd come from and I entered to find a small army of workers spooning out profiteroles, cheesecake and summer pudding into dessert bowls. No one looked up for at least a minute and then a tall, angular woman, clearly the boss from the orders she was giving, noticed me.

"Can I help you?" she asked sharply.

"Only if you're Joanna Bailey."

"I am."

She was dressed in a smart, formal suit and a hint of lace at her throat struggled to soften her features. Her dyed auburn hair was scraped back into a knot and the pull on it had so drawn her face that she might have had oriental blood in her somewhere. What hadn't been smoothed out, however, were the time lines of tough living, most of it done without support. The blue eyes were uncommonly still, as if the merest flicker might be a waste of energy.

"I need to ask you a few things about Teresa Stillman."

She thought about that, without much change in her expression, then said, "I'm extremely busy."

"I can wait."

She wanted me to leave, of course, but instead I made for a canvas chair and sat down to watch the hustle and bustle. A few moments later she came over to me.

"What sort of things?"

"Well, if she's missing I'd like to find her. If she's dead I'd like to know who killed her."

She looked me up and down before asking, "Police?"

"Friend of her father."

She ran through her options, then called out in a voice that could halt a regiment, "Jason, take over!"

"Right, Ma!" said the lad I'd seen tasting the chocolate sauce.

Joanna grabbed a half-full wine glass and led the way out of the field kitchen, through the rear flap.

Parked by the lake was a Transit van, declaring in Gothic lettering that it belonged to Fully Functional Caterers. Weddings, anniversaries and conventions were the firm's business. All you had to do was ring the number, the one I'd rung that morning, or go to the website for more details. Joanna put a tea towel over the rear bumper of the van and sat back on it.

"You know my name," she said, "I didn't catch yours."

"Nathan Hawk. What exactly is this shindig about, Mrs Bailey?"

"Teachers, toffs and other ranks meet at the end of each academic year. Lunch out here, weather permitting, then speeches in the Hall. At five o'clock we do tea and sandwiches for anyone still standing."

And at that point she set about assuming the persona Jim Kelloway had spoken of. Back in the kitchen, I fancied I'd seen a moment of horror when she realised that the real Joanna Bailey, the one feeding the five thousand, was hardly the flitting butterfly she'd fooled Kelloway with. She took a sip of her wine and seemed to raise the glass to a pair of swans who had paddled across the lake towards us.

"They mate for life," she said. "Don't you think that's terribly romantic?"

"It saves a hell of a lot of time and effort, I know that. Were Tom and Teresa an item?"

"I suppose they were." She nodded at the swans. "But I'm not sure how long it would have lasted."

"Only most people are murdered by someone they know well, the main candidate being a spouse or lover."

"That means I'm safe then. I have neither."

"Don't count your chickens. Another five per cent are murdered by their kids. Jason's one of your boys, I take it? Any girls?"

"I have a daughter, yes. She married a rather... indifferent man. But then so did I. Would you like a sandwich, Mr Hawk?"

She'd made the offer to stop me asking more questions about her family. She reached back into the van and pulled a large metal container towards her. She unsnapped the locks, took out a polythene tub and peeled off its lid.

"Chicken, ham or roast vegetable?"

I took the ham.

"Did they ever fight? Or fall out?"

She pretended for a moment that she'd forgotten who we were talking about. "Tom and Teresa? Well, yes but their arguments were a bit one-sided. Teresa was one of those people who make you feel better, Mr Hawk. Ten minutes in her company and you came away feeling... positive, optimistic. Tom took advantage of that." She looked away, out across the lake and frowned. "We all did, I suppose, but Tom worst of all. He... what would be the right word, I wonder? He drained her and that upset me."

Her pace had slowed, her voice had softened, the steady stare had mellowed into a preoccupied gaze.

"Tom wanted her all to himself, you see, and if he couldn't get his own way he sulked. He was sulking that Friday. He wanted her to go down to the coast for the weekend, to his mother's."

"Wanted them to meet, maybe."

"More likely he wanted to keep an eye on her."

"Jealous type, eh?"

We were interrupted by a lad emerging from the marquee and hurrying towards us. He was a skinny, conventional type with a short back and sides and check trousers under the whites. My eyes went straight to the moustache that hadn't bushed out yet and showed little sign of ever doing so. When he saw me looking he chewed his top lip to hide the fuzz but I guessed my gaze wasn't the only thing distressing him.

"We've forgotten the raspberry coulis for the cheesecake!" he said.

There was anguish in the voice, which itself was half an octave higher than it should've been. Joanna smiled at him and said, calmly, "It's in the cool-box behind me, darling. I kept it apart in case some bright spark mistook it for gravy."

Her gentle manner clearly puzzled the boy. He'd no doubt expected a drubbing and here she was, all smiles and sweet reason. He grabbed the cool-box and hurried back to the marquee.

"My other boy, Kyle," Joanna said.

"When Mary Harper took you on, didn't she mind that you had a record for bending plastic? That credit card fraud got you a suspended sentence?"

She smiled, without a hint of embarrassment. "Oh, dear, my colourful past. Will it always be with me? Mary didn't mind because I decided not to trouble her with it."

"So where did you get the money to start Fully Functional?"

The smile was still in place. "It wasn't the seven thousand pounds Teresa had on her that day, if that's what you're wondering. I had money from my divorce."

"So, off with the gardening gloves, on with the apron. Quite a change."

"Yes, well, Kyle and Jason were struggling and with Mary's death I needed a change of direction."

"Jim Kelloway described you as having a butterfly mind that flits from bloom to bloom. He said you couldn't focus long enough to murder someone."

"Well, that's very reassuring…"

"It's also bollocks. No one but a Sergeant Major could run a business like this. Certainly not the drippy tart you fobbed Kelloway off with."

She didn't exactly snap back to the woman I'd seen marshalling an army of workers, but she had the grace to acknowledge her failed attempt at deception. She smiled, then rose and folded the tea towel she'd been sitting on.

"Right, well, unless you've more questions for me, I'd like to return to the parade ground."

She pulled her jacket into shape, adjusted the knot in her hair and strode off back to the marquee. She'd answered all my questions, certainly, but she'd made one or two tactical errors, apart from trying to kid me that she was a butterfly. She hadn't questioned the notion that Teresa was dead, for example, let alone that she'd been murdered. In her shoes I would have done.

Given that she had four or five hours' work ahead of her I thought a quick look round her house wouldn't go amiss.

-8-

I parked the Land Rover and walked down the alley separating Carmody Place from the houses backing onto it. Number 23 wasn't hard to pinpoint and, obligingly, the back gate had been left unbolted. More helpful still was the absence of Archie Conroy, the old boy I'd met earlier. He was probably indoors, laying a table for the slap up meal of leftovers that was on its way.

From the state of her back yard it appeared that Joanna's gardening days were indeed well and truly over. There'd been a few tubs and hanging baskets at the front door but here there was fence-to-fence gravel with a concrete path leading up to the kitchen door. The door was locked. The French windows beside it were more promising. There was no handle on the outside, the windows being of an old fashioned design with a rod inside running top to bottom, disappearing into the lintel and lower sill. I put a penknife between the two frames and levered back the catch. The rod shifted and the door groaned open on rusty hinges. With a last look round to make sure I hadn't been spotted, I stepped into the dining room. It hadn't had a meal served in it for years. Central to it was a large drop-leaf table at full stretch bearing the office paraphernalia of a thriving business: a phone, stationery, notepads, a computer – the day-to-day trappings of Fully Functional Caterers.

On the walls were framed photographs. I'm understating. On every available piece of wall in Joanna's house there was a photograph, mostly of the family in happier times.

Over the mantelpiece was a record of the kids' progress, in Jason's case, from baby high-chair to VW Golf driving seat. At two years old, as now, he was square built and powerful. According to the photos, Kyle's was a more delicate advance, from first appearance in a school play to first prize in some kind of dancing competition. The daughter was there too, snapped on the day of her wedding to the… inadequate man.

Above the wedding snap was a holiday photo of Joanna on a beach, younger, prettier and about a stone lighter. She was laughing as the boys dragged her along, one on each hand, while the daughter pushed from behind. It was taken in Scotland, I thought, right up north somewhere. No place to take small kids. I've done it. The sea's freezing cold, it rains every day and if that doesn't get you the midges will.

I started to go through the contents of a steel filing cabinet which occupied the fireplace. The files were immaculate, the correspondence in date order, the credit card invoices marked, each item accounted for. There was a file of instruction booklets for things like ovens, radios, fridges. Another file, fat and misshapen, was labelled 'divorce'. Others were for insurance, mortgage and cars. I supposed that most people ran their lives that efficiently, always able to find the latest bank statement or bill. I've never been able to.

I went out into the hall. The photos here were of grandparents, from both sides of the family, together with uncles, aunts and cousins, I imagine. There were school photos from way back. A couple of sepia soldiers, Second World War. In the cupboards were the usual things. I say usual because the house, due to its layout, not to mention the profusion of photos, reminded me of my own childhood home. Joanna kept her hoover in the cupboard under the stairs, for example, just as my mother had done. Above it, on shelves built for the purpose, both women kept a sewing machine.

The kitchen was spotless. It was hung with more photographs, but yet again the drawers revealed no secrets, the cupboards no skeletons, the chalk blackboard no misfit messages, only a crude roster. Jason was down for Tuesday and Thursday, Kyle for Wednesday and Friday, Joanna Monday, Saturday and Sunday. Trust the woman to get the lion's share of whatever had to be done.

The parlour, as my mother would have called it, held no secrets either. The furniture was new, the television large and flat-screened, the sofa deep and velvet. The photos on the wall here had been poshed up, some of them tinted in a vain attempt to bring the faces of long-dead relatives into the twenty-first century. As if they might want to come. In one corner there was an upright piano, Japanese and therefore having perfect pitch. At home a blind tuner came to us once every five or six months to sort out the Kirkman grand. I don't remember his name, I don't really remember what he looked like. It isn't easy to bring a face to mind when the eyes have died. But I do recall that he charged half a crown for his work. My father swore the bastard was shafting us just because he was blind.

Up on the landing I opened the first door I came to and walked into Joanna's bedroom. It was one of the tidiest rooms I've ever seen and that in itself is reason to be suspicious.

I haven't known many women in my life, certainly very few whose lingerie I've audited, but none of them had half the underwear Joanna Bailey had. There must have been fifty pairs of knickers, two dozen bras of various colours, all neatly folded and precisely stacked.

At the back of another drawer, beneath a pile of T-shirts, lay a well-thumbed brown A4 envelope. Using two pairs of knickers as gloves, I removed it and drew out the contents. As I did so I realised that my journey to Bath had not been wasted. I'd found something that Jim Kelloway had missed. Not just misread, like Joanna's fundamental character, for example, but downright missed.

I closed the drawer, left the room, taking the envelope downstairs with me.

I called Ellie from the phone in the kitchen and knew immediately that somebody was with her. She was laughing as she picked up the receiver.

"Hi, there!"

"Ellie? It's Dad. How are you?"

"Terrific! How's yourself?"

"Er, fine. Listen, I'm phoning because I won't be home till later than I said. Something's cropped up."

Ellie chuckled. "Who is she, Dad?"

"That's very flattering, but not the case, I'm afraid. You sure you're okay?"

"Struggling through." She knew I'd realised that she wasn't alone. "Heh, Dad, guess who's turned up?"

I ran through the rest of my children, in shortest of money order. "Con? Fee? Jaikie?"

"No," she said, laughing again. "Rick. American Rick, the guy I met on the plane coming back from L.A. Is it okay if he stays the night?"

I wanted to tell her that it wasn't but heard myself say, "Of course. Put him in the box room. Clean sheets in the airing cupboard."

"Okay, Dad, thanks. See you later."

"Yeah, I'm not sure exactly what…" But I was talking to the dialling tone.

American Rick. He may have been American, he may have been called Rick, but he was making the most serious-minded of my children laugh.

I found a tumbler and filled it to the brim with ice from a tray in the fridge. I covered the ice with scotch from a bottle in one of the food cupboards and sat down to wait for the Baileys to return.

***

I must've dozed off at the kitchen table, head on the backs of my hands, and woke up to find myself staring sideways at the whisky tumbler, inches from my nose. The ice in it had melted and a bloke who was the spitting image of me, only convex and far away, was peering at me asking the same question I was: where am I? Bath, we answered in unison. Joanna Bailey's house.

There were at least two voices beyond the kitchen door, a man's and a woman's. In the baffled world of coming to I heard Joanna say something about needing the loo. Then there were footsteps on the stairs. I sat up in the chair and took a swig of the warm, diluted whisky.

Jason Bailey entered the kitchen and stopped. If he'd inherited anything from his mother it was facial stillness in the light of unsettling things going on around him.

"What the fuck are you doing?" he said, eventually.

"Drinking your whisky."

"I meant why are you here?"

"Then that's what you should've have said."

He called out above our heads, "Ma, that bloke's here!"

The voice from above was muffled but not alarmed. Without taking his eyes off me, Jason went over to the fridge (which, just for the record, he was twice the size of) and took out a Becks. Given his general appearance I expected him to rip the cap off with his teeth and spit it across the table at me. Instead he levered it off with the handle end of a tin-opener.

High-pitched Kyle entered with a carrier bag of fish and chips. "Who were you yakkin' to…?"

I raised a hand in greeting and he said to Jason, as if I weren't in the room, "It's that geezer from this afternoon."

Above our heads the toilet flushed and a minute later Joanna entered, still drying her hands on a towel.

"Archie, you don't give us much time…" she began, and stopped when she saw me. "I thought you'd be Archie, from next door.

"No, but if you listen carefully you'll hear his stomach rumbling, I shouldn't wonder."

"Did he let you in?" asked Jason.

"I let myself in. French windows."

Joanna looked at the two boys, no doubt wondering if they'd be up to the task of chucking me out. "Well, you can just let yourself out again, Mr Hawk."

"I've a few more things to sort out with you."

"You heard what she said," Jason added. "Go! Or we'll fucking kick you out."

He set his Becks down on the unit behind him in preparation for the rumble to come.

"You're a cook," I reminded him, "not a bouncer and I'd rather we stayed friends. Besides, you know what they say? If they don't hit you within the first minute they aren't ever going to. Why don't you sit down, all three of you."

He carried on staring at me for a moment or two and then, with a full-bodied roar, hurled himself at me, regardless of the table between us. I shoved it towards him, rising to my feet as I did so. It caught him at hip level and he folded in half towards me. I stuck my elbow in his neck and leaned down heavily. His face lengthened against the grain of the wood, his lips parted wide enough to be used as a sink plunger. I turned to Kyle.

"And what are you going to do? Hit me with haddock and chips?"

He was biting the moustache again, glancing at Joanna for a solution to the current problem.

"Okay, please let him go," she said at last. "Then we'll talk."

I put my mouth close to Jason's ear. "Right, I'm going to lean off you, son. You're going to stand up, unwrap your fish and chips and start eating them. Kyle, you do the same. Joanna, salt and vinegar, please… whoever heard of fish and chips without them?"

I leaned away from Jason and he unfolded, stretching his neck and shoulders back into shape.

"Don't worry, I used to win fights for a living," I said. "Given my time over again, I'd rather be able to make a decent sauce, like you."

He retreated to a chair at the end of the table, taking his injured pride with him. Kyle divvied up the fish and chips onto plates his mother had taken from a rack over the sink. The boys began eating them with their fingers. There was a third portion intended for her, but when I put two pairs of knickers over my hands her appetite seemed to fade. It disappeared completely when I produced the contents of the A4 envelope I'd found upstairs. It consisted of a single sheet of paper with letters cut from tabloid newspapers and glued to it. I read it aloud.

"I know what you did to TS. Maybe the rest of the world should know."

Joanna's face remained as impassive as ever.

"What is it?" said Jason, tilting back his head and dropping a grab load of chips into his mouth.

"Is he usually this slow?" I asked.

"It sounds like a threat," said Kyle. "Why's it been sent to you, Ma? Are they saying you killed her?"

"So it would seem," his mother replied.

"Is there a follow-up letter?" I asked her.

"No, no, that was it."

"Did you report it to the police?"

"Maybe I should have done…"

"No maybe about it. If you're innocent."

Jason pushed his supper to one side and went over to his mother. "Jesus, Ma, you didn't kill her, did you?"

"Of course not."

"Then who the hell sent you this?" She shrugged. He turned to me for a better answer. "Who sent her this?"

"Did I say it was sent to her?"

I fancied I could hear his brain lumbering around in his head, all to no purpose.

"I don't get it," he said, eventually.

"Your mother wrote it," I explained. "Your mother is planning to send it."

He got it now alright. Kyle was there long before him. "Jesus, Ma!" he said. "Who to?"

In her own time, Joanna said softly, "The person who killed her."

Jason smiled with pride. "You don't piss about, do you, Ma!"

I slapped the table to disabuse him.

"She is planning to blackmail someone, you fool! Dangerous game! And apart from being against the law, it makes her a bloody humbug for cashing in on Teresa's murder!"

"Sor-ry," said Jason, as if I'd made a mountain out of a mole-hill.

Joanna patted Jason's arm and looked across at me. "What now, Mr Hawk?"

I got up and went over to the fridge. "I suggest the boys leave us alone to talk things over."

"Yes, do please make yourself at home, Mr Hawk," Joanna said, more icily than the cubes I dropped into my glass. "Jason, bung my chips in the bin, they'll have gone soggy. And go fetch the leftovers, some for Archie, some for Mr Hawk and me. The Belgian pâté, salmon, some of the duck. Plenty of salad for Archie. Dress it up a bit, you know how he likes it." She glanced up at me and with gentle sarcasm asked, "Cheesecake for dessert, Mr Hawk? I'm afraid we ran out of summer pudding."

"Cheesecake'll be fine."

"Off you go, boys. I'll be okay."

Belgian pâté, salmon, duck and cheesecake for afters. It didn't sound bad to me.

***

"Right, so, who's the letter for?" I asked as we started on the gourmet feast.

Joanna sighed, as if I were bothering her with unnecessary details. "A woman called Darcy Morrell."

"Who is she?"

"She anchors a television programme called From Plot to Platter."

"Doesn't sound like my cup of tea. What's it about?"

"Gardening. Vegetables. Then cooking them." She smiled briefly. "And you must be the only person in the world who's never heard of the bitch."

She reached for an open magazine on the chair beside her and shoved it across the table to me. The face occupying a full page was certainly a striking one though I wouldn't have called it beautiful. She was in her late twenties, dressed in designer old clothes and even designer wellies. She was crouched in a vegetable plot on some very English allotment and behind her were several old men, leaning on spades, smiling down at her as she demonstrated the correct way of planting out cabbages. As if they'd been doing it wrong all their lives. She was looking straight at the camera, sporting a girl-next-door smile. Her teeth were television white, her tan was sun-bed beige, her dark hair pinned up sensibly. She wanted us all to like her – young, old, male, female. In my case she failed.

"Darcy's days were evidently numbered, as far as the programme went," said Joanna, "and the people who make it were looking for a successor. Because all roads in the gardening world seemed to lead to Mary Harper, they homed in on her pet suggestion, Teresa. And why not? Class, brains, beauty all rolled into one? How many gardeners can you say that about? Not Darcy, for sure. She's left blood and guts all over the gardening world, clawed her way to a half million salary. And she plans to hang onto it! She drove up one morning, dressed like an ad for Scottish Widows, cape and dark glasses to match, and warned Teresa off."

"Was Darcy on her own?"

"No, there was a man with her. He stayed by the car."

"What did he look like?"

"Oh, I don't know… six foot tall, blond hair."

"Long? Ponytail, by any chance?"

"Long-ish. He was fifty yards away and it wasn't really him I was interested in."

She offered me more whisky, which I declined, and poured herself some of the wine she'd rescued from the posh end of the marquee.

"So what did you hear?"

"Darcy told Teresa that if she accepted the job replacing her, she would regret it. She fired off a barrage of B-movie threats, ended by saying there was nothing she wouldn't do to protect her interests."

"Which you took to mean that she'd kill her if necessary."

She looked at me in disbelief. "Well, how would you have taken it? Teresa didn't scare easily and the producers kept coming back, offering more money. A hundred and fifty thousand at the last count. Twenty-two years old, for Christ's sake! I told her she was mad not to take it. I think in the end she would have done."

"So Darcy killed her. Or got someone to do it for her. Thereby presenting you with a nice little earner."

Her face went rock hard at the accusation.

"Don't you go all righteous on me, Mr Hawk. The girl was dead. Why shouldn't I get justice for her, in my own particular way?"

"How much were you hoping for?"

"I was going to start with fifty thousand…"

"And the fact that she might have killed Teresa didn't make you… consider your own safety?"

"I intended to post it from London, next time I was there."

She looked away, dismissively. I picked up the blackmail note and asked if she had an envelope.

"Why do you need one?"

"I'm going to send this to her. From somewhere on my way home. Swindon, maybe. I always had a soft spot for Swindon."

***

As I passed Plum Tree Cottage late that same night, I saw that a light was still on in Laura's sitting room. I pulled over onto the path leading to the church and phoned her. She took a long time answering.

"Were you asleep?" I asked.

"Yes."

"Ah, well, your downstairs light is on, so I assumed…"

"For goodness sake, Nathan. Come in."

I walked over to the cottage in time to hear the bolt on the front door slide back. She stepped aside as I entered and quickly re-tied the dressing gown she'd bought in Los Angeles. It had fallen open as I brushed past.

"You want tea?" she whispered. "Or something stronger?"

"By which you mean?"

"Well… horlicks, chocolate, slippery elm."

I winced at the thought of all three. "You've nothing against tea this late, I suppose? Ordinary tea? Decaff?"

Five minutes later she brought in two mugs of it and settled beside me on the sofa, drawing her legs up.

"Cheers!" she mouthed.

"Cheers. Why are we whispering? Is someone dying in the next room?"

"Out of deference to the night, I suppose." She swung her legs round and put her slippered feet into my lap.

"How's your day been?" I asked.

"Good. Annie MacKinnon gave birth at 2.15. A girl

weighing 8 pounds 2 ounces. Looks like Donald and her name is Fiona. Fiona Roberta MacKinnon."

"She wouldn't be a Scot by any chance, would she?"

She laughed, the fruity laugh that made people's heads turn in public places. "Well, now you mention it she does look like a set of bag-pipes but then most babies do."

I ran my hand slowly up her leg, to the back of her knee. She put a hand on mine and held it there against her thigh.

"Have you been home?" she asked.

"No, but I know why you're asking. American Rick."

"Ah, well, I've renamed him. 'Terrific' Rick. You'll soon realise why."

"Tell me now."

"Life to Rick is brilliant, awesome, amazing, fabulous, excellent and wicked… but most of all it's terrific."

"What's he like?"

"Charming. He'll charm even you."

"Don't count on it."

I freed my hand and ran it down her leg. She took hold of it and guided it back in the other direction.

"Before we turn to other things…" she began.

"Other things?" I said. "You know at your age, and in your profession, you really should learn to call it by its proper name…"

"Ellie came round this morning, before I went to the surgery. She borrowed fifty pounds off me."

***

I got back to Beech Tree Cottage at about eight the next morning and crept in through the back door like an errant teenager. The first thing I noticed, not because it was in the way but because of who it belonged to, was a tall rucksack leaning against the kitchen table. It had America stamped all over it in the shape of various badges and transfers, but at least it was in the kitchen. It hadn't made it upstairs. Its owner wasn't thinking of staying. Dogge stretched and came towards me, half-heartedly as if to say, "So this is how we do things now? You go off on your own for days at a time, I stay here and mind the shop?"

I made coffee and took it out into the garden, crunching my way over beech nuts the wind had dislodged. I settled beneath the long branches and watched Dogge chase the dragonflies as they helicoptered up and down the stream that carves the garden in two. She never seemed to catch any. Maybe she'd heard the old wives' tale that they only live for a day so she didn't try very hard.

Ellie appeared at the kitchen door, wrapping a silk dressing gown around her. She came over to me, no slippers on her feet, stepping between the beech husks as best she could.

"Hi, Dad. What time did you get in? Only I didn't hear you."

"Don't remember. How's Rick? Has he surfaced?"

"No. I thought he might be out here, giving it gee, your house is so historical."

"He means hysterical."

"Used to be, didn't it. Not here, but the old house. When we were all together."

I slipped my arm around her shoulders and drew her towards me.

"You miss it?" I asked. "All that noise?"

"I miss Mum, I know that."

"If you want to see her, go and look in the mirror."

She beckoned for a sip of my coffee and I handed it over, mentally waving it goodbye.

"Poor Daddy. Everyone's left you."

"They're all a day's journey away. That's all."

"Don't you miss her? Only you never say. And I just wondered if Laura had…"

She turned to me for an answer to her unspoken question.

"Had taken her place? No."

Ellie nodded. She crossed one leg over the other and began to flick the husks from the sole of her foot.

"Must be hard for her too," she said. "Being second."

"Especially with me being such a great catch, you mean?"

"You're not too bad, given the age and mileage."

"Yes, well, any wear and tear is down to you four. What are your plans for today?"

"I was going to take Rick to Oxford, round the colleges. More gee-ing and wow-ing, I expect."

"I can drop you off." She gave me a thumbs-up of appreciation. "There's a badge on his rucksack says M.I.T…"

"Massachusetts Institute of Technology."

"I know what it stands for, but is it for show or did he really go there?"

"That's where he went. Did Computer Science."

"Isn't that like Electric Kettle Studies or Washing Machine Theory?"

"Dad, you are so far behind," she scolded. "Rick wants to be a teacher. Maybe you should join his class."

"Teach here?"

"India. Well, Nepal, really. He's going to work for some charity there." The word charity must have reminded her. "Dad, favour to ask. I borrowed fifty quid from Laura yesterday, said I'd pay her back today."

"She told me."

I withdrew my arm from around her shoulders and looked sidelong at her.

"What exactly is this money for, Ellie?"

She knew instantly what I meant. "Dad, honestly!"

There was gentle reproof in the voice for me thinking the worst of her, sympathy for my needless concern, all tinged with amusement at my old-fashioned attitude.

"And when do you start at The Gazette?"

"Next Monday," she said.

I nodded. "My wallet's in the kitchen drawer."

"Thanks, Dad. You're a star."

She downed the rest of my coffee, pulled the dressing gown around her and tip-toed back to the house, leaving me to wonder if I was now buying Rick's weed as well.

-9-

Michael Carter's office was in Summertown, just north of Oxford and I was taking a chance that he'd be there. Kelloway's notes said that he was in the import/export game, which, to most coppers, is a blanket description of any dodgy business you care to name.

It turned out that Carter imported classic wines, mainly from Europe, and sold them all round the world by mail order. Michael Carter Wines occupied one floor of a steel and glass nonentity in Summertown on the Banbury Road and I'd caught him the day before he was due to move offices. They were re-locating to St Giles, the receptionist told me, where Mr Carter had bought two houses from Somerville College. If I didn't mind the chaos today she was sure her boss would be happy to see me, even though he'd only returned from France late last night.

I found myself a packing case, perched on it and wondered. Wine? Michael Carter? A man who'd done time for manslaughter? It had such a contradictory ring to it that it could almost be true. Then again, if the place was a front for something heavier, there was no sign of it. Okay, so that's the purpose of a front, to create a false impression, but you can usually spot a few giveaways. Arms or drugs? I asked myself. It sounded corny in my head, especially for Oxford, but these days nothing surprises. Maybe they were all in the packing cases. Maybe I was sitting on them...

Carter arrived at about ten o'clock together with his wife, Yoshie, and the five or six people in the place came to an inner attention. The blokes followed Yoshie with their eyes, the girls followed Michael with theirs. A good-looking man, Kelloway had said in his notes with typical irrelevance. He'd gone on to demonstrate his envy of Carter by describing him as arrogant, above himself, snotty and moody.

The receptionist pointed me out, Carter thanked her and came over to me, hand outstretched.

"Mr Hawk? I'm Michael Carter. You've come to help us?"

"Do you need any?"

He looked around, pleased with what he saw.

"No, we're all done, I reckon. This is my wife, Yoshie."

Yoshie held out her hand and smiled in that oriental way where the face moves but fails to light up.

"Nice to meet you," she said with a slight bow.

"Likewise. I have a daughter, lives in Asahikawa. Do you know it?"

"Yes," she said sharply. "I was born near there. Can I get you tea or coffee?"

"Thanks, coffee."

She turned and walked off. Carter led the way to a boxed off room in the corner, more glass than wall. Again it was packing cases, a bare desk and no chairs.

"You must forgive my wife," he began.

"What for?"

"Her abruptness. She misses Japan. When people talk about it she … reacts. Would you like me to get you something to sit on?"

I gestured to the floor. "I'll go Japanese if I need to."

He leaned back against the abandoned desk and clasped his hands together in a classic defence pose. The gold at his wrist slipped down to the heel of his hand.

"So, what can we do for you, Mr Hawk?"

"Teresa Stillman," I said.

His former politeness ebbed away, leaving behind a stony reluctance to co-operate. "If you're a copper, forget it.

I've said all I'm going to."

"Not a copper. Was a copper."

He smiled, if you could call his particular twist of the mouth a smile. "That's like saying an omelette used to be an egg. It still is one, whichever way you cook it."

"I'm working for Teresa's father," I went on. "Trying to find her."

"Private eye stuff? Well, the man you want to talk to's called Richard Crane."

He turned away, as if suddenly wishing he hadn't brought Crane's name into the conversation.

"Why him?" I asked.

"Wasn't Crane the last person to see her alive?"

"I've no idea."

He shook his head in bewilderment. "So you come back to me because I'm the guy with a record. Fair game. What is it with you lot? Round and round in the same circle, hoping that at some point the story'll change, the killer will stick his hand up."

"You agree with me then. She's been murdered."

He blew out his lips like a horse might after a heavy race. "Well, she's not walking round Oxford, playing hard to get. I can understand that sort of thinking from her father but…"

"You've spoken to him?"

"No, but I'd be happy to."

"The man who sent you down for manslaughter. Jesus, Michael, everywhere we go in this conversation there are dead bodies."

He didn't like being pressed. He took a packet of Gauloises from his pocket and lit up with a gold lighter, which he stroked for a few moments before returning it to his pocket.

"We see ourselves in our elders, right? Ourselves in years to come. There's even a bit of you I might be like in ten years time, Mr Hawk." He looked me up and down. Whatever reflection he saw, a decade from now, seemed to amuse him. He became serious again. "But not John Stillman."

He went on to tell me that, ten years ago, when given a date for his trial, his solicitor had become anxious. The prosecutor was going to be John Stillman QC. Carter knew who he was, of course, he'd seen him on the news, his picture in the paper. He was early sixties, five foot seven and walked like a duck hurrying towards water. He was bald as a bullet and not blessed with good looks. No one would accuse John Stillman of being handsome.

"And then there was the cough," Carter said. "He'd have had you believe that it had crept up on him recently, never mind the 60, 70 fags a day. The man is solid nicotine. He must've crossed over from where it's killing him to where it's curing him, at least in the culinary sense."

He looked down at his own cigarette, hardly smoked, and went over to an outside window. He flicked the long butt down onto the car park below.

"So, I went into court believing that I was going to be cross-examined by a joke. After five minutes on the stand, nobody was laughing, least of all me. He convinced that jury, with words out of my mouth – that was the clever bit, words I had used – that I'd seen my victim join the M40 at Hanger Lane and over the next 20 miles, as he cut me up, overtook me and gave me the finger, I planned to kill him. He fixed me with those beady little eyes and chip, chip, chipped away and by the time he'd done with me, the joke was on me." He paused. "Now, instead of the fearsome creature he was that day, he's running round, handing out leaflets, I hear, begging people to listen to him."

"You sound sorry for him."

"Aren't you? Ten years ago, when you snapped your fingers, the men in your team jumped. Who jumps when you walk into a room these days?"

I was meant to be winding him up, not the other way round. But in spite of the long black hair being right for grabbing, the cleared desk a perfect landing place for the head, there was something about Michael Carter that told me to hold off. It wasn't his physical being, though I judged him to be no more than reasonably fit. It wasn't a commanding presence, though Jim Kelloway believed he had one. It certainly wasn't that I liked him. It was to do with him mentioning Richard Crane and then wishing he'd kept his trap shut.

Even so, I still didn't like the fact that I couldn't make people jump when I walked into a room. I gestured politely for him to step away from the desk, giving me a clear surface on which to spread out The Map. He watched me from the sidelines. When all the pieces were assembled, I closed my eyes and brought my finger down on Tokyo. My daughter was there this week but had picked up my email of yesterday morning and responded to it.

"Dad, don't be a wally," she'd said with her usual tact. "Ellie is not smoking fifty quidsworth of weed a week. Jesus, she couldn't carry that much round with her. Well, she could but you know what I mean. As for her being on something else, you could always ask her. Love you, Fee."

The email from Con, who for some reason best known to himself had travelled north to watch Caribou migrate, had been similar in tone, but shorter. "Dad, you're losing it, mate. Get off her back." There was no request for money, either. Maybe you don't need it in Alaska.

Jaikie was more sympathetic. "Dad, of course Ellie smokes weed but has it done her any harm? Of course not. By the way, get yourself a copy of this week's New Yorker. There's an article in it about British Imports, I'm number 67 on the list. They say I'm propping up the US economy!"

I see, boy. A month ago you were just a film star. Today you're the Federal Reserve. I folded up The Map and put it away again.

"What was that?" Carter asked. "Some kind of anger management device, to keep the lid on?"

I nodded and he nodded back in recognition.

There was a tap on the door and he went over to open it. His wife had brought us coffee.

"Do you take sugar, Mr Hawk?" she asked.

"No, just milk."

She set the tray down on the desk and gestured for me to help myself.

"There are no biscuits, Michael. The girls have packed them. So sorry."

She left the room with a slight bow. Carter took a box of sweeteners from his top pocket and clicked one into his coffee.

"Are we done?" he asked.

"I doubt it. You killed a man because he cut you up at some traffic lights. You rammed his face with a steering wheel lock, broke his neck. John Stillman got you eight years. Don't tell me you never thought about revenge."

"Then why kill his daughter? Why not kill him?"

"Killing her was a much better idea. It gave him a living death."

He was adamant. "You don't get it, do you. John Stillman changed my life. He made me see exactly what I was capable of. I had planned, way back at Hangar Lane, to go head to head with my victim and, if it came to it, kill him. I wasn't aware of it at the time but as Stillman broke my journey down, thought by thought, it was like he'd been there in the passenger seat, reading my mind. Part of me keeps him there to this day."

***

An odd thing happened later that afternoon. I drove into the centre of Oxford and parked, just along from Brown's, since I wanted to check out Michael Carter's new offices. The front door was open and a man was putting the finishing touches to some limed oak. He thought I must've been something to do with Carter Wines so he didn't challenge me. I walked over to the stairs and went up to the first floor.

My mother always said that if you want to know the kind of people you're dealing with, pay a visit to their toilets. Evidently a toilet speaks volumes about standards, aspirations and self-image, not to mention how much money there is floating about. My mother would've loved the Ladies' loo at Carter Wines. She would've loved the Gents' too, furnished as it was with expensive porcelain, gold plated taps and hand-made mirrors. This was powdering your nose in style, she would have said. The toilets, the whole conversion, the property itself had clearly cost a bomb. Michael Carter was a man of substance.

I came out and walked back towards Brown's. Ahead of me I suddenly caught sight of Ellie and American Rick. They were holding hands, which didn't please me, but I was immediately distracted by a figure I recognised way beyond them. It was Tom Gibson, standing at a corner. He turned and waved. Ellie waved back, presumably thinking that she was the object of the greeting, but Tom seemed to ignore her. He carried on waving until I acknowledged him. Ellie turned, saw me and gave a yelp of joy.

"Great timing, Dad," she said. "Lunch is on you."

Rick was already stretching out his hand to me, a suitably nervous smile on his lips. He was a bit chiselled, my mother would have said, with a longish, bony face. He was dark, his hair jet black and boyishly cut, his eyes were brown and deep-set, his nose long and slender. His grasp was firm and practised, of course, and when I asked if they'd had a good morning he said it had been terrific. Further praise was cut short as Tom Gibson passed us and patted me on the shoulder, leaving his hand there in far too matey a fashion.

"Mr Hawk, how's it going?"

"Fine," I said, shrugging his hand away. "You know my daughter?"

He smiled at her. "Hi! Tom Gibson."

"Nice to meet you," she said, offering her hand. "I'm Ellie, and this is Rick Bettuccio."

A good old American name, I thought. Tom and Rick shook hands and silence fell. The silence of strangers waiting for small talk to suggest itself. None did. We carried on to Brown's and as we entered I glanced back. Tom Gibson had disappeared.

-10-

Laura and I went to The Crown that evening to wet Fiona Roberta McKinnon's head. Rick and Ellie came with us and it turned into a ... terrific evening. The usual crowd was there, armed with boxes of chocolates, teddy bears or Mothercare stuff and when the baby was passed round for each of us to hold, I suffered what Ellie described as 'an old git moment'. Seeing her holding Fiona flung me back, twenty-something years to The Bat and Ball at High Beech, Epping Forest. Maggie sitting there, on a warm night just like this, Fee in her arms, two weeks old. And a day later, here I was...

I got the first round of drinks in – not to mention the fourth and fifth – and watched Rick struggle with his first pint of English beer.

"You like it?" I asked him.

"I've never had it before, Sir, but it looks fabulous!"

He decided against raising it to his lips, there and then, presumably out of fear that he would spill it under my critical gaze. However, for all that he was nervous, being in a foreign country, in a pub no less, and three feet away from the father of a girl he fancied like mad, he made a pretty good fist of it. I guessed he'd been brought up that way, to give of his best in every situation. The American way.

"And what about England and the English, Rick? What's your verdict?"

"I have had a terrific few days, Sir." He couldn't have been more anxious for me to believe him. "I was only planning to stay here forty-eight hours but meeting Ellie on the plane, well..."

"She invited you to come and stay?"

"Yes, Sir, and I'm really, really grateful for your hospitality."

And there was I thinking he'd turned up out of the blue, not that my daughter had booked him in a week ago. But I did like the 'Sir' thing. I'd been called it for the last twenty years as a copper, as a matter of form, but not by kids like Rick who did so because they meant it.

"What are your plans, then?" I said, gently warming to him. I meant, of course, when are you leaving?

"I'm heading off to Nepal, Sir".

Good answer. Nepal was a long way away, hardly a place Ellie would follow him to. A bit short on the creature comforts for our girl, though cannabis probably grew by the roadside. I turned away to greet a neighbour and Terrific Rick took the chance to duck down and slurp half an inch off the head of his pint. When I turned back to him he was holding the glass in his hand, pretending he liked what he'd just tasted.

"This Nepal trip," I said. "Any particular reason for it?"

"My mother's cousin runs a charity there. It's a school for kids she takes straight off the street. I plan to teach there for a while."

"Will she pay you? I mean, what'll you do for money?"

"Dad…" said Ellie, warning me not to be nosey.

"No, no, it's a good question," said Rick, leaping to my defence. "Bed and board, that's what I'll be working for but my father's promised to stake me if I need it."

"That is… that is terrific," I said.

Laura pinched me under the table. I pinched her back.

She and I left The Crown at about half ten, her witching hour if she has morning surgery the next day. I had a pretty heavy day lined up as well.

***

According to the production company who made From Plot to Platter, Darcy Morrell was filming an episode of it in darkest Hertfordshire.

The programme had taken over a spread of allotments in Chorleywood and I decided to surprise her. After all, it had been three clear days since I'd posted, first class, Joanna's letter accusing her of murder and, as far as I knew, Darcy had done nothing about it.

I parked in a field alongside sound trucks, a catering wagon and dozens of cars, kids' cars, the kind that are always stuck to your rear bumper when you're taking it easy. I walked over to the allotments, which, according to the Secretary of the Chorleywood Allotment Association, had first been assigned to locals in 1940 to help them to feed themselves. Some of the men working the plots looked as if they'd been there since day one. Most, however, were anxious thirty-somethings, work-at-home family types with economy conscious wives and a weakness for the latest health scare. They knew how dangerous most of our fresh food is, how expensive the organic alternatives are, and had persuaded their husbands to go native. Periodically, from early spring till now P to P, as From Plot to Platter was affectionately known by those who worked on it, had been filming there alongside the allotmenters, with Darcy Morrell strutting her stuff. You name it, peas, runner beans, cabbages, cauliflowers – take a walk round the veg section of any supermarket, Darcy could help you grow whatever was there bigger, better and cheaper. She was the expert and she was twenty-six.

How exciting can vegetables be? For me the answer shuffles between 'not at all' and 'hardly ever', so how come people watched P to P in their millions? Well, it may be an overly cynical view but I thought I knew the secret of Darcy's success. She kept it in her dressing room. It was her bra, which she never wore on camera.

Which meant that she knew how to work a crowd. Good for her because it isn't easy. I've been on telly a few times myself. Don't get me wrong, I'm not making a bid for stardom, I'm just saying that murders are big news and the people who solve them have their fifteen minutes of fame. Then the crimes pass into history and other people make documentaries about them. Older, greyer and heavier, those detectives regurgitate the facts, usually with a more heroic spin on them. In my case, I was always polite to the people asking the questions. I never lost my temper. Why would I have done? I had the facts, somebody else wanted to hear them and was willing to pay me for the privilege.

Darcy Morrell, however, was far from polite. I couldn't make out what her problem was. I doubt if many of the people she was yelling at could, either. It was something to do with another take being needed because the kid on sound had screwed up. He looked about twelve and stood resolute, mouth shut, while she had a go at him. His boss asked Darcy to take into consideration the lad's newness to the show, his nervousness, his general lack of experience. She said she wasn't used to working with amateurs. The cameraman exchanged a glance with his assistant and Darcy wanted to know what the glance meant. The guy said it meant nothing and that really got her going. They were all fucking bastards, she said. She'd seen the unedited version of the show that was going out on Sunday. It was shite. Half the shots were out of focus, the eye shadow that stupid bitch had used on her made her look like a panda, there was even a fucking plane going over in one shot that no one had noticed.

The producer went over to her, with deferential body language hanging from his every gesture. This was Tristan Baker, a studious looking man who should've had train tracks on his teeth as a boy. Mind you, he only looked about fourteen now, so it wasn't too late. Darcy was gaining momentum and past grievances were being aired. Three weeks ago she'd been promised a Winnebago of her own. Where was it? Why did she have to share a clapped out caravan with guest gardeners? She was pulling in five point seven million viewers, for Christ's sake. Didn't that mean something? Of course it meant something, said Tristan, but...

After watching her throw this extended tantrum at a crew of forty men and women all doing their best to make her look good, I didn't feel so bad about spoiling her day. I beckoned to a subdued girl in sweater, jeans and headphones. She came over and lifted one of the cans from an ear.

"Hi!" she mouthed. "Can I help you?"

"I'm the one who can help," I whispered.

I tore a small piece of paper from the girl's clipboard and, using her felt tip, wrote two words – Teresa Stillman. I folded the note and nodded for her to take it across to Darcy. She went as far as Tristan and tapped him on his elbow. Darcy, in mid-flow, snatched the note, opened it and read it. Silence mysteriously fell. Tristan took the note and read it for himself and after a few more words with the girl messenger, he called out to the spellbound crew, "Right, everyone, thanks for the morning so far. Good work. Why don't we break for lunch now, back here at two. Two o'clock start."

No one moved. No one wanted to move. They were still enjoying the silence. Inevitably, though, one or two shuffles prompted whispers, whispers developed into full-blown talking. There was even laughter from one quarter. God knows what Darcy would've said about that if she hadn't been in shock. Tristan beckoned me. I beckoned him in return. He came over, with Darcy one pace behind.

"Good morning," he said. "My name is Tristan Baker. You are?"

"Nathan Hawk."

He glanced at Darcy, to see if she recognised the name. She shook her head briefly.

"And, er... what can we do for you, Mr Hawk?"

"You can tell me why the name Teresa Stillman has had such a calming effect on Mrs Titchmarsh here."

"Why should that be of interest to you? Are you a policeman?"

I explained that I used to be but now I was working for Teresa's father. Neither Tristan nor Darcy could see any potential harm in that. In fact Tristan agreed that Teresa's disappearance was a most puzzling affair and he wished me luck in finding her. Darcy was made of sterner stuff, told him to stop wittering and squared up to me.

"You still haven't told us what you're doing here?"

"I'd like to know why you've done nothing about the note you received the other day? 'I know what you did to TS. Maybe the rest of the world should know'."

You could've heard a carrot drop.

"I think we should continue this in my trailer," said Baker.

***

Darcy Morrell sat tight-lipped and resentful, knees together like a sulky schoolgirl who'd been caught smoking behind the bike sheds. I sat opposite her on the shorter of the cushioned bench seats while Tristan Baker fixed us drinks from his fridge.

"I take it you know who sent Darcy that crude, threatening note, Mr Hawk?"

"Yes, but don't ask me for names. A refusal to grass often gives offence."

He smiled. "I've got a feeling you're rather good at giving offence."

He handed Darcy a gin and tonic, which she went to snatch from him. He withdrew it and set it down on the fake mahogany surface beside her.

"Let's put it another way," he went on. "Do you know what the unnamed person's interest in the matter is?" The teeth definitely bothered him. He had to grimace his top lip back down over the incisors whenever he stopped speaking.

"They think Darcy killed Teresa," I said. "The purpose of sending her the note was to smoke her out. I mean I know it's a Catch 22 situation. If you'd gone to the police with the letter they'd have said, well somebody thinks you killed her, maybe we should think so too. If you hadn't gone, which you didn't, some bloke like me would bowl up and ask if you'd got something to hide. Which I am."

Tristan handed me a scotch, exactly as I'd asked for it. Ice to the top of the glass.

"We didn't respond because we thought the letter came from a crank," he said. "You have to work in television, Mr Hawk, to realise how many bozos are out there."

"You're talking to an ex-copper. I can match your nutters, kernel for kernel. Did you go to a house in Woodstock Road, Oxford, Miss Morrell, on Friday the 21st of April this year?"

"Why would I have done?"

"Because a young woman called Teresa Stillman, who'd built a garden there, was in danger of stealing your show. Out with the old, in with the new. You went to warn her off."

"I most certainly did not," she snapped with absolute certainty.

"You sound very sure. I think I would've had to check in a diary for something to be so certain."

"I have never been to a house in Woodstock Road. I've certainly never met anyone called Teresa Stillman."

I turned to Tristan, who was clearly hoping to God I had nothing up my sleeve apart from an elbow.

"You've met her, though, Mr Baker. When you offered her Darcy's job."

He took a deep breath and said, "Yes, yes, we met. She wasn't quite right for the show, I'm afraid…"

"Wasn't right? Then why did you offer her so much money?"

"How much?" asked Darcy. "More than me?"

Tristan braced himself for the inevitable consequences and, when they came, they were impressive. Darcy rose to her feet, nipples erect with sudden anger. The glass in her hand looped back and went flying across the trailer, the gin and tonic spilling out ahead of it. Tristan Baker put both hands over his head and ducked, The G and T hit the wall and spread, the glass itself shattered and fell to the floor.

"You did!" she screamed. "You absolute bastard!"

Baker sighed and gave me a painful look but it was cut short by Darcy flying at him, hitting him like a windmill in a force nine and shrieking non-verbal anger at him. Again he ducked. When she'd run out of energy he poked his head out from the cocoon he'd fashioned with his hands and arms.

"Why take this man's word for it?" he said to Darcy.

"You utter sod," she said, slumping back into a seat, the make-up now dissolving down her face. "How could you do that?! Offer that bitch more than me."

"And what's more," I threw in, "he didn't have second thoughts about her. He wanted her. She turned him down."

Darcy had no more energy left to attack him with. She merely whispered, "I will fucking kill you for this!"

"Seems like a good moment to ask if you killed Teresa Stillman as a warm-up exercise?" I said.

"Of course I bloody didn't!"

"But you did go to see her? You did threaten her?"

"I may have had a few word…!"

"Who drove you there?"

"I don't know. One of the contract boys. Don't ask me their names."

I turned to Tristan. "I expect you can find out for me, can't you?"

He nodded.

As I walked away from the trailer Darcy marshalled her invective and then launched a second verbal attack on her hapless producer. He began the long, obsequious task of placating her for an afternoon's work.

***

As I walked in through the door at Beech Tree Cottage later that evening, the phone started ringing. It bristled with a kind of urgency, or so I fancied, as if the caller had been trying to get hold of me for some time. Ellie and Rick weren't there. They'd gone to stay the night with another school friend of hers in Banbury.

"Mr Hawk, it's Yoshie Carter here."

"Oh, right. Nice to hear your voice."

As opposed to one of my children's voices, which, at this time of day, would mean they were in trouble. Good news always waits until morning.

"I phone before and leave a message. I'm sorry to be so troublesome."

I could see from the incoming call display that this was her third call.

"You speak to Michael the other day, about Teresa?"

"Yes, I'm looking for her." I tried to put a smile into my voice. "Is it you I should have spoken to?"

"I have terrible feeling Mr Hawk that she is dead. That something dreadful has happened to her."

"I tend to agree."

I thought for a moment she'd turned away from the receiver, her voice went so quiet. "I think it is my fault, perhaps…"

"How so?"

She composed herself for a moment or two. "This Richard Crane, he phoned Teresa, yes? I think it is me who gave him her number. A man came to the wall by the garden, you see, three days before she was missing. There is a footpath runs beside. He leaned over and we started to talk about the garden, how beautiful was the workmanship and who had designed it…"

"So you told him?"

She took a deep breath to prevent herself from faltering. "I am afraid so. I gave him one of our business cards, wrote down her number on the back of it."

"What else did he say?"

"Not much. He looked at the name on the card and asked if Teresa was the tall, blonde lady who had made a Japanese garden at Chelsea Flower Show two years ago. I said no, this was the first one Teresa ever made. Besides, she was short and dark."

The daft bitch had given the man an address, a phone number and a physical description.

"What was this man like?"

"Ah, well, there you have problem, Mr Hawk. You know how Europeans think all Japanese look the same? All Japanese, we think Europeans look the same. All I can say is light colour hair, to the shoulders."

I put her mind at rest, as best I could.. I meant it, too. She'd explained why her husband had regretted mentioning Richard Crane when he and I met in his office. Whoever Crane was – the man Roberto saw at Giacometto's, Darcy Morrell's driver, or someone still unknown – Yoshie Carter had told him two crucial things about Teresa. What she looked like and how to get hold of her.

Just about all you need if you plan to kill someone.

***

I woke next morning to someone banging on the front door and Dogge going berserk at whoever had disturbed her beauty sleep. I threw on a bare minimum of clothes and went downstairs to find Sergeant Jim Kelloway fully charged with anger. It was directed at both me and the front page story in the rolled up newspaper he was carrying. He strode in.

"We had an agreement," he said, glaring at me as he moved.

"Did we?" I said.

He unfurled the tabloid with a flick of his wrist and I had to step back to read the headline. 'TV's Darcy in Murder Inquiry.' Around an unflattering photo of Darcy Morrell was the story of her being sent a threatening letter, accusing her of murder.

"I didn't think she'd do it," I said. "Tell the papers, I mean."

"She didn't. We think it was someone she's upset on the production."

"Plenty of them to choose from, by God. Always be nice to the little people, Jim."

"Yes, well, be that as it may, what pisses me off royally is this!" He snatched his glasses from the inside pocket of his jacket and put them on. "Says here 'the cops are baffled'. That'll be me. 'The threatening letter was brought to public attention by the man re-investigating the disappearance of Teresa Stillman, ex-Detective Chief Inspector Nathan Hawk.' That'll be you."

I shook my head. "Jim, they've got that from John Stillman, not me."

He clenched his fist round the corner of the paper and shook it at me. "You said I'd be the first to know if you found anything."

"That's right and I haven't."

"You found this bloody note to Darcy Morrell!"

"Yes, well... Look, I haven't had any breakfast yet. I doubt you have..."

"Bugger breakfast."

"Suit yourself."

I turned and went through to the kitchen and he followed me. I tried to make him sit down at the kitchen table but he was too rigid with fury to bend at the waist. I dropped four pieces of bread into the toaster and put the kettle on while Kelloway re-assembled his paper on the units.

"Next stop the Sundays, eh? Auction your story?"

"How much would you ask, if you were me?"

He looked at me with utter contempt. "When you said that in The Swan – that I could have the kudos, you'd take the money – I thought it was a joke."

"It was," I growled. "And so is the idea of me going to the Sundays."

He hadn't shaved this morning, anymore than I had, and he was wearing yesterday's shirt. There were grubby marks around the cuff and the collar was creased.

"Who hauled you out of bed, Jim?"

"My guvnor, Chief Superintendent Howard Merton."

"What's he like?"

"He's a bad-tempered, unhappy little prick who never comes down off the ceiling. Be that as it may, who sent this letter to Darcy Morrell?"

"How do I know?"

He came over to me and stood close. Too close. "You may have a track record matched by none but this is my neck on the line. I like my neck. It has a pension attached."

I held his gaze and after a moment said quietly, "Step back, Jim. Out of my space."

He looked at me for a moment longer, then stepped away and went over to the window.

"I'll ask you once more," he said. "Who sent the note to Darcy Morrell?"

He expected another smart answer but I said, "Okay, Jim, have it your way. I sent it."

He sniggered wearily. "Yeah, like hell you did."

That's coppers for you. They never believe you even when you're telling the truth.

-11-

The weekend was given over to Terrific Rick who was heading for Nepal at midday on Sunday. Ellie went quiet round about Saturday lunchtime, which was always a bad sign so I called in Laura to make some noise. I can't say I was too keen on what I heard, though.

"I remember my first real love," she said, as we sat beneath the big beech, eating a scratch lunch.

"Love?" I said. "The boy's only been here five days. That can't be love."

"I don't know what else you'd call it. I mean you must have seen the way they look at each other, heard how they laugh at each other's little jokes. Like minds, in good-looking heads."

I'd noticed it all.

"I still wouldn't call it love. Come with us to the airport tomorrow?"

She nodded.

***

We drove Rick and Ellie to Heathrow the next day, said goodbye to him an hour before his departure gate closed and left the two of them to it.

I glanced down from a balcony at one stage, or rather Laura pointed them out to me as if to prove that they were in love. They were kissing. They weren't climbing all over each other, they'd both been too well brought up for that, but they were… kissing. Like lovers. Like people who weren't sure when they would meet again, but meet they would.

The drive home was subdued. That's how Ellie copes with mini-hells. In silence. The rest of the day was quiet as well and she buried whatever sadness she felt beneath preparations for the following day, her first at The Oxford Gazette. She went to bed early. I thought I heard her sobbing at about half ten but I didn't go up. Maybe I should've done. Her mother would have done.

I rose early to make sure that she wasn't late on her first day. She was already up and super-charged for the day ahead.

"It's Fee's," she said of the outfit she was wearing. She'd expected me to recognise it. "There's a whole cupboard of her stuff on the corridor, hardly worn. The money that woman must have spent!"

I sat down at the table and sipped at the coffee she'd made me.

"You're all set then?" I said.

She nodded. "Looking forward to it. Clare Parker's picking me up at the bus-stop. Did I mention that?" I shrugged. "You know Clare. Yes you do, you always used to like her. You said she could talk to grown-ups – that thing Mum and you prized so highly? I'll have to give her money for petrol but it seems like a good deal."

"Ellie, calm down a bit."

"I am calm. I'm just excited. What's wrong with being excited? Bloody hell."

"I'll walk up with you."

"What for? I know where the bus-stop is. No one's going to attack me on the way. Oh, and if there's an emergency, phone Clare. I've written her number on the notice board."

"Dinner tonight?"

"Come off it, Dad, I'm not thinking that far ahead. You see to yourself, I'll do something later for me."

She paused for much needed breath.

"Heh, pretty mean of me, yeah?" she said in her normal voice.

"What?"

She smiled. "Sure I'd like you to walk up to the bus-stop with me."

"No, really, if you'd rather…"

"Don't start that. Two minutes." She hurried away in the direction of the stairs and paused as she reached the foot of them. "Thanks, Dad. For yesterday. You played it just right."

"You're welcome."

She glanced at her watch for the umpteenth time and hared off up the stairs.

***

Like most bad news it came in the middle of the night. I woke to the sound of the phone ringing beside my bed and I reached out to grab it. A withheld number.

"Hallo!"

Unlike me, the bloke at the other end was wide awake. "Mr Hawk?

"Yeah, who's this?"

"My name is Richard Crane."

I was awake now, by God, and the caller was waiting for me to react. I didn't oblige.

"Still there?" he asked.

"Yeah."

"Good. It is exactly 3.17 am so you've plenty of time before the world gets into gear. Have you a pencil and paper to hand?"

It was a courteous voice, mid-thirties at a guess and its rough-sided owner was aspiring to be someone beyond his reach. Someone posh. I reached out for the pad on the bedside table.

"What's all this about, Mr Crane?"

"I'm going to give you an Ordnance Survey map reference. Are you ready?"

I didn't answer. He repeated the question more forcefully, still calm but less polite.

"Are you ready?"

"Yes."

"SP 673064." I wrote the figures down. "Read it back to me, if you'd be so kind."

"SP 673064."

"You'll see that it's just off the Tiddington Road, couple of miles beyond Thame. There's a stream there which runs underground for about 20 yards. Near where it emerges again there's a derelict barn, quite small. Stand in its doorway and at roughly North East, ten paces, there is an oak post. Beneath it is buried what you're looking for."

"What am I looking for?"

"Teresa Stillman."

I'd known what he was going to say, of course, from the moment he asked me to confirm my name. Even so, it was a chilling thing to finally hear.

"Now just a second…" I began, forever the copper.

The man had rung off. And then the image of John Stillman, sitting across from me outside Giacometto's, begging me to search for his daughter, floated into my mind and settled there. I had an uneasy feeling that at last I'd found her.

***

You need two things for digging up a grave, especially one whose exact position you aren't sure of. You need a good spade and an even better dog. I wrote a hasty note to Ellie, saying that I'd been called away, wishing her good luck on her second day, asking her to phone me about dinner that night. That seemed like enough fatherly fuss to allay any fears she might've had about my early morning absence.

There was no traffic on the road to Oxford, which gave the journey a sense of driving through a bad dream. I was thinking of Teresa, trying to bring her face to mind from the few photos I had seen. The father in me wanted to meet her at the appointed place – the derelict barn – to shake her hand, to exchange pleasantries, perhaps even to embrace her like a long lost friend. The copper in me said that wasn't going to happen. In the ten-mile drive I was travelling from the last hope of her being found alive to the near certainty that she was dead. I should've phoned Kelloway, I knew that. The reason I didn't reflects badly on me, but I wanted him to take his rightful place in the pecking order since I'd achieved, on my own and in roughly twelve days, what he hadn't come close to in three months. I had spoken to Teresa Stillman's killer. And in talking to me, albeit so briefly, he had given me a whole new angle on his victim's death…

With dawn breaking to reveal low, fast-moving cloud, I parked up on a verge just west of the grid reference I'd been given. I guessed that the derelict barn lay in a small copse the other side of a field of barley, as tall as it would ever get, but a full two months away from harvesting. The boundary hedge was laden with green blackberries, strung out between overgrown shoots of hawthorn and hazel, all in need of the sun to ripen them. I climbed over the metal gate and, spade over shoulder, walked the edge of the field with Dogge running ahead of me.

At the trees a barbed wire fence divided the field from the no-man's-land of the stream my caller had mentioned. I pressed down on the wire, sidestepped over it and then, using the spade, hacked through a wall of nettles, their sting at its most potent with the advance of summer. Beyond them, twenty feet away, stood the jagged remains of the stone barn.

I made my way to its entrance and turned north-east to face a stone wall. My caller was a tall man if all it had taken him to reach the oak post before me was ten paces. I went over to it. It had once held a gate through to the next field. Now it marked the last but one resting place of Teresa Stillman. The ground at my feet showed no sign of recent disturbance. Three months of rain and warmth had seen to that and the grass all around was clumped and well-rooted. I settled Dogge at a slight distance from me and trod the spade in. Once through the stubborn turf it sank with comparative ease into damp earth. I lifted a spadeful and carefully laid it aside.

"Here girl," I muttered to Dogge, with forced excitement. "What do you make of this? Come on, have a look."

She trotted over to where I'd scarred the ground, sniffed once and looked up at me for explanation. I sank the spade in again, beside the first cut, and lifted another chunk of earth. I chopped at the surface I'd laid bare and tried to enthuse Dogge again.

"What's this, then? Come on, what's this, what's this?"

She came to where I'd dug and twitched her nose, seemingly unimpressed. Then, as I removed a third spadeful, she changed her mind. Her ears pricked up, her nose went down and she did a sweep of the immediate area. After a few seconds of she sat down and looked at me for a reward.

"Good girl, yes," I said, taking a small biscuit from my pocket. "What is it? What have you found?"

She had found the remains of Teresa Stillman.

***

Later that day I drove down to Mayfield House to break the terrible news to John Stillman. I had found his daughter's grave at roughly 4.30 that morning and within an hour the place had become a crime scene, the burial site had been tented over and the men and women in white coats had moved in. Alone for the first time since just after dawn, I could mull over my feelings about Teresa and her sudden materialisation, albeit as a corpse and not a living person.

Kelloway had told the assembled company that Teresa was now no longer a missing person but the subject of a murder inquiry and in a strange kind of way that brought her more firmly into being. The fact that her remains were to hand gave her dimension, a physicality that previously she had lacked in my mind. By her death, if you will, she had come to life.

The opposite would be true for John Stillman, of course. While she was missing she'd been very much alive in a thousand scenarios that had simply taken her out of his sight. Now he would be faced with evidence that he would never see her again. At the moment that evidence was largely circumstantial and therefore arguable. Within the week it would be irrefutable. I'm not sure whether I was elected, or if I volunteered, to be the one to tell Stillman the news. Kelloway had made some vague objection, based on procedure, but he hadn't put up much of a fight. Nor had his boss.

At Mayfield I parked the Land Rover under the cedars and as I did so the front door to the house opened and Mrs Jenkins immediately gathered from my expression that all was not well.

"What is it?" she asked, as I approached.

"Is Mr Stillman in?"

"Yes, he's in the kitchen. Why? What's wrong?"

As she led the way down the hall so Stillman emerged from the kitchen, cigarette poised. We both stopped and he took a good lawyer's look at me and knew instantly why I was there. Nevertheless he tried to delay the awful truth, struggled to give himself a few more precious moments of believing that his daughter would walk in one day with her rational explanation of the last three months.

"Ah, Mr Hawk, how are you?" he said. "And how is your good lady? I must say I found her absolutely charming… how is she?"

"John, I have to tell you something…"

He was listening but refusing to hear. He was hell-bent on talking about Laura.

"I do like women with brains and beauty. I like height as well, you see, having so little of it myself. I like stature, both physical and intellectual. You are a very lucky fellow…"

"John…"

"Come into the kitchen, my dear chap. Mrs Jenkins'll fix you up with some coffee."

He turned and scuttled back the way he'd come. Mrs Jenkins looked at me, baffled by her employer's delaying tactics. I gestured for her to follow me into the kitchen. Stillman had opened a fresh packet of cigarettes by the time we entered. He stood by the kitchen range, hand trembling as he poked a wooden spill through the grate and lit it from the glowing coals. He straightened up and turned to us, displacing every thought in the room with lighting the cigarette and blowing out the makeshift match. After a moment of silence he closed his eyes and said, in the smallest voice I'd ever heard him use: "Please … please don't do this to me."

"I've found her body, John."

"How can you have done? It's been two weeks, that's all! How come you and not the police…?"

"John, listen to me!" The sharpness in my voice brought him round. "I found her body this morning, in a field outside Thame. The police are there now. They'll take her to the mortuary, they'll do tests to find out how she died."

"Are they sure it's her?" said Mrs Jenkins.

I nodded. "Her bag was buried alongside her. The seven thousand pounds was still in it."

Stillman looked at me and began to sway on his feet. I took him by both shoulders to stop him falling, and eased him down into one of the chairs at the table. Out of pure habit Mrs Jenkins pushed an ashtray along to him. He nodded his thanks to both of us then looked down at the cigarette in his hands.

"I'll just finish this. It'll be the last one I ever smoke. Do you think that's a good idea, Mr Hawk?"

"I do."

"Can I see her?"

"There's nothing to see."

"Is there any clue as to how she might have…?"

He shook his head, hands wide, as if pleading with me one last time to say that I'd got it all wrong, there'd been some ghastly mistake.

"She was shot. Through the head."

Behind us, Mrs Jenkins's nerve failed her and she broke into stifled sobs. Stillman looked up at her, reached out to take her hand.

"Do they know why?" he asked.

"No, they don't," I said. "But I think I do."

He looked at me with a touch of the fire I'd seen before in his eyes. I raised a hand to calm him.

"Now isn't the time to try and make sense of it, John, but we will, soon."

"Do they know who?"

"No."

"Do you?"

"No."

He nodded, then crushed out the half-smoked cigarette and waved both his housekeeper and me away from him. We stepped back, he took a gasping breath and flopped forward across the table in howling tears. Mrs Jenkins went to comfort him, but I barred her way. Reluctantly she followed me out through the back door and we left Stillman to his inconsolable grief.

***

I sat in the garden with Mrs Jenkins for the next hour listening to John Stillman's anguish coming from the house. It gradually subsided and for the final twenty minutes there was almost perfect silence. That in itself unnerved my companion. Several times she made to go back into the house, fearing for her employer's safety if left alone. Each time I laid a hand on her arm, easing her back down onto the garden bench we'd occupied.

In time John Stillman appeared at the back door. We rose and turned to him. He seemed, somehow, different. He had put on fresh clothes for a start. He had shaved, though I hadn't heard the sound of an electric razor. He had clearly showered, though I hadn't heard water running down drainpipes.

"Ah! There you are," he said, almost cheerily. "I wondered where you'd got to."

His demeanour had changed as well. The manic hope was no longer there and with it had gone the bird-like responses, the willingness to distort the simple words of those around him into evidence that Teresa was still alive. It was clear that there would be no more handbills in the street, no fifty pound tips to unscrupulous waiters, no imagined sightings of his beloved daughter. He had survived the initial shock of his worst fears being realised and was back in the colder, harsher world of reality.

As he came over to us, I saw in his face something of what Michael Carter had meant. Stillman was a man you would laugh at or cross at your peril. He turned to his housekeeper and spoke like a lawyer, calm, easy and to the point.

"Mrs Jenkins, you've been the backbone of this family since either of us cares to remember. I thank you for it."

He turned to me and I took the offered hand.

"Mr Hawk, this last fortnight you've been a tower of strength. I knew you would be, I knew you'd sort this business out one way or the other."

"I'm sorry it ended as it did," I said.

He nodded, slowly, deliberately. "It hasn't ended, though, has it." He smiled. Even his smile was different.

Less immediate, less easily drawn. "Maybe your work will inspire the police to new efforts. On the other hand, why don't you find Teresa's killer for me? I believe we agreed on fifty pounds an hour."

He was back in the land of fine detail and small print. With him being a lawyer I thought it was a good sign.

-12-

I reached home at about six o'clock. The place was deserted. There were, as yet, no reporters wanting to throw money at me, no Ellie waiting to help me catch it. She'd left a message on call minder saying thanks for my note that morning, she'd had a good second day and was going out that evening to Jongleurs, a comedy club in Oxford, with some of the kids at The Gazette. Her breeziness, not to mention her plans to visit a comedy club, seemed so out of place when set against the events of the day.

I dug out a bottle of Bells, took a bag of ice from the freezer and went up to the cabin. If I couldn't touch base with Ellie then I'd email my other kids and do so quickly, before the whisky blur set in. There were messages from all three of them waiting for me. Reassuringly, they were poking their noses into one of their sibling's affairs. The message from Fee simply said,

"Dad, who's this Terrific Rick you went on about last email? Full report please. F."

God help you Rick, I thought, the heavy cannon is pointing at you now. Try breaking the big sister, little sister bond, you'll pay with your balls.

I filled a glass with ice and added the scotch. Took a swig. Rick's okay, I wanted to say to Fee, albeit grudgingly. Good family, well-educated, polite and best of all... he's moved on. I would have added, since such things were important to Fiona, that he was good-looking.

Jaikie's message was ... well, more like Jaikie, I suppose.

"Hi, Dad. Hear that Ellie's got a new bloke. What's he like? I mean do I have to fly over there and kick butt or can you manage? The previews are going well, by the way, and Sophie Kent's become the darling of Hollywood – which isn't to say that I haven't! Remember Sophie? Old mate from drama school…?"

Having reminded me, quite unnecessarily, who Sophie was he moved swiftly on to how well his performance in All Good Men and True had been received. And whereas Jaikie could ramble on forever, providing he figured largely in what was being said, Con's developing style was brief to the point of verbal anorexia.

"Dad. Terrific Rick? Okay?"

He didn't even ask me to lend him money. Since our trip to LA, that privilege had been passed down the line to Jaikie. I hoped.

I didn't reply to their messages. Answering trivial stuff about Ellie's love life seemed small beer in the light of what had happened. My mind swung back and forth between intense sorrow and guilt-heavy relief. My gang was alive and well, all pointing in the same direction, still minding each other's business. John Stillman's only daughter, or what was left of her, was lying in a mortuary. A couple of drinks later I phoned Laura and she took longer than usual to answer.

"Doctor Peterson," said the low, husky voice.

"Hi! Have you got someone with you?" She took it the wrong way, derailing our conversation before it had even started.

"What if I have?" she asked.

"Well, nothing. I just meant have you because if you haven't I'd fancy a chat. I've had the mother and father of all rotten days…"

"My own hasn't been much to write home about," she cut in.

"I found Teresa Stillman's body."

Down she came off the high horse, nearly breaking her neck in the fall.

"I'll be right over," she said.

The phone went dead and I smiled down at a doodle of myself on the blotter, one of Con's, from five years ago. God knows why I kept a blotter. I hadn't used a fountain pen for twenty years but where else would those who used my office to email or fax from leave their mark? Among the smiling faces and matchstick men with bubbles coming out of their mouths, there was a brand new imprint in Ellie's scrawl. A single made-up word. Lovesmith. A meaningless word with lots of meaning. Full of implications, the kind you don't want to go into if it's written in your daughter's hand and a boy called Rick Bettuccio has recently turned her head. Lovesmith. I went into the house to forget about it and to wait for Laura.

She arrived by car about ten minutes later and the first thing she did as she entered was safely in character. She pointed at the bottle on the table. She'd lectured me so often about the evils of too much scotch that she'd run out of fresh things to say about it.

I said for her, "Just because someone's been murdered doesn't mean you have to get pissed? Is that your opinion?"

"Have you eaten?"

"No."

She laid a hand on my shoulder. "You should. I'm a doctor. I know about these things."

She went over to the fridge, yanked it open and looked in. She wasn't impressed. She pulled out a casserole dish with half a shepherd's pie in it, all crusty and shrinking away from the glazed sides.

"How long has this been here?"

"Twelve years," I said. "The moment it reaches its teens I'll chuck it out."

"Yes, well, it'll have to be a cheese sandwich with old salad, I'm afraid. If you've got bread."

I pointed at the bread bin and she went over to it.

"So, you were right, then," she said. "I was wrong, Ellie was wrong, John Stillman was wrong, we were all wrong except for you. You said she was dead."

"You've got the 'ump because I'm drinking. Well, the reason I'm doing that is because I'd almost come round to Stillman's way of thinking – the whole thing would end happily ever after."

She put the bread knife to the three-day-old loaf and cursed under her breath when it skidded off. She went to the sink and ran the tap gently.

"Washing the bread?" I said.

"I'm going to soften it." She passed it quickly under the trickle of water, turned off the tap and put the loaf in the Aga.

"Three minutes. It'll be like new."

She took a bag of salad from the fridge and began sorting the rotting leaves from the usable ones.

"Have you seen her father?" she asked.

"Yeah. He a patient of yours?"

"He's registered at the clinic. Hasn't been seen by any of us for years. That's partly to do with him smoking, of course."

"It keeps him fit you mean?"

"We operate a no smoking policy."

I looked at her to check that she was serious. She nodded and Dogge slunk away under the table at the sound of approaching trouble.

"That is outrageous," I said. "A man smokes, you refuse to treat him?"

She glanced at the whisky bottle, still on the table. "We're thinking of applying the same rule to heavy drinkers. Why should we help people who're determined to kill themselves?"

"That's like saying…" I didn't really know what it was like saying but I came up with something. "That's like saying why should the police find a killer when his victim's already dead!"

"It's nothing of the kind. Now tell me about Teresa."

"I found her in a scrappy little copse beside a field outside Thame. A grey-green sticky mess with smell to match. And that poked through face they have at three months dead, the skin drawn back, teeth everywhere like someone's just told 'em a bad joke."

I threw more ice into my glass and added whisky until it ran over the edge.

"It's your liver not mine," she muttered. "It may end up as big as a bull's but you're the one who'll have to carry it round…"

"Laura, I didn't ask you here to pull your face about whisky, or give me household tips, or make me a bloody sandwich!"

I slammed the glass down on the table and felt it crack in my hand. As I let go of it the glass fell apart and ice and whisky rolled in all directions.

"Hand?" Laura said, eventually.

I showed it to her. Satisfied that I wasn't injured she began gathering up the larger shards of glass, dropping them into the swing bin. She then picked out the ice cubes and slung them into the sink. She put her forefinger under my chin, lifted my head until my eyes met hers.

"Shall I sponge up the whisky and squeeze it into another glass for you?"

"No need. I've a whole case of it in the scullery."

"Why doesn't that surprise me?"

I sat quietly at the table while she mopped the surface of it, then rinsed her hands and went back to her sandwich construction.

"So, why did you get me round here?" she asked.

"To rent more brain space off you. No squad to haul me out of blind alleys. No means of getting at the truth – no foot soldiers, no data-base junky, no records – just all the mistakes I've made in the past thirty years…"

She stopped what she was doing, salad-wise. "And the things you got right. twenty-eight of them."

I'd asked for reassurance, like boozers do when they're down, and she'd given me some.

"This'll be number twenty-nine, if I get there before Kelloway and his BAs in Criminology. It's a murder now, officially, but to solve it no doubt the police'll go right back to the people they first interviewed."

"Shouldn't they?"

"Hardly a motive in sight, not even the seven thousand quid now. it was in the grave, good as new, still in the plastic wallet Carter gave her. Bodies rot, money doesn't."

"What about his motive, Michael Carter' Revenge against John Stillman, you said the other day."

"Yes, but if he'd killed her wouldn't he have taken his money back?"

"Unless leaving it there says he can't possibly be the one?"

I shook my head, more than I needed to. "That assumes he knew the body would be dug up one day. No murderer hides a body on that premise."

She nodded, went to the Aga and pulled out the washed bread. She turned to me, squeezing it like it was fresh.

"Then there's Joanna," I said. "If Joanna had killed her why would she try and blackmail Darcy Morrell?"

"What about Darcy herself?"

"Vain, stupid, self-important. Her kind doesn't commit murder. They just shout at the hirelings."

"And Tom Gibson?"

"He's not so easy to lay aside. Besotted with Teresa yet didn't do a thing to find her. That bothers me…"

She stacked the old salad onto the cheese, put the lid on the sandwich and pressed down. It sprung back to its former height the moment she let go. She nudged the plate it was on across the table to me and said, "Looks nice. Eat it. And tell me how you actually found this poor girl."

"A man phoned me in the middle of the night and gave me an Ordnance Survey map reference."

"You mean Teresa went missing, the police searched for three months and got nowhere? You came on the scene and within a fortnight someone told you exactly what you needed to know?"

"Not just someone, Laura, I think it was the man who killed her. Richard Crane, he calls himself, though whether that's his real name, I've no idea. He saw the story in the paper, the Darcy Morrell thing, it said I was looking for Teresa."

"So?"

"Something he read... prompted him, disturbed him, I don't know."

She sat back and gave that some thought, then said, "Why would the man who killed Teresa Stillman suddenly tell you where to find her body?"

I snapped my fingers but they were slightly too full of alcohol to make a clicking sound.

"That, my darling, is the crux of it. Not so much a new lead as a new can of worms. And, by the way, I'm heartened that you haven't thrown a bucket of cold psychology over his actions, stuff like he wants to be caught and punished for his crime, so he gets on the blower."

"I may yet do that."

"What happened after he phoned me? Exactly what he thought would happen. I went to the grave and checked his story. Me and Dogge." I looked round. "Where is she?"

Laura nodded under the table and I encouraged Dogge to come out and be praised. I slipped her a piece of the sandwich.

"Unsung heroine of the day. No procedure, no paperwork, just solid nose, eh, girl? Jesus, did Kelloway have a field day with that! Fancy taking a spade and a clapped out dog to a crime scene, he said."

She smiled. "Did you keep your temper? Think of a poem?"

"Ah, yes, that must be what did it. Anyway, by eight o'clock this morning the dump site, as the Americans are so fond of calling it, was alive with scene of crime flunkies, police photographer, pathologist, forensic orthodontist and they said, between them, that what me and my furry friend had dug up used to be Teresa. By the end of the week they'll be able to prove it with DNA, dental records, the whole kit and caboodle..." I looked at her and got her full attention before adding, "And that is what Richard Crane wants to know. He wants to know who he's killed."

"You mean he didn't before?"

"Try again."

She thought for a moment and then voiced the awful truth I'd realised earlier in the day. "You mean he thinks he might have killed the wrong person?"

I tried to snap my fingers again and this time succeeded. "And you know the really nasty thing about that? I'm going to have to go to John Stillman sometime and say this bastard killed your daughter believing she was somebody else. She died by mistake. She was murdered unnecessarily. You have lost her in error. You will never see her again because some evil, blundering bastard fouled up when..."

Laura pulled out a chair and sat down opposite me. "When you say he made a mistake, wrong person, what exactly do you mean? She had a doppelgänger, a look-alike."

"No, look-alikes are easy. You get a photo, you hold it up against the target's face, if it's right you pull the trigger. Did I say she was shot?"

"No."

"Through the head. From the side. They think he probably stood her over the grave, like in some Nazi newsreel, then killed her."

"If she wasn't a look-alike then what was she?"

"She was a name-alike," I said. "I think Richard Crane took her to Giacometto's to check that she was the right Teresa Marie Stillman, the one he'd been paid to kill, or

157

wanted to kill, for whatever reason."

"There can't be many, surely," said Laura.

"Dead right. Type the name into Google you get nothing. I tried it."

"Then how come, after talking to her, he got it so wrong?"

"To answer that I would've had to be there in Giacometto's, ear-wigging the conversation but what if it went something like this? Initial chat, introduction, Roberto the head waiter oozing around on the edges of it. Then at some point in the small talk Crane tries to check her provenance. Does your family live round here, Teresa? She goes all cagey. She can't help it…"

"Why can't she help it?"

"Because policemen, lawyers, judges, we teach our kids from an early age to avoid questions from strangers. You never know who's doing the asking. So, Teresa skimps on detail. My mother's dead, she tells Crane. My father's a lawyer. Do you have brothers and sisters? Crane asks. Why's he asking this? Teresa wonders. I thought he wanted my professional services, not to write a bloody book about me. No, I don't have any brothers and sisters."

I paused and reached out for the whisky bottle. Somehow Laura had made it disappear without me noticing. It didn't matter.

"What does that sound like to you, Laura? Mother dead, no other family?"

"Convenient," she said.

"Right. Nothing to double check on, except the father. But even he's pretty amorphous, being a lawyer. Now, I accept that I'm trying to turn the ugly facts into a beautiful theory that Crane shot the wrong girl. I want him to have come away from Giacometto's believing, by virtue of learning nothing to the contrary, that Teresa was the person he was after."

"Well, for what it's worth, I think it's entirely feasible. Where do you go from here, though?"

"I told John Stillman I'd find whoever's responsible. Best way of doing that is to find the girl Teresa was mistaken for. If nothing else, she needs warning that Richard Crane might want to put right his mistake."

***

I was asleep in bed and dreaming. It was one of those dreams you feel partly in control of and, given the subject matter, I kept trying to shift away to something more palatable. I was at the small copse where I'd found Teresa's body, and she was standing over her own grave, looking my way, though I don't think she really saw me. She had grey masking tape over her mouth and half a reel of it binding her wrists. I switched channels to something erotic. Laura walked into an LA hotel room and started to undress in front of me, nothing too garish or fanciful just… getting her kit off. Then she saw the whisky bottle on the kitchen table – which for some reason we'd taken on holiday with us. She started buttoning up again and I was back at the grave. Only it wasn't Teresa this time, it was Ellie, crying, unable to call out, trying to be tough, family style. She caught sight of me and it made a difference. Somehow she managed to yell,

"Dad, Dad!"

I ran towards her but there was no strength in my body.

"Dad, hi! No, no, it's okay…"

I woke up with her hand gripping my shoulder, holding me down against the pillows.

"Sorry, Dad, I didn't mean to panic you."

I was in bed, on my own, middle of the night. "What time is it?" I asked.

"Two-thirty. I've just got in."

"Right. Who brought you home?"

"Clare. You got my message? Jongleurs?"

I hauled myself into a sitting position and waited for my mind to join me there. "How is Clare? I don't mean her health, I mean her driving?"

"She drives fine."

Ellie sat down on the bed beside me and leaned back against the head board. She had a mug of tea in her hand and slurped from it.

"I take it you've heard?"

"About Teresa? Yes. It was all the talk at the club – well, ten minutes' talk. Someone said you were the dude who found her."

"And The Oxford Gazette wants the story, I suppose?"

She smiled. "It's not really our kind of thing. Or rather it is but a week after the event and watered down so as not to frighten the horses. I've got something for you, though, at least I think it's something you should know."

I reached out and took her hand. "Who drove you home?"

"Dad, we've done that bit. The other day in Oxford, remember? You'd been to see Michael Carter, I'd been showing Rick the sights. We met Tom Gibson on the corner of Clarendon Street. You introduced us."

"I remember."

"Tom and I made out we didn't know each other?"

"I remember that too."

"It wasn't true. I do know him. Tell me what he's got to do with Teresa's death."

"I'm not sure he's got anything. I mean they were certainly an item, which makes him a suspect, but apart from that... How do you know him?"

She turned away from me and gathered her courage.

"He goes to The Bell in Thame most nights of the week. He deals weed. And other stuff."

"To you?"

She couldn't have been quicker to answer. "No, no, course not to me!"

In other words yes.

"Last Friday I took Rick there to meet some friends and Tom was there, usual seat."

"Dealing?"

"Dad, get past the dealing thing." I nodded my willingness to do so. "He was pissed as a rat and he had that… dangerous thing about him that some drunks have. Look at them the wrong way, they're up on their hind legs spoiling for a fight. Anyway, he saw me, called me over, then started having a bloody go at me."

"What about?

"About you, Dad. He said you'd stirred it all up again – the Teresa Stillman thing – with all your questions, playing it like a hard man. He'd just about come to terms with her dying when you showed up and brought back all the guilt."

"He used the word guilt?"

Ellie nodded. "And then he burst into tears and out came a load of maudlin old fanny about Teresa being the only woman for him, him being the only man for her, and so on. Made a right dick of himself. Then, and this is the relevant bit… you properly awake?"

"Fresh as a daisy."

"Then he pointed at me, like he was going to threaten me, but what he said was 'Tell your old man to watch his step. There are people at the bottom of this who won't stop because some retired copper has come onto the scene.'"

He had said something vaguely similar to me when I'd visited him by the river at Chapel Farm. Ellie rose from the bed. I reached out and caught her by her free hand.

"Ellie, do me a favour. Stay out of his way for a couple of weeks."

She didn't like that. "Heh, I'm not scared of him, Dad!"

"Pretend to be, just for my sake. Try and avoid him."

She pulled an eloquent face that said I was worrying unnecessarily but she would indulge me nevertheless. She leaned forward and kissed me on the forehead. "Can I have my hand back?" she asked. I let go of it. "And can I go up to your cabin, check my email? My iPhone's messing me about."

"Help yourself. It's been a rough day, what with finding Teresa, telling her father. Why so urgent, the email?"

"I'm expecting something from Rick."

He'd left us in body but not in spirit. She downed the rest of her tea, set the mug down on my bedside table and went off to continue their relationship. Albeit virtually.

-13-

I woke the next morning to Dogge going nuts and Ellie's raised voice, telling someone to piss off or she'd call her Dad. There was some combative muttering, male voices with a female one thrown in, and then Ellie saying that she'd had enough.

"Dad!" she called out in her best banshee. "Dad, get down here! Reporters!"

I'd made the mistake of drinking two pints of water before going to bed. Laura's hangover cure. Maybe it works, maybe it doesn't but I know for sure that it stops you jumping out of bed. I struggled into a dressing gown and went into the bathroom. By the time I arrived downstairs there were six people in the hall, one of them a girl of about twenty-six, instantly describable as long. Long hair, long face, long nose, long body... long neck. She did most of the talking for the other five and pitched in straightaway with questions about Teresa Stillman. What did Richard Crane sound like? What were his actual words? Would I be trying to find him? Did I think the police had done a good job or, like the tabloids said, had they cocked it up? Was it me who'd dropped Darcy Morrell in it? How much was John Stillman paying me? Why did I go to the dump site on my own? Is that the cadaver dog...?

I went over to the dresser drawer and took out Laura's poetry book. I flicked it open at a random page and turned to them. As I began to read, they fell silent, no doubt wondering what they'd done to deserve a poetry reading.

"If I should die, think only this of me;

That there's some corner of a foreign field
That is for ever England. There shall be
In that rich earth a richer dust concealed..."

I looked at them, gesturing for someone to carry on from there. No takers. Perhaps it was the way I'd read it that had unsettled them. Eventually the long girl said, cautiously, "The Soldier. Rupert Brooke."

I nodded. "And it was meant to calm me down but I'm afraid it hasn't. So you guys need to be the other side of my front gate within ten seconds or someone'll be writing a poem, in the same vein, about you."

I snapped the book shut as if it were some winged creature snapping at flies, and almost in unison they began to back away, then turned and left. Witness the power of war poetry. It can move people. Off your property.

***

Chapel Farm had been suffering from the recent lack of rain. The ground had been hard enough when I'd driven across it a fortnight previously. Today it was like stone with a fine dust on the surface, which the occasional breeze scooped up and flung at the Land Rover.

I parked at the gate to the meadow and made my way, through recently fleeced sheep, down to the river. The water was slow moving and shallow and at the bend in the distance there was no sign of Tom Gibson's tent. For a moment I thought I'd come on a wild goose chase until I saw his rucksack. He was in the process of moving out. As I approached I saw him down at the water's edge, retrieving his keep net. He looked across at me.

"You found her then," he said.

"Yeah. You off?"

He climbed back up the bank on his side, standing with the net poised as if he would run towards me and catch me like a butterfly. He began to fold it instead.

"It's all the talk at The Bell, I gather."

I slid down the bank on my side and stepped into the water. It seeped in, slow and lukewarm, through the seams of the boots I'd so carefully waterproofed before leaving the house. At the other side, Tom didn't stretch out a helping hand as he'd done on my previous visit. He left me to it.

I looked round at his camp. The tent was rolled up and strapped to the rucksack. He had cut down the flowers and vegetables. The fire was still glowing. He'd been burning stuff he didn't want to take with him.

"Where are you heading?" I asked.

"I don't know."

"More interesting question is why… why leave now?"

"I'm sick of the neighbours dropping in all the time, asking questions."

"The ones I've got today will take you two minutes. You knew all along Teresa was dead, right? If you killed her, you certainly did."

"I didn't know anything, not for a couple of weeks." He shrugged. "After that, what else could she be other than dead?"

"Did you really go to your parents that weekend? Or did you set off, turn back, have a row with Teresa and murder her?"

He gestured with hands outstretched and splayed fingers, his voice rising, "I went to Manningtree." He calmed a little. "Teresa wouldn't come with me. If she had done, if I hadn't got arsy with her, if I'd stayed to keep an eye, she'd still be alive."

He meant it. He believed that he might have been able to save her.

"You talk like she needed a minder," I said.

"Needed something, didn't she."

He went over to his rucksack, crouched down and started to fasten the net to it.

"And what do I need? I'm out of my depth, according to you. 'There are people at the end of this who won't stop because some retired copper has come onto the scene.' What people?"

"Listen, you found Teresa's body, that's what her father wanted. Job done. Go home."

"He wants me to find out who killed her."

He straightened up. "Leave it to the cops."

"Fat lot of good they've been so far. You know, I always thought it odd that nobody tried to find her, dead or alive, except her father. Police didn't, friends and colleagues didn't. You didn't. Yet she was the love of your life, you said."

And as if that notion had some intrinsic power, the dying fire beside us suddenly came to life again, fuelled by a breeze. The charred willow started to crackle and spit. He looked at me.

"When Teresa disappeared I was... in bits. I thought it was my fault, that she'd had enough of me, I was too moody, too demanding... all those things you blame yourself for when a relationship ends. I spent two weeks feeling sorry for myself, then decided to do something. I broke into her digs in Cuxham. Nothing had been touched. There were even coffee cups in the sink growing mould, stuff in the fridge gone rotten. I took her laptop, rigged it up at my place and sent a mail-shot to everyone in her address file. More than three hundred names. I made the email big and in your face, 'Teresa Marie Stillman. Somebody must know something. Where is she? When did you last see her? Who was she with? I'm desperate to know. Get back to me'."

His voice had sunk to a whisper as he relived the events, the response to his mail-shot.

"Four days after I'd sent it, this bloke turned up on my doorstep. My first thought was army, the way he carried himself. I should call him Jack, he said. And he had this... edge to him. You know they say that if you join the SAS they give you a rabbit as a pet. You have to groom it, feed it, clean up after it, get it to trust you implicitly. Then they make you kill it, skin it, cook it and eat it. Jack could have done that without batting an eyelid."

"What did he look like?"

"Late thirties, sort of auburnish, corrugated hair. Pasty face, freckles, eyes like the proverbial piss-holes. Not a big man, but who needs to be big if you can do that to your pet rabbit?"

"What did he want?"

"He came in, uninvited, searched my flat like I was some kind of terrorist, then asked me a string of questions. How did I know Teresa? When had I last seen her? What made me think she'd gone missing? Then he asked me to describe her. That's when I bit back. You sound like you know her, I said, why come to me for the finer details? He swung round and punched me in the stomach. I've always thought I could handle myself but I didn't see that one coming. Next morning I woke up, blood on the pillow beside me, I'd brought it up in the night. I couldn't eat properly for three weeks. Every time I took a piss it was agony."

I nodded. "Knew what he was doing. But you don't think he knew Teresa?"

"All I know is he told me to stop looking for her. When I asked him why, I thought he was going to thump me again. 'You'll know why on Tuesday', he said. Sure enough, Tuesday came and in the post was a whole bunch of photos. Mum, Dad, my brother, sister, her three kids, her husband. And a slip of paper that said 'Don't go looking'. The message couldn't have been plainer."

"So you gave up."

"You make it sound like I chickened out…"

I shook my head. "You did the right thing. Did you tell John Stillman about it?"

"I couldn't. He so wanted to believe she was still alive. I knew she was dead."

The fire had died down again. He separated the embers with the toe of his boot and reached for a water bottle to finish the job properly.

"I've got a few other questions," I said, over the rising steam. "About my daughter."

He was quick to respond. "I don't know her."

I was even quicker. "She says you do. I say she buys weed off you."

"What does she say?"

"Does she or doesn't she?"

"Couple of eighths in the last three weeks."

"How much did that cost her? Twenty quid a time?" He nodded. "Did she buy anything else from you?"

"Listen, man, I don't push stuff at people. I get them what they want, okay?"

"So what did she want?"

"Dope!"

"Nothing else?"

"Not from me. Listen you'd be far better off asking her these questions…"

I'd have been far better off knowing what the other £110 of my hard-earned pension had been spent on.

***

The next morning I drove over to see John Stillman who, true to his word, hadn't smoked another cigarette since I'd found his daughter's body. We sat in his kitchen, in ancient armchairs, when we could have chosen what seemed like a dozen other rooms to talk in. With hands steepled together, forefingers supporting his chin, he fixed his gaze on a crack in one of the floor tiles and listened intently as I outlined my theory that Teresa had been murdered by mistake. I'd expected the proposition to unsettle him but instead it brought some measure of relief. He was glad, he said, that she hadn't had enemies. He was even more pleased that his own enemies had not sought their revenge by taking his daughter's life. Even so, he was more determined than ever that I should find her killer.

Back at Beech Tree I went up to the cabin to make a phone call. The disinterested voice at the other end said, "Yeah?"

"That's polite for you, Steve. Not going soft in your old age, I hope? Nathan Hawk."

He chuckled as he'd always done, like an old Harley, ticking over but ready to zip past you and leave you standing.

"How you doing?" he asked.

"Fine. You?"

He didn't sound sure. Steve Yates never sounded sure about anything, just in case you held him to it years later.

"Slogging on. One year to go."

"Then what?"

"Ah, well, you know… plans."

"It's me, Steve, not the Devon Gestapo."

He paused for a moment. "We're going round the world. Me and Steph. On the bike."

It was my turn to laugh. "What?"

"See, you're like everyone else. They think I must have a bolt missing…"

"I don't think you're mad, I'm just surprised."

He sniffed. "Why?

"Because we used to have trouble getting you to leave the manor for half an hour, never mind go off round the world. Remember that trip we made to pick up that bastard from Schipol?"

And we were off – his kids, my kids, his dog, my Dogge, his new wife Stephanie, my new… friend Laura. Eventually I heard a sing-song voice in the background call him for Sunday lunch and he brought the conversation back into line.

"So what is it this time, Nathan? Something to do with Teresa Stillman?"

"You've been reading the papers again. Yeah, could you run the name through all the mangles, see what you come up with? I know it's not as easy as it used to be, trouble if you get caught with your hand on someone's details…"

He chuckled again. The Harley had warmed up a little. "No one catches me, Guvnor, you know that. What's the name you want checked?"

"Teresa Marie Stillman." I spelt the three names for him. "Thing is, I've actually found her, or rather I've found what's left of her. For a shedful of reasons that I won't bother you with, since your dinner's on the table, I think she's been killed by mistake. Someone shot the wrong girl."

"And you want me to see how many others there are? Okay, give me a couple of days. I'll try our own database first but it so happens I've got a body, washed up on the shore three days ago, no ID. Middle-aged woman, nothing suspicious but I've every reason to go poking round in the new NHS computer."

The voice in the background summoned him again, telling him the soup was going cold. Soup? The man really had landed on his feet.

"I've got to go," he said.

"Sure. What kind of soup?"

"Leek and potato," he said casually, and rang off.

I turned to check my email. The account that came on screen first wasn't mine, it was Ellie's. That feeling of dread you sometimes get in a bad situation caught me just below the sternum. I wasn't really sure why. All I know is that my hand hovered over the keyboard, withdrew, went forward again and then clicked the mouse. A box appeared, asking for a password. I didn't know it. Or did I? I paused again and looked round, presumably to see if anyone had slipped into the cabin without me noticing. No one had. I typed in the word 'Lovesmith'. I clicked the open button and there they were, four emails in her Inbox, five in the Sent folder.

Feeling small enough to crawl under any key on the pad, I opened the first message from Terrific Rick, and read: "Hi, Ellie, thought I shouldn't waste any time checking in with you…"

He went on to say what a terrific place Nepal was and how much he thought she would love it. I skim read down through his reasons and wound up at a paragraph beginning, "How goes the struggle, eh, kid? Believe me, it is worth it. Like I told you that day in Oxford, I'm here because I flunked out of college. Why did I flunk? Stuff, man. Gear. I'd been smoking since the eighth grade and I'd become, well… the guy who was always caned. I was the one who had to take a breath in the middle of a word, not just a goddam sentence, because I didn't have the mental energy to spit out all the syllables in one go. Look, I'm sorry, I'm giving you a hard time…"

More than anything at that particular moment, I wanted to read Ellie's answer. I clicked over to the Sent folder and opened the first message.

"Hi, Ricky my sweet…"

Stung by guilt at even being there, in her personal correspondence, I skipped to a new paragraph.

"As for the dope, well, I'm giving it my best shot, which is like saying no, not yet, but I will. I've been using less since, well, since my old man started getting suspicious…"

The cabin door opened and I hit the power button, crashing the computer. Ellie walked in and paused. We could both hear the screen crackling as it cooled.

"Hi, Dad. You using the computer? I'll come back."

"No, no," I insisted, rising from the chair. "Have it now. I've just finished."

***

Steve Yates rang me back a few days later, Thursday to be precise. He had scoured just about every database he could access, legally or otherwise, and had come up with three Teresa Marie Stillmans. The first was John Stillman's daughter. The second was a woman of 87, living in Falmouth. The third was more hopeful. She was 23, Steve told me, known as Terri more than Teresa, and lived near Blackburn in Lancashire. Number 4A Mellor Brook Close, to be precise. He'd found her details via the NHS Strategic Tracing Service, he said, then sucked in air like a plumber giving a tricky estimate.

"That noise used to mean you had a problem, Steve."

"It's nothing, I'm sure."

Which meant, of course, that he thought it was something.

"There isn't a great deal of info on her, as medical records go, and I've got a theory about that."

"Let's hear it."

There was more taking in of air. "Well, she had all the usual jabs at childhood, right — mumps, measles, whooping cough, whatever else they have but that's it. There's a blank between then and a year ago, when she broke her right arm. But that's all. Childhood inoculation, last one at eight years old, then nothing for twelve years."

"So what's your theory?

"She's been living abroad. I'd say she went as a kid with her parents and came back to university or something. Stayed."

"Sounds good," I said.

He paused. "Be nice to see you again, Nathan, to meet up sometime. I know we say it every time. I know it won't happen. But it would be nice."

I wanted to say that I agreed with him, but he'd already put the phone down.

-14-

A couple of days later the Coroner released Teresa Stillman's body for burial. Her father organised a service for her in the private chapel at Mayfield House. It was a dignified affair attended by some of those who'd been close to her. There were no hymns, no homilies, no poetry readings, just a few prayers and a bible reading that Tom Gibson delivered with some style.

Joanna Bailey was one of the mourners. I wanted to ask how she reconciled her presence there with having wanted to use Teresa's death as an opportunity to blackmail the person she thought had killed her. But we steered clear of each other.

There was an assortment of Teresa's old school friends, some kids from the design course at Greenwich and a sheepish looking Jim Kelloway. Most impressive of all, however, was Michael Carter. In a display of genuine mutual respect, he and Stillman shook hands over the past and chatted like old friends.

There was no sign of anyone answering to the description of Richard Crane, nor was there any sign of the man who had chauffeured Darcy Morrell the day she threatened Teresa. The auburn haired man who'd thumped Tom Gibson to such good effect had steered clear as well. I hadn't really expected him to do otherwise.

Teresa was buried alongside her mother in the small piece of consecrated ground beside the chapel. A last attempt at reconciliation. Mrs Jenkins had laid on food for the gathering but there was no pretence of this being a celebration of Teresa's life. She had barely had one.

There was no bid to jollify the event with witty speeches or reminiscences. It was a solemn and subdued recognition of a terrible tragedy.

***

As life would have it, one or two domestic problems leaped out at me over the next twenty-four hours, stopping me in my tracks. The worst of them happened on Wednesday night when some ancient plumbing in the loft chose to spring a leak and brought down some plaster in the back bedroom. Alan Potton sorted the pipe work out for fifty quid and half an hour's chat the very next day. Danny Price saw to the plasterwork on Friday for roughly the same amount so I reckon I got off lightly. I wish I could say the same about the vet. Dogge's booster jabs came up on the computer and I took her down to the surgery. Two minutes' work, hundred and twenty quid. I sound like my father again but at those prices he would have had reason to balk. And I'd certainly inherited his weakness, his fondness, his predilection – I'm not really sure how to describe it – for worrying about his children. It's a curse that bedevils most parents who believe, in time, they will overcome it. It's wishful thinking of the highest order.

The main reason for my lack of sleep at the moment was Ellie. She'd been living in Paris for over a year now, during which time I'd worried about her once every ten days or so. Now that she was home with me, I was worrying three, four times a week. And I wasn't entirely sure why. However, I woke one night with the name Rick Bettuccio being whispered in my subconscious ear and after twenty minutes of trying to finish a ten-day-old crossword, I got out of bed, slipped on a dressing gown and went downstairs. I made a cup of tea, took it through into the living room and switched on the television ready to settle back and be stupefied by the nocturnal fare of a hundred or so satellite channels.

As luck would have it, the first channel I chose was showing a documentary in which an addict was about to inject himself and thereby set my teeth on edge. He was tapping away at a well used arm to bring up a vein and, under instruction, was positioning the hypodermic at exactly the right angle, having first squirted any air out of the needle. In it went, the plunger went down slowly, out the needle came again. The boy folded up his arm to the praise of his instructor. The camera pulled back to show us that we were in some kind of rehab clinic and it wasn't heroin being doled out, it was methadone.

The nurse turned next to a girl who was also having difficulty preparing her arm. She was becoming anxious, defeatist and the nurse stepped in with encouraging words. She took the girl's hand and together they sought the elusive vein, just above the crook of her elbow, and tapped it into profile. The nurse handed the girl the syringe and turned back to the boy.

He was holding out his hand. The nurse gave him a small round plaster. He removed the plastic cover under her watchful eye and placed the plaster over the needle prick in his arm to stem the oozing blood.

Sudden realisations in the middle of the night never quite have the clarity of their equivalent in the cold light of day, but that doesn't soften their impact. Quite the reverse. I knew those plasters. I'd seen something similar a week or so previously. Complete with red blood spot dead centre. In Ellie's rubbish bin...

The part of my mind that could just about reach forward into the daylight knew for certain that my daughter hadn't been injecting anything, let alone heroin or methadone. Nevertheless, there in the semi-darkness, isolated from the real world at three in the morning, with my imagination about to run riot, I wanted to know chapter and verse on those plasters in the bin. I wanted to know what the money my daughter had cadged off me had been spent on.

I went upstairs and knocked on Ellie's bedroom door. There was a muffled groan from deep inside the cocoon she always made with her duvet. She must have broken through it in order to ask what time it was. I said it was just after three. She groaned again, this time more forcefully.

"Dad, what the fuck…?" she began.

"I need your help with something. Downstairs."

"Can't it wait?"

"No."

A few moments passed and then, through the gap under the door, I saw a light go on. I turned and went downstairs again.

The very act of moving about the house had brought sweet reason back into play. Common sense was filling the vacuum left behind by departing panic. Of course there wasn't a problem here, apart from the suggestive power of television and my copper's mind seeing the worst in everything. None of my children would be so self-destructive, so feeble-minded, as to fall into the heroin trap, even with the social pressures in a place like Paris… Would they?

Ellie stumbled into the kitchen a few minutes later, wearing an old dressing gown over an even older sweater, neither of them hers. She flopped down at the table opposite me and muttered, "This had better be good."

"It isn't," I said.

She squinted at me for a moment, thinking back over what had passed between us in the last few days, what I might have discovered to her embarrassment. According to the cautious smile she gave me, there wasn't much. She half closed her eyes again and tilted her head back to keep me in view. She didn't look like a heroin addict, but I don't suppose many heroin addicts do.

"Well?" she asked eventually, in her challenging way.

"Show me your arm."

If any part of her had still been asleep it woke up then. She opened her eyes fully and gazed into mine and for those first few moments all I could see was full-bodied guilt.

"Oh, Dad… I'm so sorry," she said, quietly. "I didn't want you to find out like this, I wanted to tell you in my own time…"

She pushed her chair back and folded her arms, gripping each above the elbow with the opposite hand.

"You mean I'm right? That's where the money you cadged off me, off Laura, has gone?"

It must have been my obvious distress that warned her. "Dad, you make it sound like I've…"

I rose quickly, walked round the table and stood looking down at her. "I've seen the plasters in the bin, Ellie. I saw them last week…"

"What?!"

She was on her feet too and horrified, not by her own predicament or my anguish, but by the fact that I'd obviously been through her rubbish at an earlier time. And there we were again, moving round a table, Ellie backing away, me in pursuit, only this time there was no doctor in the house to see fair play or separate us if the need arose.

"That is outrageous, Dad! You've been through my room, through my rubbish…?"

"If I hadn't, when would this have come to light? Jesus, I'm supposed to be going to Lancashire, day after tomorrow!"

"What's to stop you?"

"Well, first we have to get you help."

She stared at me in horror, then pulled back the left side of the dressing gown until the shoulder and arm of it fell away. She pulled up the sleeve of the sweater as far as it would go and exposed, right there in the crook of her elbow, a fresh plaster. "Is this what's set you off?" she demanded.

I turned and she followed, caught up with me at the sink, grabbed my arm and spun me round to face her. She was trembling with rage and could hardly get the words out. "You stupid, stupid man…" she managed. "You thought I was shooting up? That is some opinion you've got of me, Dad!"

"A hundred and fifty quid, Ellie, that's how much you've had off me in the last couple of weeks."

She laughed but not in mirth. "You think that would pay for a smack habit?"

"I wouldn't know…"

"Of course you know, you were a bloody copper! What you mean is you didn't think it through properly. You just jumped on the first bandwagon that came along."

"So what should I have thought?" I snapped.

"Anything but the worst! I'm your daughter!"

With that heartfelt reproach the tables had turned. She had become the aggrieved party, I the overbearing tyrant. And with all my training in the mysteries of leading a suspect by the nose, I was left waiting for any explanation she might care to give. She pulled out a chair from the table.

"Dad, sit down," she said, quietly.

"I prefer to stand."

"Then fucking stand!" she yelled, in a momentary relapse.

She calmed herself with a simple Yogic hum, more parody than approved technique. It was a trick she'd learned from her mother and in spite of its impurity it always seemed to work. She led me to the table and sat me down. Once I was settled she showed me her arm again.

"Dad, these aren't needle marks. Well, they are, but they're nothing like what you think. They're jabs, vaccinations – Typhoid, Malaria, Yellow Fever."

"What do you need them for?"

She made me look her in the eye. "I'm going to Nepal."

She held my gaze until I responded. All I could think of to say was, "Terrific Rick?"

She nodded. She went on to explain that the idea of her joining him in Nepal had been mooted way back on the flight home from Los Angeles. She'd told him that she wasn't returning to France, no matter how much pressure her family applied, but at the same time she was looking for something useful to do with her life. Or at least the next few years of it. Rick had mentioned his Aunty and her orphanage, that he was going out to help her and would stay for at least two years.

That was probably what did it for Ellie. Something had happened between them on that plane. It had happened in the travel agency the previous day but the plane was the proving ground. Eight hours in each other's company and they'd fallen in love yet were planning to go to opposite ends of the earth. That didn't sound like Ellie to me.

The inoculations had cost a hundred and fifty quid, in three instalments. She'd planned to pay me back out of her first pay cheque. I said it didn't matter. I was glad she'd found something… useful to do rather than just lounge her way round the world along traditional student routes like Con was doing. I didn't mean it, of course. The thing about Con was I knew he'd get bored eventually and come on home. Ellie was made of sterner stuff. She might not.

She was leaving for Nepal in six weeks' time and between now and then I was going to have to pretend that I was delighted by the prospect.

***

Shortly after Ellie left for work the next morning, or rather later the same morning, I strolled round to Plum Tree Cottage with Dogge. It was Laura's day off and I found her all set to tackle a host of chores that were long past their do-by date. I began what I thought would be the uphill task of persuading her to leave them a day longer, only to find that she was a pushover. Within twenty minutes we were heading across open country, up towards The Ridge, roughly in the direction of a pub called The White Feathers. According to Laura it did a remarkable game pie lunch for ten quid on Tuesdays. And this was a Tuesday.

For the first mile or so we walked in single file, the three of us, beside a vast, sloping field of struggling barley dotted with fading poppies and occasional thistles. Our conversation was gentle and halting, the small-talk of the season, about the fullness of the hedges, the glut of songbirds thanks to the absence of magpies, the dryness of the earth on this side of the valley for want of rain in the past two weeks. When the narrow path joined a bridle-way, halfway up the gentle scarp towards our objective, we walked side by side and she put her hand in mine. We hadn't done that in Los Angeles. Something to do with the kids being there, I told myself. We hadn't done much of it back here in Winchendon either, but I didn't have an excuse for that...

I told Laura about Nepal. Ellie's decision didn't surprise her, in fact I wondered if perhaps I was the last person to hear about it but I didn't pursue the matter. Then I told her about the proposed trip to Lancashire, ending by saying, "Keep an eye on her for me, will you?"

-15-

I wasn't quite sure what I hoped to find at 4A Mellor Brook Close, Blackburn, the address Steve Yates had given me, other than a girl called Teresa Marie Stillman. And if this was the version of her that Richard Crane had meant to kill, but had murdered John Stillman's daughter by mistake, she would at least give me some hint as to Crane's motive.

Top of my list was Love, in all its splendid and terrifying aspects, driving people to take horrific action. Had someone hired Richard Crane, maybe, to avenge Teresa passing them over, cheating on them, stealing away a cherished boyfriend? If so, wouldn't there have been a photo for Crane to check his target against? Wouldn't the injured party have known three months ago that Teresa was still alive and struck again? The Love idea began to lose its bite. If you love someone, you may not know all about them, but when you come to kill them there isn't much room for error. The same goes for jealously, envy and good old-fashioned hatred. You know the person who's the cause of those emotions. That's the whole point. You can't get them out of your mind. So, again, when you come to kill them there aren't many identity errors you can make.

How about theft, then? The whole spectrum. You can steal an awful lot from people these days without knowing them, without ever meeting them. Had Teresa scammed somebody so badly and for such a vast amount that they'd sought revenge? Were we talking stocks, bonds, computer transfers, theft of ideas, straight robbery – theft in all its glorious colours? Against that were two things. First, she was female, second she was only twenty odd. There aren't many big-time robberies committed by people of her age and sex. Better still, in her defence as it were, if she'd stolen a lot of money what was she doing living in the top floor flat of a small, Lancashire house?

How about approaching it from the Steve Yates angle, then? She'd been living in another country as a kid and came back a couple of years ago to attend university? Did someone abroad have a grudge against her? I mean was it somewhere with a culture so different to our own that the merest slight is punishable by murder? Iraq, Columbia... Northern Ireland? It was bottom of the barrel stuff, I admit, and I kept coming back to the one big question. Why didn't whoever killed her know anything about her, including what she looked like?

It was a good question and, in place of an answer to it, Tom Gibson's view of the situation kept ticker-taping across my mind. There are people at the bottom of this, he'd said, who won't stop because some retired copper has come onto the scene. We'd see about that.

***

Say Lancashire to most people and what do they think of? The accent, Blackpool, Pendle Hill and its witches? I went there once with Mum and Dad, to visit my grandparents on my mother's side. I must have been ten at the most and I looked forward to the trip for weeks beforehand, not least for the train journey that took us there. A steam train, noisy and lumbering, alive with people and smells from the buffet carriage. We took our own sandwiches, of course, but that too was reason for delight. My mother made good picnics. My father pointed out the places we passed – I can't remember them now – but he was almost as childlike about them as I was.

At about five in the evening we reached Crewe and the train stayed in the station longer than scheduled. There'd been a derailment on the line ahead, we were told. My father came to the defence of the guard who gave us the news when others in the compartment complained as if it were his fault. We moved on slowly, stopping and starting for the next three hours, with people hanging from windows to see the possible cause of our delay, withdrawing their heads to tell us the colour of the signals and to castigate British Rail, not to mention a certain Doctor called Beeching. And as time passed, so my first view of Lancashire was obscured by the approaching night. It didn't matter. I had a picture so firmly in my head, so evocatively drawn from the books my mother read to me, that darkness could only improve my imaginings.

At Doncaster a man got on the crowded train and opened the door to our compartment in search of a free seat. He was slightly drunk, though I didn't know that at the time. He smiled at my mother who said, "Go sit on Dad's knee, Nathan, there's a good lad. Let the gentleman have your seat."

The man thanked her, thanked me, and sat between my parents. I remember that everyone had to shift up a little, so broad were the man's shoulders. He talked mainly to my mother and made her laugh. I can't remember what they discussed, though my father said the next day that the man had been 'pissed as a rat and too bloody forward by half'. Evidently my mother hadn't minded. She smiled as they chatted, used words I'd never heard her use before and somehow that made her seem more sophisticated, I would say now, more alive, more interesting to those around her, but then she just seemed… different. She told Dad that the man had been far too handsome for her to care if he was pissed and forward, or sober and backward. My father made to slap her on the backside and deliberately missed.

That man, however, with his large frame and good looks, his easy manner and beautiful voice, rising and falling in the local argot, running words together and rounding his vowels, was everything I expected Lancashire to be in human form. He was the lush green grass on the banks of the Ribble, he was the rain that fed it, the snow that swept from moorland roads down to isolated farms. He was the stone walls that marked out the land, he was the sudden hamlet you came upon when cresting the brow of a hill. He was the place he came from. And the next day I could hardly wait to get my fill of it.

When the morning light surged into my grandparents' house in Preston I woke and ran to the window, threw back the curtains and looked out. I couldn't believe how wrong my imaginings had been. My grandparents lived in a street of chalet bungalows, on a hill certainly, but that was the only thing that made it different from the street we lived in ourselves. Admittedly my disappointment was soon tempered when Nan and Grandad took us into the Trough of Bowland, to a place called Dunsop Bridge, and we walked in the Lancashire I'd expected to find at their front door. We walked beside a stream. I wanted to drink the water from it but Mum wouldn't let me. She said the sheep on the hills had peed in it. I didn't believe they would be so unmannerly.

These days, as I pass the sign on the motorway that tells you you've reached Lancashire, I think of two things, rain and stone, but not in any romantic sense. I've yet to visit the place when the one hasn't been falling in stair rods and the other hasn't looked even greyer than it did the last time I was there. The moors are still beautiful, I'll concede that, if bleakness and biting winds are your bag. The Trough of Bowland is still a great place to picnic in, providing you choose, as my grandfather must've done, the one sunny day in the year. But who decided to cut the landscape to ribbons and run great roads through it? Someone who hates grass, loves concrete, obviously. And loves roundabouts too. When one Lancastrian road meets another it does not do so with a polite junction, but offends all sense of decency and proportion with some of the biggest merry-go-rounds in Europe.

Before checking into the place I was staying at, I decided to visit the address for Teresa Stillman that Steve Yates had found on the NHS Computer. 4A Mellor Brook Close turned out to be one of a gaggle of newish houses, set in a loop just off the road between Preston and Blackburn. The houses were terraced, in the modern way, and off-set from each other in both plan and elevation.

Given the narrow width of the street, I parked up on the kerb and went to the front doors, there being two of them side by side, 4 and 4A. I rang the bell to Teresa's top floor flat. Waited and rang again. This was Lancashire. Curtains were already twitching.

A man of about 60 on a sit-up-and-beg pushbike was coming towards me from downtown Mellor Brook. He had a cyclist's hunch, with his flat-capped head disappearing into raincoated shoulders and to that extent he couldn't have been more Lancastrian had he been wearing a red rose in his buttonhole. He slowed down to tell me that Terri was away. My response didn't please him.

"Are you sure?" I said.

He put a booted foot down on the kerb to steady himself and looked me over. "Course I'm sure."

I gentled my tone. "You wouldn't happen to know where she's gone, would you?"

"No idea. Freda's your man for that." He nodded at the ground floor of the house, flat number four. "Nowt goes on round here that she don't have the genetic code for." I turned to ring Freda's bell. "She's away an' all."

"Not my day, is it."

"She's only down on t'market," he said, as if I'd blamed him for her absence. "She's a stall there, sells bags that fall apart soon as you look at 'em."

"She'll be back soon, then?" I said, hopefully.

"Bingo." This old boy and I were destined never to fully understand each other. I thought he'd meant bingo as in yes, I'd got it right. He'd meant Bingo as in the game. "King's

Head. She's won Caller's Pot three times on the bloody trot."

Nursing that grievance he wound back a pedal with his toe and cycled off. I called after him.

"Where does Terri work, do you know?"

"Bowler's, in town. Canal Street."

That would be my first port of call in the morning.

***

Very eventually I found the place I was booked into, The Millstone, and promised myself, for the umpteenth time that year, that I would chuck my RAC Book of the Road and get myself acquainted with Google Maps. Trusting it, believing what it said to me, that would be the tricky part.

The hotel had once been a mill, no doubt about that, but nowadays beer, wine and spirits flowed where once water had driven a huge wheel. Across from reception was the lounge, indistinguishable from a thousand others of its kind, a strange mixture of oak panelling and flashing slot machines begging you to feed them. Doing just that were a couple of blokes, one mid-twenties, the other pushing forty. They stopped and went over to the bar when a good-looking woman entered and ordered a vodka and tonic.

I went to my room on the third floor to unpack. Lying dead centre on the carefully folded shirts was the poetry book Laura had given me. She must have slipped it into the suitcase as I went to say goodbye to Ellie for the umpteenth time. I smiled and placed it on the bedside table.

My window looked out over a stone slated roof that ran the entire length of the kitchen. The roof fell steeply to the rear car park, turning in a right angle way over to my left, where it capped a row of old stables. That would be my escape route if the place caught fire.

I showered and changed, went down to the bar and ordered a big whisky on a glassful of ice. The two blokes and the vodka tonic lady were still there, the girl now telling a story, every word of which the two men were hanging on. When she finished it they laughed, though there followed some doubt as to whether they were supposed to. They apologised for not seeing the ambiguities in her story and tried to shift their ground, making a real hash of it. Finally they decided to call it a day and returned to the fruit machines. The girl caught my eye and came over to me and I prepared myself to sympathise, unnecessarily as it turned out.

"Hi," she said, chirpily. "Are you staying here or have you just popped in for a drink?"

"Staying. You?"

"I'm the assistant manager, Penny Swarbrick. I should be wearing a name brooch, I know, but it's tacky, is that. Welcome, anyway."

She smiled, professionally, and offered me her hand. It was cold and slightly damp from nursing the vodka and tonic.

"Many staying?" I asked.

"Fifteen. Not bad for mid-week."

I nodded at the two blokes, yanking down on the tight-fisted machines. "Who are those two?"

"Car salesmen, passing through. Regional director and his assistant. Or so they say."

"Don't you believe them?"

She smiled again, her own smile this time. "Not hundred per cent.

"You mean where are the suits and the smarm?"

"Exactly. Out in the morning, denim jackets and jeans, back at five. Couple of lasses in for dinner the night before last, but mainly you'll find them at the bar."

They sounded like coppers to me.

***

Up in my room, an hour or so later, I phoned Laura regardless of the fact that it was long past her witching hour. It rang eight or nine times before she answered. "Hello, Nathan. Did you have a safe journey?"

I flopped back onto the bed the better to savour the voice. "Laura, hi. What are you up to?"

"Just on my way to bed."

"I like the sound of that. You know, if you were here…"

I broke off and she laughed, her prescription laugh, the one that made you feel better.

"Go on," she said. "If I were there what?"

I thought for a moment or two. "I can't. I'm fifty years old with four grown-up children. It'd sound so daft. But that doesn't mean I wouldn't like to."

"Fifty-two," she reminded me. "Your age."

"I still wouldn't know where to begin…"

"What are you wearing?"

"Chinos, the black shirt you bought me in LA…. cream jacket."

"Not you. That's what you ask me. What am I wearing?"

"Sorry. What are you wearing?"

And now she was the one who paused. "No good. The moment's gone. I had dinner at The Harrow this evening with your daughter."

"What was she wearing? The usual array of hand-me-downs?"

"You're lucky, Nathan. She's a good kid. Thinks the world of you."

"I know. When I get back, can we go somewhere, Laura? You and me, just the two of us, couple of days. I've things to say about the future."

"Sounds interesting. Nothing, by the way."

"What do you mean, nothing?"

"That's the answer to the question you couldn't ask because you're 52. I've just stepped out of the shower…"

There was a knock on the door. Mine, not hers. A man's voice and, as you can imagine, it annoyed the hell out of me.

"Mr Hawk? I'd like a word if I may."

"Who's that?" said Laura.

"I don't know." There was another knock. "I'll get rid of them…"

My visitor couldn't wait. The locked door burst open, shoulder-barged by a powerful man dressed in a brown leather jacket, grey polo shirt and jeans. He was mid-thirties, at a guess, with an auburn cast to the thick, ridge and furrow-cut hair. His face was picked out in the same colour scheme, with a reddish stubble overshadowed by an orange moustache, all set on a pasty white background.

"D'you mind, I'm on the phone," I said.

He came over to me, yanked the receiver out of my hand and replaced it on the cradle. "Not anymore. We need to talk."

"What the hell about?"

"Terri Stillman. Who else?"

I gave him an alternative. "Marilyn Monroe?"

He didn't even smile, not that it was meant to be funny. "Be serious," he said. "Like me."

"You're police, I take it?"

He began sauntering round the room, scanning it as coppers do for things to hold against a suspect. "Keith Daniels. Known as Jack…"

"Who d'you work for?"

"I'm SOU. Special Operations Unit. Heard of us?"

"Yeah, you grew up through the cracks left when Special Branch moved in with the anti-terrorist mob. Which makes you neither one thing nor the other."

He dropped to the floor as if a gun had been fired. He looked under the bed then sprang to his feet again with feline grace.

"Reds?" I asked.

He dusted his hands against each other. There was a sense of discipline to the man, not just brute strength but something well ordered from a former life. Army, perhaps.

"Who told you where to find me?" I asked.

He didn't acknowledge the question. He looked in the fridge.

"Help yourself," I said.

"I'm teetotal."

That figured. He moved on, glancing into the bathroom. I asked again who had informed him of my whereabouts. He turned and came over to me and stood far too close for comfort. I reckoned this was the Jack who'd prevented Tom Gibson from eating properly for a fortnight with a single blow to his guts. If I took him on I knew, we both knew, it would be no contest. Apart from the piss-hole eyes he had shoulders like a rhino and, no doubt, a headlong charge to match.

"Who told you…?" I tried again.

"This isn't a quiz game," he said. "This is a me telling you game. Terri Stillman has gone." He floated his hand away into the distance. "You will not be able to find her. I'll repeat that in case you missed it. Terri Stillman has gone. Shall I say it just once more to make absolutely certain…?"

"Gone where? Australia? New Zealand? Isn't that where you lot usually pack 'em off to?"

"It is, although Canada's becoming increasingly popular with both criminals and their victims."

He moved to the chest of drawers and started opening them, from the bottom upwards.

"So, if she's gone why are you still here?" I asked.

"Oh, this is a routine visit to make doubly sure that nothing about Terri's past remains in this Godforsaken place. Her past now includes you."

"Should I be frightened?"

"I would advise… apprehension, yes. You see, when you started looking for the first Teresa Stillman you trampled on grass that had been growing very nicely up until then."

"And then I found her. Are the two things connected, me finding Teresa's body and Terri moving out?"

It was another question he didn't consider worthy of an answer. He lifted my suitcase down from the top of the wardrobe, slammed it on the bed, opened it and felt the seams.

"How come she warrants top dollar treatment?" I asked. "What's her story? She's hardly a big time villain at her age. Is she a victim, a trial witness?"

My suggestions brought the nearest thing to a smile that he was capable of, a thin-lipped sneer. "You think you're so bloody smart, don't you. Twenty-eight murders and you're King Kong. Everything you touch just has to be a major conspiracy."

"That's all you're going to tell me?"

"That's all you need to know. She's gone. Far away. Never, ever to return, if you know what I mean. I'm leaving now, Mr Hawk. I suggest that tomorrow morning you do the same. I've taken the liberty of settling your bill, up to and including breakfast."

My mobile on the bedside table rang. I went to answer it but he was there before me. He snatched it up and glanced at the caller ID.

"Oh, how nice," he said, perfecting the arctic smile. "Your daughter. I must say she seems an absolutely charming girl."

He certainly knew how to unnerve a chap. "What the fuck would you know about charm?"

He answered the call in a gentle, oily voice. "Ellie, hi. My name's Jack. How's the new job at The Gazette?... Good, good. And you're off to Nepal, I gather... Yes, your father's right here. I'll hand you over to him."

He tossed me the phone, turned on his heel as if commanded by some sergeant major within him, and left.

"Who was that?" asked Ellie.

"Just some bloke," I said.

Some bloke from SOU. And if the two car salesmen staying here were coppers, as I'd first suspected, what the hell were they all doing swarming around Terri Stillman? Were they the people Tom Gibson had referred to who wouldn't stop because some retired copper had poked his nose in? It might have been ego on my part but had I'd wandered into something rather bigger than a mistaken identity?

-16-

I booked an alarm call for eight o'clock and bang on the dot the phone rang. Breakfast would be served for another hour and a half, said Penny Swarbrick, but if I knew what I wanted she would inform the kitchen straightaway. I ordered kippers. I never cook kippers at home because the smell lingers for a week, that's if you can get a properly smoked pair in the first place.

The restaurant was quietly busy and I chose a corner table from where I could check out my fellow guests with ease. The car salesmen were nowhere to be seen but an elderly couple from Wales were hogging the muesli and orange juice at the self-service table. A man on his own in one corner, reading a book, was waiting for scrambled eggs on toast. When it came, he propped the book up against the coffee pot and carried on reading while he ate. Totally absorbed. A younger couple, thirties, casually dressed, were discussing the day's sightseeing. A walk up Pendle to the makeshift cairn right at the top. Two women in their forties were trying not to make their relationship with each other the centre of attention. They were succeeding, with everyone except me.

Just as I was beginning to wonder why I'd ever thought of kippers as a delicacy, Penny Swarbrick came over to me and asked how they were. I said they were delicious. She glanced round and lowered her voice.

"There was a man earlier, seven o'clock, asking after you." It was the piece of news I needed to fully waken me. "Wanted to know if you were staying here?"

"What was he like?"

"Thirty-odd and tall. Fit and dishy. Long fair hair, tied back."

"Ponytail?"

She nodded. "Dressed in leathers. Anyroad, we don't give out information about clients, not even basic stuff like that. I mean if you're staying here, which you are, the people you want to know would know. For all his looks he started to get a bit pushy. Those two car salesmen came to the rescue. Told him to leave and he did." I glanced round the restaurant and Penny rightly assumed that I was looking for them. "They checked out, half an hour ago."

"Did Mr Daniels check out as well?"

She frowned, wondering for a moment if her box-file memory had let her down. Assured that it hadn't, she said, "I don't think a Mr Daniels was ever here." She topped up my cup from the coffee jug. "So who was he, the man asking for you?"

"His name is Richard Crane."

A man about whom I still knew absolutely nothing, other than the length and colour of his hair. I was surprised to learn from Penny that the ponytail hadn't been dispatched to the knacker's yard, or at least been dyed a different colour. All I really knew was that I'd spoken to him once when he'd phoned me in the night and led me to Teresa's remains. His presence here in Lancashire was worrying, suggesting that my initial theory was right. He had unfinished business with the Teresa Marie Stillman he had meant to kill in the first place.

***

A school crossing lady told me you could see Bowler Plastics from the road bridge over the Leeds Liverpool Canal and when I reached it I held up the traffic behind me for a brief spell to check her theory. She was right.

On the far side of the bridge a left turn dropped down past a row of terraced houses with roof slates shining black from an early morning shower, the brickwork deep red, almost brown and the front doors painted a heavy green. Rich colours for a poor place. At the end of the cobbled street, between the railway line and the canal, stood an old mill converted into three industrial units. When cotton was king here there would've been barges in the basin, queued up to take bolts of woven cloth down to Liverpool and away to the world. Now there was a forlorn supermarket trolley, raising a drowning arm above the water. As for the mill itself, most of the windows had been bricked up and the chimney long ago dismantled.

I parked the Land Rover on a patch beside the towpath, flattening a clump of willow herb doing its best to cheer the place up. Three Asian lads, late teens, were hoofing a ball around and it came towards me as I reached them. I put my foot on it and we looked at each other.

"Which one is Bowler's?" I asked.

"On the end," said the kicker in a George Formby accent.

He didn't say which end. His friend, a stylish type in pencil thin jeans and a sleeveless black vest, saw that it made a difference to me and pointed leftwards.

"Scrapyard end," he said, flicking back a mane of black hair.

I thanked him and kicked the ball back to them. It spun away at an angle, miles off target, and we all watched it land on an old car. One of the lads went to retrieve it.

"Not a player, then?" said the sleeveless vest, grinning.

"Shows, does it? You work there? Bowler's?"

"Aye, we're on a break," he said, as if I'd been checking his time card.

"I'm looking for Terri Stillman," I said. "Know where I'll find her?"

Mention of the name clearly caught him on the raw. The grin faded, never to return in our brief acquaintanceship. One of his mates called out to him, "Rafi, come on, man!"

The ball was back in play, but Rafi was now more interested in me than in football. He flicked back his hair again. "You won't find Terri, pal. Beggared off four weeks ago, hasn't been back."

"Your boss, where will I find him?"

He was beginning to accept that I wouldn't leave without talking to a grown-up. "Not an 'im," he said, cockily. "It's an 'er. Dorothy. Up in t'office."

His mates were still calling him to re-join the game but his heart wasn't really in it. He watched as I walked over to the factory and entered through the big double doorway.

I found myself in a time warp of at least thirty years. The machinery was certainly that old and most of the units had an air of perpetual break-down to them. A slightly built man in his fifties, dressed in a once blue overall, was emptying a sack of plastic pellets into the machine nearest me. He told the operator to try it. The woman, a tall creature with hair scarfed up above a pinched, unhappy face, closed the gate in front of her. The two halves of the machine came together and at the other end out came a block of plastic bottle tops. The operator and the foreman gave each other the thumbs-up, he turned with his empty sack and saw me leaning in the doorway. He called out, "Help yer?

"I've come to see Dorothy."

He pointed up to a large gallery office, suspended over the work area. Through the glass window I could see a fifty-something grey-blond filing paperwork in a cabinet. The foreman nodded at a flight of metal stairs on the far wall and told me I should walk round the edge of the shop floor to reach it. Health and Safety.

There were a dozen or so machines in the place, all different shapes and ages, manned by a bunch of people who fitted the same description. A couple of middle-aged women

I passed were having a mouthed conversation across two machines – just as they might've done a century ago. Then it would have been above the noise of the looms, today it was over the sound of the BBC's Asian Network. An elderly Pakistani, nodding in agreement with whatever opinion was being aired, brought the women tea in plastic cups and they thanked him.

At the top of the metal stairs I turned and looked down at the shop floor. The footballers had returned from their break and were going back to their machines. All except Rafi, who was talking to the foreman. About me.

I knocked on Dorothy's door and she called out for me to enter. She turned from her filing and looked at me over her reading glasses.

"Who are you?" she asked.

"My name is Nathan Hawk," I replied, suddenly sounding too posh for my own comfort.

She was a good-looking woman, underneath her doubts about me. She was tall and well cared for and gave off a northern air of no messing. She was wearing jeans and trainers for practicality, a white blouse to show off a good figure. Her hair had had money spent on it recently, judging by her habit of checking to see that it was still in place. She dumped the rest of her filing on a desk and placed her glasses beside it, then apologised for the excessive warmth in the office. The heat of human enterprise rising from the shop floor, I suggested. Busted thermostat, she said. Either way I took off my leather jacket and draped it over the back of a chair.

"I'd like to ask you a few questions, if that's okay," I said. "About Terri Stillman."

She nodded. "I bet number one on your list is the same as mine. Where the 'ell is she?"

I glanced down at the shop floor where Rafi was at a machine now, opening and closing the gate, stamping out fancy handles. "One of the lads told me she disappeared weeks ago," I said. "He seemed upset. Why? Does he have a special interest in her?"

She slipped a forefinger under a gold chain at her throat and tugged at it, looking me over, not entirely averse to what she saw. "Yes, well right now I'd like to know what your special interest is, Mr Hawk?"

I gave her a re-worked version of the truth and said I was an ex-copper working for Terri's family, trying to find her. "My problem is no one seems to know much about her, including her family, so I've come to you."

"Aye, you were right to do that. We're a friendly bunch here, the folk she would've turned to in a crisis."

"Was there one?"

"Not that I know of."

"When did she actually go?" I said, turning to her wall calendar.

"Saturday the 7th of June. Dates like that stick, don't they."

They certainly do. Terri disappeared on the seventh. I had dug up her namesake's remains on the sixth. That was too much of a coincidence to actually be one.

"You saw her on the Saturday?"

Dorothy nodded. She was thinking back now, not just fielding the questions. "We went to karaoke in the evening, Terri, me, some of the girls. Monday morning, no sign of her. That simple."

"Did she have a boyfriend? I mean a young girl like that…?"

She suddenly frowned and relaxed it just as quickly, probably aware that it put ten years on her. "You mean she must've been sleeping with someone for life to be worth living?"

I shrugged. "Just asking the usual questions."

"No bloke in her life, not unless you count Rafi."

It was my turn to frown, without caring how old it made me look. Which isn't true, of course. I went over to the glass and looked down onto the shop floor. "Are we talking ditched lover, do you think? Is that why he was a bit chary with me out on the front patch?"

"I'm not sure Terri would've called him a lover. Bit on the side, maybe." She joined me at the glass and looked down at her workforce with obvious affection. "She was… God, I'm talking about her as if she's dead and gone. That's because the bloody police do! She is, is, is incredibly bright. Educated. With the best will in the world, Rafi's fair to middling."

"Must've been his looks then," I said.

She smiled at the maleness of the remark, then confessed, "They'd do it for me and no mistake."

"Was it you who reported her missing?"

"I sent one of the girls round to her place, no answer. Neighbour said they haven't seen her all weekend. Not answering her mobile, no emails, no text or anything to explain, so I called the police. They were on it like a shot. They were here within forty minutes."

"Here not there?" She nodded. "What did they look like?"

A hint of irritation entered her voice. "Well, I don't know, do I! Coppers. The oldest was about forty. Your height, fair hair…"

"Denim?"

"Yes, as it happens."

I briefly described both of the car salesmen I'd seen at The Millstone and she nodded all the way. When I'd finished she added, "There was a third…"

"Auburn hair, mid-thirties?"

"Didn't say much. In fact I'm not sure he said anything, so I took him to be the boss."

"His name is Jack Daniels. Don't ask me what he is, but I don't think he's a copper. He paid me a visit at The Millstone and during our rather one-sided conversation he encouraged me to believe that Terri's dead. So no wonder you found yourself talking in the same way."

The notion shocked her, though she wasn't the sort to go to pieces over it.

"Did they question anyone about her disappearance?" I went on. "Rafi, for example?"

"They didn't get a chance. He heard them say they were police and he slung his hook."

I glanced down at the workforce again. Rafi was still by his machine, opening and closing the gate, stamping out fancy handles for England. "So no one's ever asked him what he knows about Terri, where she might be, why she might be there? Least of all the police?"

"Well, no, I suppose it is a bit odd…"

I went out onto the metal staircase. As I descended it, Rafi must've felt my eyes burning into his neck. He stopped his work. He didn't turn, he just held his ground for a moment or two, slightly hunched over the machine. Then, as I reached the bottom step and trod from metal onto concrete, he bolted, fast as a whippet, straight across the shop floor. I heard myself yell after him, "Police!"

It was habit. It was also unproductive since Rafi was already out of the doors and heading for the wide grey yonder. I can't say I made a conscious decision to chase him, I just found myself doing so. Habit again. Straight across the shop floor, no regard for Health and Safety this time. The machine operators seemed to fall away in slow motion to give me clear passage. Outside, Rafi was sprinting towards the canal, having the better of me on two counts. He knew the area and he was thirty years younger. Fit with it, not a touch of fat anywhere, and I'm not quite the skin and bone I used to be.

As I reached the towpath I could see that Rafi was pulling away from me at quite a rate. I was going to lose him and if that happened I'd waste a week finding him. He had reached a derelict warehouse, a hundred yards downstream from Bowler Plastics. It was a shell, much vandalised, with notices blaring out from every surface, warning of the dangers of entering. Rafi ducked into it.

Maggie always used to groan when people did that in films. The very last thing you would do in real life, she maintained, would be to run into a building and then run up the stairs. It was all to do with letting the villain fall to his death, she said, instead of giving the film a more imaginative ending. We missed a hell of a lot of film endings on the strength of her belief. Which was wrong, it now seemed. Here was Rafi, the embodiment of real life, pursued by a real-life ex-copper, charging into the building. I could hear his feet clattering up stone steps above me.

There was method in his madness. The warehouse on this bank was exactly mirrored by one on the other side and they were joined at third floor level by a covered walkway over the canal. Rafi was going to take that, I reckoned, go out through the opposite warehouse and melt away into the city beyond. The thought of stairs, upwards for three flights, made me pause at the warehouse door. I leaned on the door jamb, hauling in breath, listening to my pulse. I turned and kicked the door out of pure frustration and as the pain of doing so shot up my leg, I remembered the supermarket trolley.

I'd seen it in the canal when I first arrived at Bowler's, half of it above the water line. How deep could this canal be? I could still hear Rafi inside the warehouse, taking the upward stairs two at a time, reaching the door to the walkway. He pulled it open, it fell back with a boom that rang out through both buildings. A second later he was running across the walkway.

I slipped into the canal and the slow black water came cold, right up to my crotch. What breath I'd caught when I'd stopped running was whipped out of me and the shock of that propelled me forward. I waded, arms wide for balance, through the water – a misnomer if ever there was one. Oil, acid, pitch, detergent, un-named chemicals, they were the things I could smell.

As I reached the other side and heaved myself out of the water, I noticed a young woman with a small child in a pushchair coming along the path. She stopped dead, in a mixture of fear and amazement, watching water pour from my lower half as if from a punctured bag. Her small son kicked his legs in sheer delight. I entered the warehouse and she hurried past without a second glance. My jeans were sticking to me like a second skin, cold and reptilian, slimy to the touch. Above me I could hear Rafi coming down the stairs. He was at the second floor by the sound of it, though his pace was slower now. Perhaps he thought he'd already outrun me. The little bastard was about to discover that there is more to life than being young.

Like its twin on the other bank, the warehouse was derelict to the point of no return with tectonic plates of concrete flooring, fallen from above, lying tilted on broken steel joists. I picked up a piece of timber and hid behind a stone pillar at the base of the stairwell. As Rafi came hurtling down the last few steps I sprang into his path, swung back the wood and belted him on the shins. He cursed with a scream, trying to keep his balance with a windmill of arms and legs, then spread his length twenty feet away from me. I went over to him. He rolled over with a groan and looked up at me.

I hauled him to his feet by the shoulder hoops of his vest. He came up like a small dog dangling on its lead. I shoved him into a corner and leaned in over him, one hand on either wall.

"So tell me, three coppers show up at the factory one day…"

"I know nowt!" he squawked.

"Listen to the question. These cops walk in and you make yourself scarce. Explain that to me."

"My business!" he said, right in my face.

I wanted to smack him but I held back for one second and for some inexplicable reason Laura's poetry book drifted into the mental space between my fist and his face. I'd dipped into it before going to bed the previous night and now bits of the following intervened, though needless to say I didn't voice them.

Whose is the love that, gleaming through the word
Wards off the poisonous arrow, of its scorn,
Whose is the warm and partial praise,
Virtue's most sweet reward?

It was so contrary to how I'd felt, never mind what I'd done in the last five minutes, that I wished I could recall more, and in the right order.

"Look, I'm not a policeman, Rafi. I'm just looking for Terri."

"So fuckin' what?"

I stepped back from him and he peeled himself away from the rough stone surface, shaking his hair back into shape. I said, with as much conviction as I could muster, "You do know she's probably dead by now, don't you."

"Don't say that, Mister, please."

"Murdered, if you ask me."

He winced and shook his head to drive the notion away and after a few moments said, "When I saw them coppers up in Dottie's office it were a shock, only not just because of…" His eyes wandered away again.

"Stuff?" I suggested. "What else?"

"I'd seen one of them before. With Terri." He described the younger of the two car salesmen. "They were together in Thackyduck…" He remembered that I was a Southerner. "The Aqueduct. It's a pub over in Darwen."

"Did you speak to them?"

"No, I were a bit pissed off, given that she and me were meant to be going out. Didn't know what to say so I said nowt."

"You talk like they were boyfriend and girlfriend," I said. "They weren't."

He thought for a moment. "Looking back all I saw were two people at a table, having a chat, like… easy with each other."

"Holding hands, kissing?"

"No, but then Terri weren't that sort in public. If there were owt more to it I couldn't say…" He looked down at the floor and began to draw a pattern in the dust with the toe of his trainer. "You know what I think?"

"Go on."

"I think she were a copper an' all." It was the one thing that had never crossed my mind but that was no reason to dismiss it. "Which'd mean that all the time she were playing it cosy with me she were reeling me in."

"What for?"

We answered the question together. Stuff.

"It's not just me, you see," he added, sheepishly. "It's family. Family business."

Whatever his family were into I didn't want to know about it and told him so, for the third or fourth time. He twisted the shoulder hoops of his T-shirt back into shape and slapped the dirt from his jeans.

"I keep thinking back to the time she and me spent together," he said. "She'd ask me things about my Dad, cousins, uncles. Lots of things. She were really interested in 'em, she said, and could she meet them some day?"

It had the whiff of undercover work certainly, but only a whiff. "Did that ever happen? The meeting?"

He laughed. "My old man? White girl? You must be having a laugh." He thought for a moment. "You know, she didn't… fit here somehow. She were smart, smart like a copper. Too smart to be working in a sodding factory."

You don't get an endorsement like that every day. She was smart, he'd said, she must have been a copper. But a missing copper. Maybe even a dead copper. Dead or alive, it gave a new twist to finding Teresa Stillman's killer.

***

Rafi and I walked back along the towpath together. At the doorway to Bowler's, talking with the foreman, was the young woman with the pushchair whose son still thought I was good value and kicked his legs again to prove it. The other onlookers were puzzled, of course. Rafi and I had left in such a hurry, one of us chasing the other and I'd clearly been for half a dip in the canal and Rafi's limp said he'd bumped into the piece of wood I'd been holding. So why were we chatting so amiably about the canal, cotton, the warehouse and Dorothy Bowler?

Dorothy came towards me, smiling at everything about me from the waist down. "You took a short cut, I hear." I glanced over at the young pushchair woman. "My daughter, Hilary. Said she'd seen this strange creature, half-man, half-crocodile, jump out of the water and stand there dripping."

The gathering began to break up. Dorothy pecked her daughter on the cheek, fussed her grandson one last time and watched the pair of them trundle off.

"You made their day," she said, turning back to me. "But not mine. Why are you looking for Terri, Mr Hawk? What's she done?"

"Tell you what, meet me tonight for dinner, I'll tell you."

She smiled and lowered her voice. "I'd like that. Where?"

"You decide, time and place. Meantime, have you got a shower I can use?"

"Far side of the shop floor. Dry clothes, though?"

"In the motor." I squelched off towards the Land Rover to get my suitcase.

***

As I stood under the shower in Bowler Plastics, I made a resolution. Before winter set in I would get one just like it, with the same spread and force, installed in the bathroom at Beech Tree Cottage. The days of the lukewarm trickle that passed itself off as a 'power shower' were numbered, thanks to my walk across the Leeds Liverpool canal. In its place would be sheer luxury, whatever the cost. It's a resolution I've made many times before and nothing has come of it. This time, as always, things would be different.

Delight at the prospect of being able to enjoy a shower in the future soon gave way to the present possibility that Terri Stillman was a copper. It certainly tallied with the fact that no one knew much about her. She'd been keeping herself to herself, not putting out, not getting too close to the local lads. Why the factory, though? Did Rafi's suspicion that he and his family 'stuff' were a police target hold water? Yes, it did. Where it leaked, however, was in the time Terri had been working at Bowler's. Nearly a year. As Terri's police boss I'd have wanted a result long before now.

And where did Richard Crane fit into all this? Had he harboured some burning grudge against Terri the policewoman that at last he'd avenged and Jack Daniels was just... clearing up the mess afterwards, lying his way out of any embarrassment?

On the other hand, if Crane had had a score to settle with Terri wouldn't he have known what she looked like? If she'd put him away for some crime, surely he would've had her face etched onto the back wall of his mind and he wouldn't have mistaken her for John Stillman's daughter. Unless, of course, he was simply hired fire-power, working for somebody else...

Tempting though it was to stay in the shower and dwell on the matter, somebody else was paying the electricity bill. I turned off the Rolls Royce of a tap, stepped out and began to towel myself dry.

-17-

Dorothy had suggested that we meet for supper at eight o'clock sharp in a pub called The Spread Eagle. It was once a collection of farm buildings, restored and joined together to give the best food in the county, she said, and could be found on a ridge road known unaffectedly as The Tops. The view from there in the daytime was evidently spectacular, with a valley on either side falling away and then rising to distant hills. The view at eight in the evening wasn't bad either with the lights of rural Lancashire seeming to be all the sharper for a cold wind heading down from the north.

Inside, The Spread Eagle wasn't vastly different to The Millstone. An attempt had been made to indulge a sentimental attachment to the past while making sure the technology of the present was to hand. I made use of the latter after Dorothy phoned me at ten to eight and, like every woman I've ever known, informed me that she might be late. I went over to one of the three computers in a horse box of an alcove, proudly known as the business area, and once the assistant manager had dded my internet usage to the bill to come, I logged onto my account. There was a message from Fee.

"Wherefore Lancashire? Fee xx." It was followed by a tear-stained postscript, longer than anything she'd ever written to me before. "PS, I'm thinking of coming home, Dad. It's basically not going well here at the moment. I mean Yama's wonderful but he's also a pain. No, I don't mean that. He's lovely but that isn't true either… Jesus, I don't know what I mean."

Whatever happened to the old style of letter writing where you worked out what you wanted to say before you put pen to paper, instead of using the paper – in this case the email package – as a sounding board? I ploughed through her angry tale of love on the rocks and how she now believed that men, no matter what their nationality, would always let women down. Except men like me, she hastened to add. But then I wasn't really a man, I was her father. I wrote back telling her to sleep on any decision she made but if, in the end, she wanted to come home she should let me know as soon as possible.

The moment I sent my reply I began to worry about where she would live. It wasn't concern for her, of course, it was concern for me. I knew only too well where she would live. Beech Tree Cottage.

An email from Con didn't do much to cheer me up, on top of which it implied that he hadn't transferred his borrowing fetish from my bank account to that of his younger brother as I'd hoped. The message began well enough. "Hi, Dad. You've heard, I expect, Fee and Yama have split. Good. Never liked the guy anyway…" And without drawing breath he moved on to the more serious stuff. "Dad, listen mate, I don't have any money lying around, do I? I mean met a guy here the other day – we're in Tutka Bay, Alaska by the way, Christ it's fresh! – said that when he was 21 this trust his grandparents had set up kicked in. Started me thinking. Do I have a trust, or something, that nobody's told me about…?"

I wrote back fairly simply. "No."

Jaikie had a Jaikie-like slant on his sister's crumbling romance. "…feel really sorry for her. I mean love can be shit, don't you think? I was given this script to read the other day, boy meets girl, fall in love, she turns out to be criminally insane. What a part for someone like me! Well, not like me but me full stop! I mean if there's one thing I do know about it's crime. My father was a copper, for God's sake! The other thing I know about is women. And the other other thing I know about is what makes a good script…"

And so on, mainly about how brilliant he would be as a romantic hero at the mercy of an evil woman with a face and a body to die for. I wrote back saying that since he hadn't asked me how I was, but presumably wanted to know, I was fine. Thank you. Only then did I admit it to myself. I hadn't come into this so-called business area to read my email. I'd come to read Ellie's. I brought the Yahoo mail page up on the screen. ID: Eleanor Hawk. Password: Lovesmith. The message from Terrific Rick began, "Hi, Ellie. Miss yer? Does the Pope crap in the woods? Listen, straight to the point, this country is beautiful and the people are terrific…"

I leaned back and a huntsman in a print on the horse box wall caught my eye. No sympathy. Quite the opposite, in fact. What are you doing, he said, hovering over your daughter's first love affair ready to swoop down and kill it? You're a fine one to talk, I said to him. What has that fox ever done to you? But at least I skipped to the last paragraph.

"How goes the fight, Hawk versus the Weed? Oh, and give my regards to your Dad. I love you. I love you. I love you. Ricky."

I just had to know what her response was.

"Hi, babe. Can't help you on the toilet habits of Popes, I'm afraid, but I sure am glad you feel the way you do about me. The old man? Hmmm! Which is short for Hmmmmm! I've told him about Nepal and he seems cool. I wouldn't feel so bad if him and Lofty Laura were going at it full stretch but they're not. I'm going to have to move it along, only I'll need to pick my moment to do it. Like, 'Heh, Dad, how often do you and Laura…?' Urgh! Purleeeease! Don't worry, I'll think of a way. As for the weed, won't say I have, won't say I haven't. Have to say, though, that I think I love you too. Ellie."

I closed down the computer. Like they say, if you listen at keyholes…

***

It was just after 8.30 when Dorothy Bowler entered The Spread Eagle, causing heads to turn, not all of them over 40 years old. She was dressed with long, black good taste, in a satin all-in-one number that didn't grip her so tightly that she couldn't breathe yet allowed the casual observer to make a pretty good guess at what was underneath. She was full of apologies for her lateness. I told her I was used to it and steered her over to the bar.

She slipped onto a stool and swivelled round to the assistant manager who had supervised my internet use. Face to face with Dorothy he immediately straightened up and began, quite unnecessarily, to pull his clothes into shape. Adrian, as he was called, then faced a brief question and answer session about exam results, girlfriends and future prospects, after which he set about fixing a gin and tonic for Mrs Bowler and another whisky for me. When he was safely out of earshot, Dorothy explained quietly, "He's my cleaner's son. I wouldn't normally have a cleaner, but you can imagine with running the factory, six days a week, eight o'clock start … why are you smiling?"

If I was smiling it was on account of her need to apologise for having a cleaner. I explained that I understood it perfectly. "It's a class thing in my case, a Northern thing, or something in yours."

She chuckled, more through her nose than her mouth, then allowed her fullest accent to express an essential truth. "Never try putting owt past an old copper, eh? Especially your dyed in the wool hang-ups."

"How come you're running that factory in the first place?"

She leaned into the bar and folded her hands together. They were perfect hands for their age, long fingers and dagger nails. No rings. She told me that Bowler Plastics had been her father's business and when he died, 25 years ago, he left it to her. It was the last thing on earth she wanted and just as she was about to off-load it, along came Jeff and swept her off her feet. Jeff was a pilot, working for one of the small charter firms, and he liked a drink or twelve. Planes and booze don't go together, as Jeff found out very soon after their wedding on a run to Holland. He overshot a tin-pot runway, just outside Rotterdam, flew whatever he was piloting into the side of a barn. No damage to life or limb, just the real estate. He was fired and, in the aftermath, set about spending Dorothy's money. Needless to say, he didn't get another job. Needless to say, he didn't stop drinking. Needless to say, he died five years later with a liver the size of Pendle Hill.

"Your turn," she said. "For the third time of asking since we met, why the interest in Terri Stillman? What's she been up to?"

I nodded at the menu on the bar. "Why don't we order first?"

***

The waitress led us to a table in an alcove lit by false, flickering candles, the effect of which was either romantic or downright gloomy, depending on your mood. I told Dottie that my friend Laura would love the place. It wasn't true, of course. Laura would have loathed it but I just … wanted to bring her into the conversation and in doing so reverted, albeit for only five minutes, to being a boring, awkward teenager, telling the girl I was with about the girl I wanted to be with. I didn't leave it there. I told her how clever Laura was, how arrestingly beautiful, how well she got on with my kids and finally how we definitely had a future together. God knows why I did it. It wasn't as if Dorothy was making eyes at me. In fact her eyes glazed over once or twice as I was speaking.

When the rabbit in mustard sauce came, along with a bottle of wine, we fell to talking about our various offspring. I tried not to hog the conversation, which was difficult, given that Dottie had just the one daughter, Hilary, whom I'd met at the factory. Somewhere in the middle of it all, with gin and red wine playing their part, Dottie made the kind of admission you'd want forgotten in the clear light of dawn. "Hilly's lovely, of course, and a good mother, but I just wish she was more … interesting, like your kids seem to be. I guess that's why I miss Terri so much. With the best will in the world I couldn't say that Hilly was…"

Hearing herself about to be disloyal, she broke off. I tried to be helpful and said, "We're all different. Thank God."

"I could talk to Terri about things. She was a good listener. I know she thought of me as a kind of mother. It makes me sound two hundred years old years old, but that's how it was." She smiled. "She could be such fun. We're pretty short on laughs in the plastics industry. She could take off anyone at the drop of a hat. Me, Rafi, politicians, Bill the Foreman, any of the girls. She could be such fun!" She gave the last word an extra kick and a couple of heads turned towards her. "Sorry."

"Did she ever say where she was from?"

"No and I never asked."

"Did she ever speak about her family?"

"Never. I assumed there'd been a falling out. And you still haven't told me why you're here."

She was right and I wasn't sure that I wanted to. For some reason I couldn't explain to Dorothy, I knew that the truth about Terri Stillman would severely damage her generous view of human nature. The irony was that, without being aware of it, Dorothy probably knew more of the truth about her missing friend than anyone aside from Jack Daniels and his car salesmen, or possibly the elusive Richard Crane. But I had to give her something so that she'd confide in me, share with me those useless details that are often the key to solving a crime. I started way back at John Stillman, with how he'd come to me and I'd turned him down, then taken up the case again after Ellie went missing for a few hours. I went through Tom Gibson, Joanna Bailey, Darcy

Morrell and the Carters. I told her how Dogge and I had found the body. I was about to tell her that I believed John Stillman's daughter Teresa had been mistaken for her friend Terri when my natural caution intervened. It amounted to the two opposing possibilities that, in spite of her charm and credibility, Dorothy was a woman I hardly knew. She claimed to be a friend of Terri Stillman but could just as easily have been a signatory to the plans to kill her.

It turned out that I wasn't the only person in the room with misgivings. When I finished speaking she reached down into her bag and brought out a clip of A4 sheets, documents that were clearly the result of a Google search. She put on her reading glasses and perched them on the end of her nose.

"Nathan Hawk. You'd be the same Nathan Hawk who was a Detective Chief Inspector in the Hamford Regional Crime Squad, till a couple of years ago?" She'd been checking up on me and I wasn't sure if I was offended or impressed. I settled for being impressed. "The Nathan Hawk who caught..." She turned over a page. "...Anthony Barber who killed four women in Chester? The Nathan Hawk who caught Barbara Hemmings?"

Feeling only marginally as if I were being interviewed for a job that it might be foolhardy to give me, I said, "Killed her husband, on holiday in Anglesey."

"Jeremy Guard who murdered... well, who did he murder, Nathan? Just so that I'm doubly sure?"

"His parents. Jim and Alice. Is there some reason you've been digging into my past?"

She folded up the document, put it back in her bag and snapped it shut. She took a ladylike sip of her wine, then changed it to a full-blown swig. "I have to be certain that you are who you claim to be. On balance I think you are, but you could so easily be pulling the wool over my eyes. You wouldn't be the first man to..."

"Why do you need reassuring?"'`

"I'm going to tell you something I haven't told the police. Don't ask me why I haven't, but there was always something not quite right about them. Especially Daniels."

"Good decision. They showed up within forty minutes of you reporting Terri missing? Too quick off the mark for regular police."

"That's kind of what I thought…"

"They didn't come to get information that would help them find her. I think they came to remove all trace of her from your factory. They came to make sure that, apart from bare essentials, you knew nothing about her!"

She nodded gently. "That certainly explains why they asked for her work records. They took them away, said they'd bring them back and I've not heard another word."

Dorothy paused for one final moment, as if still wondering whether to trust me or not, and came down in favour. "Tell me, do you think she's dead?"

"My Teresa Stillman's dead, that's for sure. Your friend Terri, though…?"

"I'm pretty sure she's alive."

She lowered her voice and explained her reasoning with great delight. It was dead simple, she said, so simple that it just had to be true. When Terri went missing she left her mobile phone behind, down on the factory floor. One of the other workers handed it in. The very next day, Dorothy was sitting at her desk when Terri's mobile rang from the bottom drawer of the filing cabinet. She answered it and the guy on the other end of the line asked, in his jumped-up-never-come-down Edinburgh posh, for Miss Catriona Baxter. Dorothy said she didn't know anyone of that name. The bloke said then why are you answering her mobile? Dorothy back-pedalled, apologised, thinking she was about to get some information on Terri. Which she did.

"For a start that her name had changed!" I said. "Catriona Baxter. Pure Scot."

"There'd been a hitch, he told me. The ferry Miss Baxter was booked on, the 9.40 from Uig, has been cancelled, due to major engine problems, but she's been re-booked on the 12.10. Would I be kind enough to pass that on and convey Caledonian MacBrayne's apologies for any inconvenience." She paused and looked at me. "You're the only other person in the world who knows that."

"Apart from Edinburgh Posh," I said. "Ferry from Uig, did you say? Where the hell's Uig?"

"Isle of Skye." She reached across and laid a hand on my arm. "Will you go and find her, see what's happened? I'll pay you, I promise."

I said that was extremely kind of her but unnecessary. Somebody else was already paying me.

-18-

I took up Dorothy's offer to spend the night on her couch and followed her back to her bungalow, which lay at the farthest point of a small cul-de-sac off the Preston Road. It had belonged to her parents and represented a triumph in their ascent of the social ladder. They had moved to it from a council house on an estate that could still be seen from the kitchen window. That one shortcoming aside, for the last ten years of her life as proud matriarch in the first house anyone in her family had ever owned, Dorothy's mother was complete.

I was a touch put out by the fact that nobody followed us home, indeed there'd been no watch kept on me since Jack Daniels' visit to The Millstone the previous evening. It meant, I assumed, that he believed I would comply with his polite request to "fuck off home and forget about her". I would have considered it a mark of respect had he left at least one of the car salesmen behind to make sure that I did his bidding, but there'd been no sign of either of them.

While Dorothy made coffee I phoned Ellie, even though it was nearly midnight, and told her that I was planning to go to Scotland for two or three days, maybe more. How did she feel about that? She said it didn't bother her in the least. That worried me. I could think of twenty reasons why she'd be pleased to have the house to herself and after tussling with the first three, I dismissed them all in favour of being delighted that she could cope without me.

"How's the Doc?" I asked, by way of voicing the fact that I could always check up on Ellie via Laura.

"You know how she is, Dad. You spoke to her this morning. No change."

"How's Dogge?"

She trimmed her response to a bare minimum. "Dogge fine. Dad, me work tomorrow eight o'clock."

"Before I put you down," I said. "I need a favour. At The Gazette you must have access to these big news providers? Reuters, Associated Press, News Global. Could you tap into them for me?"

She laughed. "Dad, I've been there five minutes and you want me to start screwing the system for you!"

"It isn't a big deal, I promise, I'm just covering all bases. I want a list of major court cases coming up in the next year. Nationally, not tin-pot local stuff. Gangland wars, big corruption cases, terrorist plots. Go back 18 months, two years, say."

"Dad, I wouldn't know where to start!"

"There must be a crime reporter on the paper. Butter him up, get him to show you the ropes."

"What am I looking for, exactly?"

"Somebody in a protection programme who fits Teresa Stillman's profile. They could be a witness, could be a victim, but I doubt if they're a villain." I paused. "Go on, say you'll give it a bash. I'll be your best friend."

Then she disarmed me completely. "Dad, you're that already. G'night."

***

When I woke up next morning it was to Dorothy standing over me, suggesting that I sit up and take the tea she was holding. Conscious that I was seven-eighths naked and believing, for some absurd reason, that Dorothy might never have seen a man in that state before, I sat up carefully and tried to pull the sleeping bag up and around me. She smiled and set the mug down on the coffee table beside me and asked what I fancied for breakfast. It wasn't a real choice, she said, she was just being polite. It was cereal and/or toast. I said they both sounded fine. She then told me she was leaving for the factory in half an hour, but I should take my time, use the bathroom, the phone, her computer, anything I fancied, as long as I made sure the catch on the front door was down and I slammed it hard behind me when I left. She went back into the kitchen, leaving me to infer from her hospitality that she trusted me with her house and everything in it. And to find Terri Stillman.

***

Dorothy left for Bowler Plastics, repeating her instructions on closing the front door, pausing only to ask that I let her know how I got on. With Terri, she said, not the door. I promised I would, thanked her for the couch and breakfast and she went. I made myself another cup of tea and phoned Caledonian MacBrayne.

I guess what normally happens, when people ring Cal-Mac to book a ferry, is the girl on the other end reels off departure times, the punter picks one, and Jock's your uncle. I was coming at it from a different angle.

"You've a ferry that leaves Uig at 12.10 daily," I said. "Where does it go to?"

"Is that one of our Island ferries?" said the posh Edinburgh voice.

"I don't know. That's why I'm phoning you."

The Cal-Mac girl didn't like being put on the spot.

"I don't follow," she said. "You have a ferry booking but…?"

"I just want to know where the 12.10 would take me if I had a place on it."

There was a pause. The tension in my voice had made her suspicious.

"Would you mind holding on for a moment, sir?"

And before I could object, Beethoven's Pastoral played on a xylophone came on the line and stayed there for a good two minutes. Eventually the music faded and a young Scotsman said,

"Good afternoon, sir. Can I help you?"

"I hope so," I replied, with absolutely no threat in my voice whatsoever. "I'd like to know where the 12.10 ferry from Uig goes to."

"Do you mind if I ask why, sir?"

I really hadn't thought it would be this difficult but I had to sympathise with them to some degree. This is the age of saboteurs, hi-jackers and suicide bombers, terrorism in all its many colours, and who knows where its perpetrators will strike next? Probably not the Scottish Islands, but you can never tell.

"Alright, I'm sorry," I said. "I should've told the young lady. I'm not a customer. It's a quiz question. Round Table."

My lies were getting feebler by the week, probably through lack of practice. Even so, the Cal-Mac boy went for this one.

"Oh, I see," he said.

I heard a few keyboard strokes and a final flourish as he hit the return key.

"Lochmaddy," he said.

"Where's that?"

"North Uist. Good luck with the quiz."

***

I spent the next hour studying a map of the Outer Hebrides. The Western Isles. I'd never looked at them before. I don't think I'd said the words more than half a dozen times in my life. Crocodile. That's the shape of them, from the toothy jaws of Loch Tuath, right up in the north of Lewis, down through Harris across to the body and tapering tail of the Uists, Benbecula, Eriskay, Barra and Mingulay. There's nothing to fear, of course. This croc is dead on the map. The flesh has been picked away, by the midges I shouldn't wonder, leaving the lattice of bones to break the water's surface as 1000 tiny islands. It lies on its side, with its back to the Atlantic, braced like some gigantic tidal barrier. Until that particular day the only claim to fame of The Hebrides, as far as I was concerned, had been a place in the late shipping forecast, inspiring a swell of imagination at the mention of sea areas Rockall, Mallin Head, North Auxerra and South Auxerra. Gale force nine. Imminent.

It rains there, snows there, freezes there, fogs there, blows like hell there… and I was heading there. Why couldn't Jack Daniels have put his foot down, if indeed it was all about hiding Terri away from public view, and sent her to the South of France?

***

My favourite saying about male drivers, probably because I'm guilty of what it purports, is that we believe anyone going faster than us is a bloody maniac, anyone going more slowly is a doddering old fool. I can provide a third element to this self-righteous fallacy, the missing link between the other two, if you will, especially after my long haul up through Scotland to the Isle of Skye. Anyone doing the same speed as us for more than two miles is almost certainly on our tail. During my journey, four separate cars fitted that bill and in each case I put up with their steady pace and sensible distance behind me for as long as I could. Then I either slowed right down or pulled over to let them pass, which eventually each one of them did.

The only point at which I took my eye off the rear view mirror for any length of time was when the Land Rover began kicking and screaming its way up Shap Fell and my father popped into my mind. One Christmas he resurrected an electric train set which he had played with as a boy. There were two engines, the Duchess of Montrose and a little black tank engine. He fixed the track to a long run of plywood in the attic and we spent many a happy Sunday making trees from old sponges, haystacks from loofahs, meadows from carpet off-cuts.

Then, six months further on, he got ambitious. He decided to build a scale model of Shap Fell, bang in the centre of what to me was a perfect layout. He explained that once upon a time the express to Scotland stopped at the bottom of Shap and a tank engine was hitched on to give extra power for the ascent. The romance of it filled my head for weeks as he fashioned this famous slope. I could see the carriages, the faces at the windows, the water being taken on by the engine, the guard and driver hitching up the shunter and then that slow surge of power all wrapped in clouds of smoke and steam. But could my father recreate all that in our attic? Could he make our train go up the hill he'd so lovingly built? He could not. And it made him as unhappy as I ever saw him.

Recalling his disappointment dampened my spirits on that June morning, forty-odd years later. The feeling was compounded several hours later by Glasgow, which, like every other city in Europe, tried to lose me in a conspiracy of lousy sign-posting. Eventually I found the road to Erskine Bridge and by mid-afternoon had reached the big Highland names – Ben More, Loch Linne, Ben Nevis, Invergarry, Kyle of Lochalsh – but, as beautiful as they are, on my long haul north they were mere staging posts and I was happy to leave them behind.

I've mentioned my concern, some would call it my fear, that I was being followed. My mother would have had the perfect truism to excuse any hint of paranoia. Better to be safe than sorry, she would have said, when my pulse suddenly quickened in a mixture of anxiety and thrill. I had stopped just outside Fort William at a place that was more coffee shop with petrol pumps attached than full-blown service station.

As I sat on the bonnet of the Land Rover sipping my coffee, checking my onward route to The Western Isles, I heard the approach of motorbikes. How many there were I couldn't tell. Two, perhaps, certainly no more than four, but whatever the number the riders were taking it easily. They brought to mind my friend Steve Yates and his wife, their plans to travel the world on the Harley Davidson, but the mental image of them was whipped away by that of Richard Crane, black leathers, fit and dishy, ponytail, mid-thirties.

Three big bikes pulled into the parking area and the riders and their pillion passengers dismounted, removing their helmets as they did so. Three couples, men and wives, or at least girlfriends, and one of the men had long hair, certainly, overshadowed by a full white beard. They greeted each other, not having spoken since their last stop at Carlisle, I gathered, and then they strolled over to the coffee shop, five of them admiring the scenery, one of them, an Auguste Rodin look-alike, noticing me. As a boy he would no doubt have challenged my stare with a coarse demand to know what I was looking at. At middle-age he settled for testing my mood with a cautious nod that broke my stare and I smiled, as thinly as I could.

"Hi, how's it been?" I asked him.

He looked back in the direction from which we had both come. "It's been good. Yourself?"

"Not bad at all," I assured him.

He nodded again and followed his companions into the coffee shop. When he was out of sight, I threw the remains of my coffee onto a grassy patch, climbed into the Land Rover and drove away.

***

It was five o'clock when I crossed over into Skye and headed for the port of Uig. The road runs parallel to the sea and up by Loch Snizort it rises one hundred metres or so and follows the contour of the coastal hill. I chose a Bed and Breakfast place, just off the road, and ten minutes later was drinking tea in a conservatory overlooking The Little Minch. On a clear day you could see Harris and Lewis, my hostess told me, but this was a misty, wispy evening. Tomorrow would be fresher, livelier, she added, but since I'd be sailing on Cal-Mac's newest ship I wouldn't notice a thing.

Later that evening, prompted by the whole gamut of meaning in the words fresher and livelier, I phoned Ellie and was greeted by a grunt.

"Translation?"

"Dad, I'm in bed."

So she was, now she mentioned it. The voice was coming from deep in the cocoon. "Jesus, Ellie, it's only nine o'clock…"

"My editor wants me in the office by seven tomorrow. Is this social, Dad?"

"Well, yes and no. Ellie it's a bit… fresh here and I've come unprepared…"

"Scotland, mate."

"…could you dig out my sheepskin jacket from the back of my cupboard and post it to me on North Uist. It's an island in the Outer Hebrides. I'm going there tomorrow. Send it the quickest way possible, next-day delivery, whatever you can find." My hostess had suggested that the jacket be sent to a friend of hers called Mrs Jane Stewart who ran the best shop on the island. She had also booked me in with another friend who ran a B & B close to it. "Got a pad and pencil?"

"Biro bedside table, old envelope."

"Mr Nathan Hawk, care of The Post Office, Bayhead-by-Lochmaddy, North Uist, Scotland HS6 5AB. Write 'to be collected' on it."

Then I steeled myself for the bit she wouldn't like. "There's something else," I said. "In that clay pot Jaikie made me at Haddenham First School, it's on the desk in my office, there's a key."

I paused. I was trying to make her irritable so that I could hang on to the moral high ground.

"And?" she snapped, falling in with my intentions.

"Well, it's a key to the safe in the wall, in my bedroom behind the oval mirror."

After another pause she asked with full-blown sarcasm, "Do you by any chance want me to take the key, stick it in the lock and turn it? Open the door perhaps afterwards?"

"There's a gun in there. I'd like you to send it with the jacket."

I heard the cocoon give way and the creature inside emerge in recognisable form. "You mean we've got a fucking gun in the house?" she yelled.

I explained, as if doing so would appease her, that it was a Smith and Wesson 38 that had saved my life on at least two occasions and had therefore retired when I did instead of being handed back to the Hamford Armourer for further service.

"Who are you going to kill?" she asked.

"No one, I hope. Wrap it up in an old T-shirt, bury it in the jacket along with the box of shells, also in the safe. Take it all down to the post office first thing. Oh, and Ellie…"

"What else?" she said. "Heat-seeking missile, out in the garage?"

I smiled. "If anyone asks for me, especially a man with a reddish cast to his complexion and corrugated hair, say I've gone to France but you don't know where exactly. Then phone me."

-19-

Come morning, I could barely see my hand in front of my face, never mind Harris or Lewis in the distance. Cloud was tumbling down the mountain behind the guesthouse and curling up at the water's edge, but at least the crossing would be calm, my hostess assured me. Provided the ship didn't bump into anything the captain couldn't see, I suggested. Such as Northern Ireland.

As if to make a neurotic fool out of me, by the time I took my place on the morning ferry, the cloud had moved on and left a cold, clear sky behind it. Standing out from a handful of late holidaymakers and the MacAskill lorries delivering to the islands was the group of six middle-aged bikers I'd seen in the service station at Fort William. The Rodin look-alike remembered me and nodded in a slightly more relaxed way than he'd done on the mainland. "Thought you might be," he said. Coming here, he didn't say but meant.

"Me too, you," I replied, meaning that I'd guessed he and his companions were headed this way as well.

The shorthand nature of our conversation suited us both and by the time we'd reached the stairs up from the vehicle deck we'd run out of things to say, reasons to nod at each other. I went one way, he went another, explaining to his friends where he and I had met before. They didn't remember me.

Crossing The Little Minch, the stretch of water between Skye and North Uist, took an hour and a half, long enough to make me feel that I was heading for a foreign land, albeit one where English was spoken, if not always understood. Behind me now the Isle of Skye seemed vast, a country in its own right, and more than once I mistook it for the mainland proper. Where the coastal hills met the sea they were scalloped at each promontory as if some great creature had savaged them. Having bitten off more than he could chew he'd spat out unpalatable rocks in the shape of a dozen small islands.

Ahead of me lay the Uists, lower in profile than I'd expected. To the south were the islands of Barra, Mingulay and Eriskay and far, far to the north, across the Sound of Harris, lay the island of that name. Beyond its imposing hills was an impression, nothing more, of the great mountains of Lewis. As we approached North Uist, the ferry wove between rocks and warning lights, finally making the small harbour of Lochmaddy. With its single quayside and lone building, it stood at the focal point of a hundred or more islands stretching away towards the south and west, like some vast sea creature. It felt as if one muffled squeak, or whatever passes for language in the deep, and this monster would thrash its tail and take to the ocean beyond.

Once off the ship I parked the Land Rover on the cramped quayside and walked across to the Cal-Mac office. I was just about to enter when I heard the sound of youth being reclaimed as the three motorbikes revved and held back, then revved and revved again their way along the harbour slip road, off into the illusory freedom of the open road. The Rodin look-alike nodded as he passed me.

In the Cal-Mac office I asked the girl for directions to Bayhead and with 'By Lochmaddy' being part of the address I expected it to be just around the corner. It was thirteen miles away, virtually on the other side of the island, proving that the Outer Hebrides is a land of long journeys that end in small destinations.

By the time I reached Bayhead, the tide was out, revealing a sweep of sand that stretched, uninterrupted, for at least three quarters of a mile across to the opposite side of the bay. Sgeir Ruadh, which sounds far more romantic than its English translation, Red Rock, was the name of the guesthouse I'd booked into. The house stood at a point where a curve of small hills, seeming to jostle for prime position, formed the head of a small sea loch. Like the dozen or so houses nearby, it had been built in the late 70s, a modern version of the stone house now lying in ruins on the same plot of land.

Mrs MacDonald was a diffident host in her late sixties, bundled up in a thick woolly jumper overlaid by an even bulkier cardigan. She was immediately suspicious of me and, when I think back, I must have seemed something of an oddity. A middle-aged man, travelling alone in a battered farm vehicle, I'd turned up out of the blue, just before the summer invasion of tourists. What on earth could I have been up to?

When she brought me a cup of tea in the porch, I tried to put her mind at rest with a lie and, although there were elements of truth to it, it sounded almost as feeble as my quiz lie to the lad in Cal-Mac Customer Services. I said I was searching, on behalf of an old friend, for his young daughter. He believed that she'd come to live here a couple of months ago and he was anxious to make his peace with her. I kept my eyes firmly to the left as I spoke, having read somewhere that if they drift rightwards it means that you're inventing. I wondered if, as a district nurse, Mrs MacDonald had read the same article.

"So you'll be one of those private detectives?" she asked, looking right at me.

"Not really. I was a policeman."

I'm not sure if that gave her confidence. It used to, with people over fifty, but theses days nobody falls for it..

"Och, I see," she said, cautiously. She asked me what I wanted for breakfast. I told her. She said it would be on the table at seven-thirty sharp.

"You wouldn't know of anyone yourself?" I said. "New to the island? I mean with you being the district nurse…"

I think her eyes flicked rightwards but I couldn't swear to it. "No, no and I wouldn't know where to suggest you start looking either."

"How many people live on the island, Mrs MacDonald?"

"On Uist? About fifteen hundred."

The population of a large English village. I'd done it before and, if the worse came to the worst, I'd do it again. I'd knock on every bloody door till I found Terri Stillman.

***

I drove back into Lochmaddy that evening and had supper in a hotel restaurant close to the ferry terminal. That isn't as bad as it sounds. As ferry towns go Lochmaddy is more Padstow than Portsmouth and even then just a fraction of the size. However, the fresh lobster I ordered was the biggest I'd ever seen and halfway through putting paid to it, Ellie phoned. We started the conversation badly, and it went downhill from there.

"Ellie, did you post my jacket, et cetera?"

"Yes, I did. Dad, I want you to listen to me very carefully. No interruptions."

"What's wrong?"

I was rising from the table, preparing for action, having detected strain in her voice, the clipped, breathless delivery, which with Ellie indicates a problem.

"Dad, nothing is wrong! For God's sake, can't we just exchange a few words, discuss the odd change to a schedule, without you going off half cock and thinking the worst…" The pause for breath heralded the expected volte face. "Alright, something is wrong, but I wouldn't have put it that way if you hadn't asked me straight off what was bloody wrong!"

"Where are you?" I asked.

"I'm round at Laura's…"

"Let me speak to her."

It was the wrong thing to say. "That is something else which pisses me off! Like, if there is a problem, why the hell can't I be the one to deal with it? Does there always have to be a so-called adult on the fringes, waiting to step in?"

I was being watched by at least four other people in the restaurant who were trying desperately not to let it show. However, they could see the fight or flight in my stance, they could hear the tension in my voice, and were no doubt curious to learn what it all meant. It occurred to me that for all their interest, for all my fatherly concern, I was no nearer to knowing what the original problem was.

Against my better judgement I paused and took a deep breath. I sat down at the table again and took a mouthful of water to counter my suddenly dry mouth. Ellie must have done something similar at the other end of the line. I was first to pick up the thread.

"Okay, Ellie. How are things?"

She acknowledged my attempt to normalise the conversation. "Thank you, Dad. We've been broken into."

My body was telling me to rise from the table again, head for the door and head for Beech Tree Cottage. My brain was saying stay where you are. For a moment it felt as if I were being tested by my youngest daughter and whatever I said next might set a course for our relationship over the next three or four days. I lowered my voice and gave it what we both knew was an unnatural calm.

"Right, well… what's been taken?"

"That's the funny thing," she said. "Nothing."

"So how do you know you've been broken into?"

I could sense Ellie at the other end, perhaps with my voice on speaker now, turning to Laura, pointing out that although I was a policeman for all those years I still didn't know that people break into places for other reasons than to steal.

"It's what they did while they were here, Dad."

"They?"

"One of them was a woman."

I asked her to explain her reasoning and, like the very best of its kind, it was painfully simple. One of the intruders had used a tissue to blow their nose on and smeared it with lipstick before chucking it in the bin. Amateurs, she concluded, and I agreed. One of the visitors, and we assumed it was the woman, also performed two small tasks while they were in the house. The first thing she did was to fill up Dogge's water bowl, the second was to pick up a jacket from the porch floor as she left…

"Whoa back, there!" I said.

"No good complaining, Dad, I dropped the jacket on my way out to work, promised I'd pick it up this evening. She hung it on a coat hanger."

"How did she get in?"

"Through the kitchen window. It's 300 years old. It doesn't close."

It was another of those jobs I'd been meaning to do since I moved in: make the windows fit properly. "Where was Dogge all this time?"

"Probably licking whoever it was to death."

I gave the points headlines: window, water bowl, jacket, tissue. "You know that tissue could be very useful, Ellie…"

"Don't worry, Dad, Laura's already bagged it up and she's sending off to a private lab tomorrow for DNA analysis."

I was beginning to feel ever so slightly redundant. "That's good work," I managed to say. "Why do you think there are two of them and the other's a man?"

She explained their combined thinking with proof to match. There was a size eleven footprint in the herb garden under the kitchen window. They hadn't gone as far as to make plaster of paris casts but they had measured it with a ruler. They reckoned – and so did I now – that a fairly tall guy had lifted his slighter companion up to the openish kitchen window. She'd slithered in over the sink, made friends with Dogge, who to be honest I would have expected to go berserk, though not if she was parched, and then she went to the front door and let her size eleven companion in.

So, who the hell were they? They weren't Jack Daniels' people or they'd have left no trace of themselves behind. They were rank amateurs. So who were they? And what were they looking for?

"Did they leave any other marks?"

"No, we reckon he took the shoes off in the porch, went round in his socks."

"Did anyone in the village see them?"

"No."

"Have you told the police? Jim Kelloway?"

"No, that's really why I'm phoning you…"

"Good girl! Don't tell him a thing. Can I speak to Laura now?"

There was a momentary lapse back to her original argument as to why I shouldn't be allowed to. "Dad, we've been through…"

I'm guessing that Laura approached at that point and took the phone out of her hand. I'm pretty sure I said all the right things, like how are you and thanks for preserving the DNA sample, but then I said, "Listen, can you do something for me?"

"When you lower your voice like that, it usually means something tricky."

"No, not at all. Just get Ellie to stay with you for a couple of days."

She chuckled, then realised that I must have a good reason to ask. "I'll try, certainly. Why, who are these people?"

"I don't know, but given that anyone poking their nose in my business these days really wants to know where Terri Stillman is, they make me nervous."

"Leave it with me."

I lowered my voice even further. "Oh, and remind her that I'm still waiting for the list. Of court cases. She'll know what it means."

-20-

The next morning I learned something fundamental about the Hebridean way of life. Mrs MacDonald had said that breakfast would be at 7.30 sharp. It arrived at a blunt eight o'clock with no mention of the time lag because clocks and watches don't figure much here. They're up on mantelpieces, or locked in jewellery boxes, deferring to the greater taskmasters of weather, light and the landscape. The latter reminds you, at every glance, of just how long it's been here and its durability isn't measured in minutes and hours but in millions of years. In such a time frame, being half an hour late with bacon and eggs hardly seems to matter.

After breakfast I drove down to the shop-cum-post office, just half a mile away. It stood at the head of the loch, commanding what passes for a prime trading position on Uist. Three roads met, none of them seemed to go to or come from anywhere, and there was no signpost to counter that impression.

The shop was a relic from an earlier civilisation, single storey and built of concrete blocks, with walls and its roof clad in green corrugated iron. In front of it, on the granite-chip forecourt, black and wet from saltwater spray, were two petrol pumps that must have given service for half a century. They stood tall and green, with small round faces, one with the word petrol written on it, the other diesel. The exorbitant price of each was written on bits of cardboard slung round their necks.

Inside, the place reminded me of my father's garden shed where a barrage of new smells, not unpleasant ones, would greet the visitor fresh every visit. Just like Dad's hideaway, the shop was gloomy, though not oppressively so. Such natural light as there was came from clear plastic panels in the roof and a couple of glass windows on the loch side. The shelves were meccano-like structures, ranging up and down the length of the stone floor. At the far end, a small booth served as a post office counter and a white-haired woman of about sixty emerged from it in the hope of serving me. She adjusted her glasses by the winged frames to get me in focus.

"Good morning," she said. "I'd say you were the gentleman staying with the MacDonalds?"

"And you'd be right. Nathan Hawk."

"Jane Stewart."

We shook hands and she gestured for me to take a basket from the stack at the unmanned check-out.

"I'm not actually shopping today, Mrs Stewart. I'm asking favours."

She pulled up the zip on her sheepskin body warmer as if adjusting armour for combat. She was going to sell me something from Bayhead Stores or die in the attempt.

"If it's directions you're after," she said, "we've maps on aisle three."

"It isn't places I'm trying to find, it's people. Or rather one person. I was hoping she might've been into the shop sometime during the last three months."

I told her what I was pretty sure she already knew from Mrs MacDonald, that I was looking for the daughter of an old friend, that she was called Terri Stillman though she was probably known here as Catriona Baxter.

"How old is this lassie?" she asked.

"Twenty-three."

"And have you a photograph?"

"No, but I can describe her to you…"

She began to close down on me and who could blame her?

"I can't remember who was the last newcomer to the island," she said. "The police would know."

They probably would, I thought. Jack Daniels would surely have informed them of Terri's arrival, though not the real reason for her being here. He would also have told them to be on the lookout for a man answering my description.

"I didn't want to bother them," I said. "I mean as an ex-copper myself I know just how busy a day can…"

I was digging a hole I might not be able to climb out of. I stopped.

"Go on then," she said, eventually. "Describe her."

She listened while I gave her a cut down version of Dorothy Bowler's description. When I'd finished she nodded and for one moment I thought she'd recognised the girl I'd spoken of.

"No," she said, finally. "No one of that description's ever bought provisions from me. Are you sure she came to this part of the island?"

I wasn't, of course. "Certainly."

She held up a forefinger. Way in the distance she had heard the sound of approaching money in the shape of motorbikes descending from the hinterland to fill up with petrol.

"Excuse me, I'm going to shout," Jane said. She'd been right to warn me, she had the power to deafen. "Hamish!" she bellowed. "Petrol!"

"He won't sleep through that," I said, when the wow and flutter had subsided.

"We do packed lunches, by the way," she said. "Did I mention that?"

"No, but…"

She had a handwritten menu in front of me before I could finish the sentence. I chose tuna and bacon with salad on a bap. She asked if one would be enough. I said she was probably right, I'd have two. She'd made her sale and turned to go out back and build my lunch.

"Just a second, where will I find other shops, Mrs Stewart? Like this one?"

I added quickly that I'd no intention of taking my custom elsewhere, I was simply trying to nail down the focal points in the community. Even so, she turned up her nose as if the shops she was about to mention were decomposing after a slow, well-deserved death. "There's Lochmaddy," she said. "People go there, though I can't say I hear brilliant reports of it. And there's Balivanich, of course, on Benbecula…"

"That's another island though," I said.

She cackled, pure Highland grouse. "Aye, but you'll not get your feet wet, there's a causeway you can drive across. As for the shop there, well…" She turned up her nose even farther. "…NAAFI supermarket. Need I say more?"

"You mean there's an army base there?"

She nodded. The bikers had pulled onto the forecourt. Through the open door I counted the six riders who were beginning to feel like old friends, the kind you don't see for years then keep bumping into.

"Excuse me," said Jane. She meant that she was going to shout again and did. "Hamish!"

The sound waves rumbled along the roof spars and fell to earth at a doorway to the back of the shop through which a young lad emerged, eating what smelled like a fried egg sandwich. He was about sixteen, I guessed, and only half awake. He walked past us, gently waving aside the possibility that Jane might speak to him. At the door he stuck the sandwich in his mouth, donned an anorak that had been hanging on a nail, and went out to deal with the bikers.

"Yours?" I said of him.

She nodded. "He's a good lad when he's awake. You have any?"

"Four," I said. "Grown up and gone but, like Hamish, not to be approached before noon."

She smiled and began to open up to me again. "Person you need to speak to is Davey Laing, the postie." I glanced towards the Post Office cubicle. "He's been and gone for the day, I'm afraid." She had paused beside a chiller cabinet and leaned in. "The bacon. Smoked or otherwise?"

"Otherwise," I said. "Where does he live?"

"Davey? Towards Hougharry."

"Last question. Has anyone else asked after her?"

"No."

"Favour. If they do would you mind fobbing them off?"

"Why?"

"I think they'll be the people who are trying to kill her."

Because of the angle she was standing at her glasses seemed to treble the size of her eye-balls. In them I read a mixture of pure fear and even purer excitement.

"My sandwich?" I said quietly, and reluctantly she withdrew to make it.

From the relative cover of the hardware shelves I watched Hamish deal with the easyriders. When he'd filled them up he took their money and came back into the shop with a bundle of notes blooming in his fist. He stopped and looked me up and down.

"They asked if the Land Rover was yours."

"What did you tell 'em?"

"Said I didn't know, it or you."

"When you give them their change, nod at the one with the beard, just like this." I showed him the nod the biker and I had developed.

At the till he held the banknotes up to the light to check for the metal strip. They were, after all, English notes. As he totted up the change, all of 35 pence, and printed out a single till receipt, the bikers fired up their engines and in the style I'd become familiar with, they revved and revved again their way off the forecourt.

"Nice bikes," Hamish said, pocketing the change they'd ridden off without. "Harley, one of them."

His mother called to him from the back. "Urge them in, Hamish. Urge them in!"

He looked at me, taking my sympathy for granted. "They've gone, Ma."

Jane Stewart appeared in the doorway through to the back. "Gone?" she said, as if at least one of them had died right there in her shop, not simply ridden off. "Gone?"

***

It was nearly one o'clock by the time I found Hougharry, following an Ordnance Survey map Jane Stewart had sold me. It had been an instructive journey. The driver of the first car I passed waved at me. I gestured back, minimally. Five minutes later a second driver passed me with a wink and a flick of his head, all very matey. And a little unnerving. Maybe he'd seen me on the ferry, I thought, or at the quayside so I waved back but with no real friendliness intended. When I then passed a beaten up old truck and the driver of it waved, smiling into the bargain, it twigged. There are so few cars on Uist that all drivers pass each other with a friendly greeting. The sheer courtesy of it had caught me off guard.

Jane's highlighting of the map had a batch of exclamation marks at the point where I needed to turn off from Hougharry and head towards the Nature Reserve. She was right to have made a big deal about it. It was a sly, obscure turning and with it being on a corner might easily have been missed.

The first house I came to was a croft and it didn't need an ex-Detective Chief Inspector to figure out that a Post Office worker lived there. A red postbus was parked on the grassy slope opposite.

Mrs Laing was a hatchet-faced woman, with a stooped and shrivelled body giving an impression of being forever in defiance of the elements. She looked up at me with eyes that offered a disturbing choice of which one to look at. I aimed at the bridge of her nose as she told me that her husband was "down with the sheep". I thanked her and walked the half-mile or so down to the machair, the stretch of grassland between the sea and the shore, and way in the distance saw a man in an orange work suit. He was driving a bunch of sheep towards me with the help of a mean-faced border collie, crouched and sure-footed.

Davey Laing was a stick insect of a man, tall and twitchy, with a face that lied about his age, but in the wrong direction. I put him at 60-plus but he'd been a small child in the 60s, he said, which made him just over 50 years old. He looked me up and down and smiled. I guess he'd seen it all before, foreigners going down to the beach dressed as I was for soft weather. He placed himself to windward of me and explained that between us and the next landfall, Newfoundland, there were 3000 miles of icy sea. When the wind blows from that direction, it blows long, hard and cold, sticking two isobars up at all before it. It was blowing now, bringing rain clouds in from the sea in a dozen shades of grey. I stuffed my hands into the pockets of my leather jacket, hunched up my shoulders and told Davey what my business on the island was. After I'd given him a description of Terri, he nodded.

"There've only been three new arrivals in the last couple of months. Two are in their forties, husband and wife, the other could well be the lassie you're describing."

He spoke with a typical Highland lilt, unmistakably Scottish, but clipped at every word. The stress is all on chosen syllables, the others being skipped over almost inaudibly.

"Where does she live?"

He stopped walking, called the dog to his side from where she eye-balled the sheep she'd been driving. They stood defiantly, face on to the Atlantic Ocean, their fleeces sparkling white, bleached and combed by the salt wind. Davey pulled the cloth cap he wore, two sizes too big for him, right down over his ears. My own were being torn from their mountings.

"Bail Iochdrach, that's where she is," he said. "I don't know that she's still there, mind. No post for her in the last week or so."

"Where's… Bail Iochdrach?"

"On Baile Sear" He responded to my blank look with a translation. "Baleshare. It's an island. Iochdrach's a kirk and five houses. Hers is the nearest one to the road. I'll show you on your map."

"How far from here?" I asked.

He narrowed his eyes and looked southwards along the coastline. "On a clear day you can see it from here, six, seven miles."

I followed his gaze southwards to where clouds were blackening by the second, corralling us from all directions and bringing on a false dusk. Any minute now the heavens were going to open and chuck it down from every angle.

"How many of them do you get?" I asked as he added a few pen strokes to the map. "Clear days, I mean?"

"Enough. If the sun shone every day the Boeings would soon fly in, property developers would follow."

With due regard to the direction of the wind, he turned and spat to show his contempt for such a prospect. The oral missile flew twenty yards before landing on a pile of kelp. I spent the next half hour reminding myself occasionally that I'd eaten in a Japanese restaurant in Los Angeles where kelp had been served as a delicacy.

"You haven't told me her name," I said.

"Miss C Baxter. I can't tell you what the C stands for."

"Catriona," I said.

"Aye, well, she doesn't have much by way of post but then young people don't. The art of letter-writing, all forgotten within a generation."

He swung his stick and pointed to the sheep, whereupon the dog belted off to gather them into a bunch again. Together we headed for the croft. Ignoring the first few lashings of rain I asked, "When did you first deliver there?"

He twisted the hard, weather-beaten lips in an effort to recall. "Three weeks ago. Aye, tenth, eleventh." He yelled in Gaelic at the dog, who had snapped at one of the sheep's heels. "You know, I wouldn't set your hopes too high on her being your friend's daughter. This lassie's from Glasgow."

"How do you know?"

"The accent, man."

I thought back. No one had said that Terri was a Scot anymore than they'd said that she wasn't. Maybe that's why she'd chosen to come here. It would've been like coming home. Except that no one here seemed to know her.

By the time we reached the Land Rover, rain was bouncing off every surface and I was drenched. Davey invited me in to dry off but in truth I was too embarrassed to accept. Before I climbed into the Land Rover, though, I told him what I'd told Jane Stewart, that Terri was in mortal danger. Whereas Jane had thrilled to the prospect, and by now had probably told every customer she'd served, Davey Laing took it with a facial shrug.

"Why?" he asked simply.

"I'm not sure but can I ask a favour of you? If anyone else enquires after her, stall them for me or send them on a wild goose chase."

The idea of lying appealed to him, if the smile was anything to go by. "What shall I say?"

"Tell 'em she's gone to Newfoundland, to sort out the weather."

***

Back at Bayhead, Deirdre MacDonald greeted me at the front door of her guesthouse with news that my daughter had been trying to get hold of me all day. She made it seem, with her despairing voice and gently shaking head, that it was my fault that the signal in this part of the world was rubbish. Even so, I thanked her.

I phoned Ellie and after a brief report on the state of things dear to us, such as Laura, Beech Tree Cottage and the dog, she told me she'd got the information I wanted. The crime reporter at The Gazette had been only too pleased to show her the ropes and furthermore give her his own personal list of big cases that had recently been tried, or were due to hit the courts in the next twelve months. She hadn't asked him to filter his suggestions and leave only those that contained reference to a girl like Terri Stillman, but even so his final list wasn't huge. I praised her initiative and her sense of diplomacy.

"There's four pages of it, Dad," she said, clearly doubting that my attention span could cope. "Shall I send it?"

"Please."

Before ending the call she told me that she and Dogge had spent last night at Laura's house and had been fine but, and it was a big but, she'd stayed there only to spare Laura an ear-bashing from me. Fair enough, if that was the way Laura had put it to her, that I would get scratchy if Ellie didn't spend the next few days at Plum Tree Cottage.

I turned in shortly afterwards and sat in bed reading the document Ellie had put together and emailed. There were five or six cases The Gazette's crime reporter had thought worthy of attention and a few others of lesser interest. Biggest headlines went to Lord John Kettridge, 46 years old and loaded, who had raped the 23-year-old daughter of his personal assistant. He'd made the mistake of doing so in front of friends who had turned against him for a variety of other reasons. He was heading for a fall, provided that the prosecution could keep his victim safe. Was that victim now called Terri Stillman? I didn't think so.

Nastiest, in Ellie's view, was the case of an off-duty soldier who had run over the only daughter of Mr and Mrs Harold Stacie in Tonbridge. She'd been returning home late at night with a girlfriend, a credible and articulate witness.

This particular squaddy's mates had already had one go at her and muffed it. Had the police stepped in and placed her in a witness protection programme under the name of Terri Stillman?

The crime reporter's favourite was the murder of a head teacher in a posh boys' school, even though it had happened five years ago. It was widely believed to be the work of a boy called Max Lakeman, then aged 17. Three months ago one of his girlfriends had walked into a police station and made an accusation. The case sprang to life again, Lakeman was arrested and placed on remand in Somerton Lea Young Offenders Institution. Was his accuser Terri Stillman? Whether yes or no, a couple broke into Somerton Lea a month later, presumably looking for Max Lakeman. They didn't get very far. The security thwarted them.

Fourth on the list was the fraud of the decade, about which nearly everyone in the UK knew something. It involved six directors of an international bank, Winslow and Hardacre. They'd forced up the share prices by buying each other's holdings and then sold them at a stockmarket high. A two-bit secretary at the bank had reeled off names, dates and amounts to the police and three directors had gone to prison because of her testimony. Three others, including a government minister, had got off. Was the girl still a threat to them? Had she been given a new existence as Terri Stillman by way of thanking her for nailing the main culprits?

The case I was most pleased to see on the list involved two London villains who should've been jailed thirty years previously and left to rot. Now ageing to the point where respectability beckoned, they had fallen out over what they knew about each other. One had informed on the other. By way of revenge, his opponent had assaulted his rival's two daughters at a family gathering. One of them died. The other survived but her small son had got caught up in the shooting that followed. He too had died. The case was soon to be tried and the surviving daughter had supplied most of the evidence against those involved. Was she Terri Stillman, now morphed into Catriona Baxter and being protected by SOU?

Crimewise it had been like most other years, then, with corruption reaching into government, the ever steady rise in crimes against children and the ubiquitous serial killer and rapist at work. A new phenomenon had emerged, of course, in the shape of imagined terrorist plots. Few if any had amounted to much.

But was Terri Stillman hidden away in Ellie's list, among the victims, witnesses and informants? I couldn't see her.

-21-

Next morning I went down to the shop and found that my parcel from Ellie had arrived. Jane Stewart was squeezing and pressing it from all angles to ascertain the contents.

"It's a sheepskin jacket," I said, liberating it from her grasp. I then resisted her attempts to sell me things I didn't need and also managed to keep from her the purpose of my day. I was heading for the address Davey Laing had given me, the last place he'd delivered mail addressed to Terri Stillman.

I stopped only once on the journey there to unwrap the parcel. Ellie had packed it well, with the Smith and Wesson, holster and shells wound in several old shirts, then buried deep in the craftily folded sheepskin. No note. I separated the pistol from the shells, one in the glove compartment, the other in a side pocket, donned the jacket and went on my way.

The drive took me through some of the bleakest small landscape I've ever known, sweeps of grazing overrun by heather, backed by rising, jagged hills, so near they felt touchable. I stopped at the causeway joining North Uist to the island of Baleshare and wondered at the technology that strings out a line of rocks in the sea, cements the sides, tarmacs the top and somehow gets it to work as a road.

Once over the causeway it was a straight road to Loch Samhia and from there I turned off and bumped my way up the track towards the kirk and gaggle of houses that made up Bail Iochdrach. To either side of me the machair was richer and wider than the norm for Uist, so much so that a small herd of Aberdeen Angus was grazing on the pasture I drove across. Ahead of me, surrounding a low, stone house was a garden sheltered by the dwelling itself and a protruding wall. I could see runner bean plants that had reached the top of a tripod but then shrivelled against the hopes of whoever planted them. A basket of spindly geraniums hung beneath the new thatch. The latter was made of heather, roped down and weighted all over with heavy, flat stones taken from the nearby shore.

So impressed was I by the sheer defiance of the house, not to mention the optimism of whoever lived in it, that I almost missed a small, single-storey cottage to my right, set in a dip and partially obscured by its own boundary wall. It was built of plain stone with a slate roof, curtains at the windows. There were no beans, no baskets, no defining features. It was trying not be seen.

I guessed this was the house Davey Laing had referred to as being the one nearest the road. I parked just beyond it. I was nervous. If Terri was here, and I felt there was a fifty-fifty chance that she might be, in a strange way it was going to be like meeting up with an old friend I hadn't seen for twenty years, wondering just how much he or she might have changed. I'd never met Terri Stillman, of course, and was anxious to see how different she was from the picture I'd formed in my mind.

I went through the gate to the cottage and down the stepped pathway. I knocked on the heavy front door and back came the dull echo from closed doors within. I knew it so well from all those fruitless house calls as a young copper. Terri, or Catriona, as I should have been thinking of her at this point, wasn't in. At least, that was the palatable version of what I feared. The less appetising one said that she'd never been here in the first place. I knocked again, even though it was foolish to think that she might not have heard me the first time.

I stood back and looked up the hill to the four-square kirk, 200 yards away. An elderly woman who'd been cleaning the windows at the front now opened the door and entered. I decided to join her for morning prayers. Mine would be simple. Please don't let Terri Stillman have moved away.

The kirk would've come as a pleasant surprise if finding Catriona hadn't been uppermost in my mind. I'd expected Presbyterian guilt to be seeping out of its stonework, but found plastered walls, painted white, with arched windows that gave out onto picture postcard views of the coastline all the way down to Barra. Just inside the door, purple drapes, floor to ceiling, formed a lobby with stairs rising either side to the balcony above. On an oak desk lay a stack of newsletters, a spray of wild flowers and the eternal collection box.

The other side of the curtains, in the church proper, the pulpit was dominant, set high enough for the minister to glare down at every lost soul who'd come to hear his take on The Big Questions. At the simple altar the window-cleaning lady was changing the cloth and turned to greet me, expecting me to be one of her neighbours, I imagine. She wasn't elderly, after all. She was pushing 50, admittedly from the wrong side, but had kept her looks. To either side of her lean, unblemished face, her long brown hair rolled rather than fell, thick without a hint of white. As a girl people would have commented upon it so she knew it was one of her best features, which is why she wore nothing on it, no beret like Deirdre MacDonald, no woollen tea-cosy like Jane Stewart. The rest of her was battened down against the capricious winter with jeans, a sweater and a heavy fleece.

"Good morning," she said, taking me for a wayside repenter. "I'll not be a minute then I'll leave you in peace."

The accent was posh Edinburgh, identified by its aloof weariness. I reassured her that there was no hurry, that she should take all the time she needed.

She smiled. "Aye, well, it's a grand little kirk, quite a rarity on this island." She lowered her voice for fear of giving offence. "Mainly Catholic, here on South Uist. Where are you staying?"

"Bayhead."

"With Deirdre MacDonald?"

I nodded. "You live here, I take it?"

"The house on the right. Ceol na Mara."

She re-set the crucifix and candles on the altar and came down the short aisle towards me. She looked me in the eyes for a moment then offered me a bony hand that seemed older than the rest of her. "I'm Marian Korting," she said.

"That's a new clan to me."

"I married a Dutchman."

You can tell many things about a marriage by the way one half of it introduces the other. She'd used the past tense. Her Dutchman was either out of the picture or she wished he were.

"I saw you knock on the door, the house opposite me," she went on. "Who did you think might open it?"

"Catriona Baxter. Is she away?"

She began to straighten the prayer books, walking sideways between the pews to do so.

"Aye, well people never stay there long. The place belongs to the Ministry of Defence, it's their Visiting Officers' Quarters. People stay there sometimes and I'm asked to clean up when they leave. This time they brought in their own people."

"Was it just Catriona living there?" I asked.

"Yes, but she had a visitor, rather dour man…"

"With reddish hair?"

She cocked her head like a gundog hearing game in the long grass. "Do I sense intrigue, Mr…?"

"Hawk."

I gave her the same story I'd given Jane Stewart. Catriona Baxter was the daughter of an old friend and, as an ex-copper with time on my hands, I was looking for her.

"A falling out, then," she said. "Over her little boy, perhaps?" It must have been the blank look on my face that made her prompt me. "Your friend's grandson?"

Having invented my friend and his daughter, I hadn't expected there to be an extended family. I pretended I'd just caught up and nodded gravely. I was about to dig for more information but she got there first.

"Who is she really, Mr Hawk? What has she done?"

As I framed an evasive answer a bell rang. It came from the direction of the houses and Marian tensed up at the sound of it.

"Ah, coffee," she said and led the way out into the churchyard.

The bell we'd heard was hanging beside the front door of Ceol na Mara and Marian's husband, far from being a thing of the past, was ringing it, yanking a rope that was fastened to the tongue. He was a big man, far too big for the house he was living in. He sported a black beard, greying at the edges, a belly with no edges at all and a less than pleasant way with him. He gave me a taste of it as I approached with his wife.

"Who's this?" he barked at Marian.

"Rolf, this gentleman is looking for Catriona."

"Nathan Hawk," I said, reaching across the wall.

Korting ignored my hand, informing me instead that he hadn't made enough coffee for three. I said I didn't want coffee. He grunted and went back into the cottage. Marian stayed, presumably to have a chat with someone who'd do more than grunt at her.

"You didn't answer my question," she said. "What has Catriona done?"

"Nothing, as far as I know. Your initial thoughts were right. A falling out."

She looked away, clearly no stranger to family disputes. "Yes, the young can be so merciless in the way they punish their elders. You have children?"

"Four."

I could see Rolf Korting through the open window, trying to make his presence felt. He was setting out two mugs on a tray, for the coffee presumably. Then I saw him carefully drop a spoon, which bounced across the stone floor, clink, clink, clink.

"Listen, I don't want to keep you, but…"

"That's alright," Marian said, quickly.

"You mentioned my friend's grandson."

She smiled. "Well, I assume it's his grandson?" She wanted confirmation but I gave her a look of mock horror that she took me for the sort to give secrets away. "It's just that I went over there one day, soon after she moved in, just to be friendly. I found her crying. Well, sobbing inconsolably would be a better description."

"You just walked in on her? Caught her by surprise?"

She nodded. "It was a fine day, the door was open, I strode in calling out her name… and there she was." She shook her head, recalling the intensity of the young woman's grief. "I did my best, apologised for the intrusion, I even took her in my arms while she pulled herself round. On the kitchen table was a photo. Of a child."

"You think that's what upset her?"

"Almost certainly. It was in a silver frame so I picked it up, asked if the child was hers. She nodded and took it from me. I told her how sorry I was."

"How old was the little boy in the photo?"

"I didn't really get a good enough look. I mean I'm not even certain that it was a boy…"

Bring a child into any investigation and the ground beneath you shifts immediately and in all directions.

"Catriona never gave you a reason as to why she was here?" I said.

"I never asked. I imagined that with it being an army house she might have had connections. A soldier boyfriend, maybe."

The noises from the house were growing more insistent. Rolf was stirring milk into the coffees, rattling the spoons against the side of the mugs. It still had no effect on Marian.

"And you reckon she's moved on?"

"Yes, mind you no one stays there very long."

It was an MoD house, that much was common knowledge, and Jack Daniels had borrowed it as a jumping off point, though not for places like Australia, New Zealand... Nepal. As much in hope as certainty, I didn't think Terri Stillman had gone too far.

Rolf Korting's behaviour peaked. He appeared at the back door, rang the bell again as if calling a school playground to order, then stood there, arms folded, staring at me.

"Do you have any other questions?" Marian asked, ignoring the summons. "I'd be quite happy to try and answer them."

"I think we'd better call it a day, don't you. You've helped me a great..."

I broke off because Rolf was now lumbering towards us, head down like some flabby old bull. We waited for him to draw level and just as he did, Marian stepped back, like a referee in a boxing ring moving away to let the fight begin.

It was the second surprise she'd delivered in the space of ten minutes. She'd suggested there was more to Terri Stillman than had met my eye, namely the possibility that she was a mother grieving for a child. And now, unless I was mistaken, she wanted me to thump her boorish husband and had engineered our conversation to that end. I had two choices. I could leap over the wall and sink my fist into the Dutchman's pot belly or I could walk back to the Land Rover and drive away.

"What you want?" Korting asked, aggressively. "My wife, daf'bitch? Take her! Coffee? Have mine. Cold anyway. Fuck you both!"

And with that he leaned over the wall, laid his hand on my shoulder and shoved me, putting his full weight behind it.

In that land of many mists one suddenly descended before my eyes, red in colour, and I was over the wall like a goat. Even as I landed, twisting my ankle slightly, though that wouldn't have made a great deal of difference, the envelope containing The Map fell out of my pocket. The poetry book was back at the guesthouse. I paused before the terrified Dutchman and his now excited wife. To their surprise and, if I'm honest, to mine as well, I stooped down and picked up the envelope. I took out the fragments and laid them on the wall I had just vaulted. I closed my eyes and brought my finger down on Asahikawa, led there no doubt by an email I'd received from Fee, just before I'd left home.

"Dad, Nepal isn't the end of the world! Well, it is, geographically speaking, But she's not going to fall through a crack in the earth's surface…" Then she changed her mind, comprehensively. "No!" she shrieked. "Forget what I just said! Stop her! She can't go to Nepal! People disappear there, get kidnapped, murdered, and she's going with a man she hardly knows! You have to stop her, Dad!"

You mean just like I stopped you going to Japan? Right away, my darling. No mention of Yama, I noticed. Was he really history?

Hard on the heels of Fee's email was one from Con. I thought I detected genuine sympathy in the first few lines. "Dad, mate, she has to do it. Yes, Nepal's a bloody long way away and you'll miss her, you poor old sod…" Genuine sympathy first, then genuine need. "Tell you what, why don't you and I meet up in Oslo next month. I'm going there with Anna to see her parents. Speaking of which, my round the world ticket doesn't cover bloody Norway. Can you believe that?"

No, I can't, my dearest boy. And, just out of interest, who the hell is Anna?

Jaikie was next, still firmly the centre of his own universe, but better informed about certain things than I was. "Dad, it's Nepal, not the bloody Moon. Ellie sent me a photo of the guy and I like the look of him. He reminds me of George's agent. Sorry, George Clooney. I only mention him because I'm being flagged to play his younger brother when the PR on All Good Men and True's over. George and I look rather alike, people say, and seeing that he's the best-looking man on the planet why should I complain? And never forget that I get it from you. Or Mum. Anyway…" Then came the better informed bit. "I gather Con's dumped Kirstie, The Nightmare Redhead, and fallen for a Viking called Anna."

So, it was pretty much business as usual in their worlds. Instructions on how to handle their siblings, a turnover of partners, shortage of cash, inflated self-esteem. What about my world, though? None of them ever seemed to ask if it was still turning. Maybe because they knew that even at such vast distances they were my world. When theirs turned so did mine. Remembering that made me feel a whole lot better about the temporary disappearance of Terri Stillman.

I gathered up the pieces of The Map, replaced them in the envelope and went back to the Land Rover without a word of explanation to the Kortings and trying not to walk with a limp.

-22-

Jane Stewart planned to take full advantage of the coming tourist season and, by way of getting into the swing of it, was keeping the shop open until sunset. At nine o'clock that evening I was one of her last customers. A very Scottish day weatherwise had given way to a calm, sharp evening. A red herring-bone sky was being swallowed up by the gathering dusk and along the coastline in both directions lights were coming on in houses that up until then had been indistinguishable from the landscape, so scattered were they, so perfectly at one with their surroundings.

Hamish was minding the shop for his mother, who had gone to visit a friend in Benbecula but she'd left him her sheepskin body warmer, which I envied. He looked up from a game he was playing on his smartphone. A sting of music from it told him he'd lost a vital limb, or something, and no doubt he blamed me for it. I was wrong. He abandoned the game because he wanted to speak to me and indicated as much by pointing, singling me out in a crowd of one. I raised my arms in surrender.

"Mr Hawk, I've got something for you."

I thought I detected his mother's style and he was about to try and sell me something, especially when he reached under the till and brought out a magazine. It was called Innse Gall.

"Local magazine," Hamish explained. "The words mean Outer Hebrides."

"They would," I said.

"It's the new one, this week's." He was flicking through the pages and stopped halfway in and bent Innse Gall back on itself. "This lassie you're looking for, Catriona Baxter? Would this be her?"

He handed me the magazine. Dead centre of the page was a photo taken outside a blackhouse. Blackhouses are the traditional dwellings on Harris and Lewis, a place where grown-ups, kids and cattle shared the same kitchen, bedroom and bathroom. Until recently they were regarded by the islanders as little more than hovels, with their stone-faced peat walls and turfed roofs. And then, in the 1960s, Historic Scotland gave them a marketable curiosity value, by which time most of them had been torn down and replaced by four-square modern equivalents.

There were three people in the photo, two facing the camera, arms round each other and a third a yard or so distant, just about to turn away. The caption underneath gave the names, left to right, Gillies MacIntyre, Una Fulbright and… Catriona Baxter.

I was about to pull him towards me, prior to hugging him, but the moment gave way to the familiar sound of motorbikes approaching along the coast road. Hamish tutted. The last thing he wanted at that point was another customer, but dutiful son that he was, he braced himself for business and went towards the door.

"It's the same girl who stayed down at Bail Iochdrach," he said, turning to me as he went, walking backwards. "Where you went today."

"Are you sure?"

He stopped. "Aye, course."

"See to business first, then we'll talk."

He went outside to wait for the bikers and I started reading the item surrounding the photo in the magazine. Gillies MacIntyre was an artist living on Harris and was beginning to make a name for himself in Europe and America. He had a gallery in a loosely adapted whitehouse on the coast road up from Leverburgh. Una Fulbright was described as a friend, although the way they had their arms round each other spoke of more than friendship.

The bikes were pulling onto the forecourt, only it wasn't bikes, plural. It was a single bike. I stepped behind the cover of some shelves and carried on reading the article in Innse Gall. Gillies had just taken on a Girl Friday to front the gallery, to answer the phone, deal with emails and generally help to flog his paintings and sculptures. Her name was Catriona Baxter, early twenties, and from the date of the paper I reckoned she'd been in the job two weeks at the most. About the same amount of time Terri Stillman had been gone from Bail Iochdrach.

On the edge of my attention, out on the rapidly darkening forecourt, I heard Hamish being polite. "Have you just come off the late ferry?" he was asking.

"Yes," said a woman's voice. "Fill her up, will you."

It wasn't my nodding friend from the gang of easyriders, then, if they'd just got off the boat. I could afford to ease my way out from behind the shelf. Hamish began to fill up the bike. I couldn't see either of the riders, but I heard the man yawn, loud and long. Some instinct born of a lifetime reading grunts and groans, body language, attitude, even silences, made me find a straight line between me and the two new arrivals. As if to help, the forecourt light triggered into life as the man took off his helmet. He was indeed good-looking, just as everyone had told me to the point of trying my patience. He was over six foot tall with a purposeful gait, arms swinging from the shoulders and, of course, there was that full head of hair. As for the woman, she was tiny with an ill-used face, pinched and drawn before its time, her dark hair mussed from wearing the helmet. Both of them wore black leathers. The bike was more forthcoming. It was a Goldwing, a packhorse on two wheels, overflowing with its riders' travelling needs. A tent was strapped to the rear pannier.

"You looking for somewhere to pitch for the night?"

"We are," said the man.

"Hougharry. Name of Davey Laing."

By God, that Davey Laing sure knew how to turn a bob or two. The post, a croft and now a campsite.

"Where's that?" the man asked Hamish. "When you've done, show me on the map."

I won't say that my blood ran cold, but I know what other people mean when they use the phrase. I'd only ever heard his voice on the phone, but out there on the forecourt was the man who had called me in the middle of the night and told me where to find the remains of John Stillman's daughter. It was a courteous voice then, it was courteous now, though rough-sided and trying not to show it. The woman spoke again, pointing across the forecourt to the edge of it. I fancied I knew her voice as well but that might just have been my fancy.

Without realising I was doing so, I made my way to Jane's household section where I picked up a frying pan. I paused to consider just what I might do with it, should the need arise, should Crane come into the shop and find me. Cook him, perhaps? I replaced the pan. Farther down were kitchen knives, good old-fashioned steel carvers, but even here in a land of negligible crime they were locked in a glass cabinet. The hardware section was more user-friendly. I picked up a claw hammer and went back to my listening post.

The woman asked Hamish, "That Land Rover, does it belong to Mr Nathan Hawk?"

Something about the way she asked the question told me she knew the answer.

"Aye, that's right," he began. "Friend of yours?"

The man and woman looked at each other. "In a manner of speaking," he said. "Is he staying here?"

It seemed as though Hamish was about to say no, then tell them exactly where I was staying, but some canny instinct must have intervened. He raised his voice slightly, for my benefit. "I've no idea where he's staying. I mean I know he's gone off for a walk, asked if he could leave the motor there."

"Walk in the dark?" Crane asked.

Hamish grinned as if a joke had been made, then glanced at his watch. "He went before lunch. I was getting worried. If he's not back soon I shall call Sergeant Burns."

"Police?" the woman asked.

Hamish nodded and finished filling the Goldwing. The woman had the exact money in his hand before Hamish could even read the figures on the display. Her companion, however, clearly wasn't sure about the walk in the dark story. He took a step away from the pump and peered into the shop through the open door. With the glare of the forecourt light, against the 40 watt gloominess of the shop interior, he couldn't see much and was apparently considering walking over to check it out.

"Shall I tell him you were asking after him, when he comes back?" said Hamish.

Crane turned back and leaned over him, trapping him between the pump he'd just used and the Goldwing he'd just filled. Crane's voice dropped a couple of degrees celsius, became business-like and vaguely threatening.

"We don't want you telling him anything at all."

Even though Hamish wasn't about to argue the point, Crane took him by the front of his mother's body warmer with just one hand and drew him even closer before spelling it out.

"Have I made myself absolutely clear?"

"Aye," said Hamish, as bewildered as he was terrified.

The woman patted her companion on the shoulder and he released his grip on the body warmer. They climbed back onto the Goldwing, fastened their helmets and within seconds had disappeared into the darkness.

***

Hamish locked up the shop, took two beers from the chiller and we settled opposite each other on the floor in one of the aisles, leaning back against the shelves. Still bemused by his encounter with the two bikers, he wanted to know who they were.

"He calls himself Richard Crane."

"And who's she?" asked Hamish. "Only she's not his wife. No wedding ring."

He explained that when she'd thrust the money at him it had been with her left hand. He'd had perfect sight of all her fingers.

"That doesn't mean they aren't married. And Richard Crane probably isn't his name, either. He just uses it when he kills people."

Looking at Hamish, I at last understood the meaning of the word agog as he thrilled to the idea of having been threatened by a murderer.

"You did well out there," I said as I got to my feet. "Keeping him at bay."

I'd always thought that Richard Crane and I were in some kind of macabre race, trying to reach Terri Stillman first, he in order to kill her, me to prevent him. According to Penny Swarbrick he'd asked after me at The Millstone in Blackburn where Jack Daniels's car salesmen had seen him off, telling him that I'd gone back home to Beech Tree. So what had brought Crane and his lady pillion passenger to The Outer Isles? Had he somehow picked up my trail again? If so, how? And far from being a race, was he plain following me, relying on me to lead him to his target?

I went down the aisle a few paces, stooped and picked up the copy of Innse Gall I'd abandoned half an hour earlier. I homed in on the photo of Catriona, Gillies MacIntyre and his friend Una.

"What exactly is a whitehouse?" I asked Hamish who had followed me. "Says the gallery is one. I know what a blackhouse is, what's a whitehouse?"

"Kind of opposite to a blackhouse." Ask a silly question. "It's proper, with an upstairs and down. Old, yes, but with taps and baths and toilets."

"There's posh. You sell webbing clouts?"

"Probably. What are they?"

"Nails with big flat heads, usually galvanised."

"What's that?"

"Rustproof, but I'll take the nearest thing you've got."

He led me to a shelf in the hardware section and took down the very thing, a box of a hundred.

"I'm impressed. Carpet tape?"

He produced a roll of that too and awaited further requests.

"I'll have that box, if you're not using it." He reached down to an empty cardboard container and thrust it at me. "What time are the ferries to the Isle of Harris?"

"To Leverburgh? Twenty past seven, eleven and two in the afternoon."

"Two's the last?"

"Aye."

And then, as is often the case when you divert your own attention, befuddling details fall away and leave you with a cold, clear through line to the bleeding obvious.

"The parcel!" I said.

"What parcel?"

I turned and slapped a nearby packet of nappies. "The one my daughter sent me the other day. This."

I pinched the sheepskin at the sleeve but Hamish was none the wiser, and I kept him that way. The parcel was surely the means by which Richard Crane had caught up with me. Ellie had written down the shop's address, on the back of an old envelope probably, left that lying around Beech Tree for Crane to find when he broke in. With his lady pillion. I looked at Hamish, who was still agog, and winced.

"I don't suppose there's the remotest chance that you got the number of the Goldwing?"

He paused, looked up at the roof spars and closed his eyes for a moment. I thought he was despairing of our combined negligence, then he lowered his head again and said, "KE 09 WXF."

I patted his face with both hands, perhaps a little harder than I needed to. "You little beauty!"

He grew two inches taller, right in front of my eyes.

***

Back at Sgeir Ruadh I scrounged a pair of scissors from Mrs MacDonald and, up in my room, sat cross-legged on the floor and refashioned the cardboard box into a single strip about five feet long and ten inches wide, carpet-taping it together where necessary. I then pressed the webbing clouts through the cardboard, a couple of inches apart, and a hundred nails later had constructed a very passable tyre-burster.

So, if Richard Crane, or whatever his name was, planned on following me – which the more I thought about it, the more I reckoned was feasible – I was about to put some distance between us. I studied the Ordnance Survey and found the perfect spot to throw him off my trail.

-23-

Next morning I drove down to Bayhead Stores and stayed in the Land Rover while Hamish brought me my sandwich lunch then filled up the Land Rover. When it was done he came to the open window and I could see that the increased height he'd gained last night had been reduced a little.

"She's been asking all morning what the nails were for," he said, glancing back at the shop doorway. "I keep saying I don't know, but she won't have it…"

"Tell her they're for a bed to lie on, the carpet tape… you never know when you might need to tape somebody's mouth up. Listen, I'm heading south. Seems from the map that, at the junction just before Creagorry, I can double back on a different road."

I offered him the folded back Ordnance Survey map, but he didn't need it.

"You can. The B892."

I nodded. "So if Richard Crane asks where I've gone, tell him… Benbecula."

He looked at me, uncertainly. "You know Harris is north…"

"I know."

I smiled at him and he became part of a conspiracy, though he wasn't sure of its details. He nodded slowly. "I see. Will he ask though?"

"They've followed me all the way to your front door, Hamish, they won't give up now." I lowered my voice. "My guess is they're watching us right now." He spun round to challenge the onlookers. "No, you daft bugger, they're not here on the forecourt. Up on that ridge maybe."

The ridge in question was a good three quarters of a mile away, but the best place from which to see the comings and goings at Bayhead Stores.

"Talking of being spied on..." He jerked his thumb to where Jane had emerged from the shop with a cloth and was now polishing the glass in the door while trying to overhear our conversation. I paid for the petrol and the sandwich and thanked him for his help.

***

I drove out to a high point about three miles away in order to get a decent phone signal. I can't say for certain that I was followed, but in a landscape like The Outer Hebrides, one of long open views, whoever is watching doesn't have to do so from close range.

I phoned Jim Kelloway at Thame nick and, when I eventually got through to him, he sounded pleased to hear my voice. His own was soft and easeful, that of a man winding down his career and with each of my questions, my requests for help, he resisted all chances of cranking it up again. I outlined the progress of my inquiry and he listened patiently. At the end of it he said,

"Well, you don't seem to have got much further than I did. I mean, yes, you found Teresa's body and we're all grateful for that. I'd have got there myself, if I'd had the manpower."

I wanted to disabuse him, point out that I'd got this far all on my own, but I needed his help so any straightening of the record would have to wait. I moved on to Richard Crane and again he listened without interruption. When I paused for him to speak, he said he couldn't accept the link between Crane giving me details of Teresa's grave, then following me up to Blackburn, his breaking into my house and finally his presence there on North Uist. They were loosely connected bits and pieces, he said. There was no proof that he was the same man Teresa had met at Giacometto's. Quite a few men have ponytails. I put the phone in my right hand and felt for The Map as a precaution.

"What about the woman travelling with him?" I asked.

"Well, yes, I hear what you say, Nathan, but proof that she broke into your house too? Jacket hung up, dog-bowl? Thin stuff."

I hadn't told him about the tissue I'd found in the bin. It was the one piece of hard evidence I had and it should have been passed onto him. I sighed with as much resignation as I could muster. "Yeah, maybe you've got a point, Jim. All the same, would you be kind enough to check a number for me?"

He chuckled with relief. It seemed like I wasn't going to pursue the matter too vigorously and get him to do some real police work after all.

"Course I will," he said.

"It's a bike, a Goldwing. KE 09 WXF. I'd like to know who owns it."

"Shouldn't take long. Phone you back soon as we can."

The next call I made was to Gillies MacIntyre's gallery in Horgabost. The phone rang and was picked up almost immediately. A woman's voice said, "Good morning, how may I help you?"

A young voice, Scots accent, more Glasgow than Highlands.

"Morning. I'm phoning to ask about opening times. Have the summer ones come into force?"

"They have. 9.30 to 6.00 pm, every day except Sunday."

I fancied I could tell what sort of person owned the voice. Young, keen, new to the job, trying to make a good impression.

"Fabulous. So if I drop in one day next week, will Mr MacIntyre be there?"

"He'll certainly be available, should you wish to discuss any of the work on show."

I adopted a half nosey, half apologetic tone. "Sorry, is that Mrs MacIntyre?"

The voice didn't flinch. "No, I'm Mr MacIntyre's personal assistant. Catriona Baxter."

For the second time in four weeks I'd found a Teresa Marie Stillman. And this one was still alive.

***

I stayed put for the next half hour and for the first time since arriving in The Outer Isles, I could see why so many yards of purple prose had been written about them. The weather girl that morning had told us, with an element of surprise in her voice, that it was a fine start to the day. A clear blue sky above was dissolving at the horizon into a golden haze and below me, to left and right, the loose knitted fabric of the land seemed to float on the water. I wasn't sure if, in terms of mass, the land or the sea had the advantage. In time it would be the sea but for the present the grass was doing its damnedest to grow although what little of it there was lay twisted and beaten by the elements. There were no trees, occasional flowers, but few gardens surrounding the one or two houses I could see. It was a truly ungenerous landscape of bare essentials, calm today, and quiet but for the gentle fall and retreat of waves beyond the machair.

In the distance I could see right across the Sound of Harris to the island itself where Catriona Baxter was hard at work selling Gillies MacIntyre's paintings, pushing them to a wider public who would turn him into a household name. Clearly Una Fulbright thought he would take the world by storm and that probably explained her arm around him in the Innse Gall photo. Taken at face value, his arm around her was to do with her youth and beauty, but what would they make of Catriona Baxter, once they knew the truth about her? And if that truth turned out to be terrible, would it alter their view of the place they lived in? Would it alter mine, that of a mere visitor just beginning to fall for the seductive isolation of the place?

When Jim Kelloway called back he was full of apologies, presumably for bearing news that he thought would disappoint me.

"The Goldwing's registered to a Luke Edward Taylor," he said. "Age 34, address 7 Whitsbury Lane, Rockborne, Hampshire. Not known to police. Not even a speeding fine. Sorry, Guvnor."

As I pulled away from my vantage point, I fancied I caught a small flash of light half a mile away, the sun on glass, as if binoculars had suddenly been lowered. I wanted them to be more than pure fancy. I wanted them to belong to Richard Crane now renamed Luke Taylor in the overcrowded address book of my mind.

If you'd asked me then I would have denied it, but I was playing with fire. Certainly I had to find the girl in order to know why Taylor wanted her dead but I didn't want him getting so close as to have a second chance. That was something of a balancing act and I decided to call in the B team, in the shape of Jack Daniels and SOU once I'd found Catriona. Timewise it might be a close-run thing, but it gave me a real boost to think that I'd be calling the tune and Daniels would have to dance to it.

***

The drive to Creagorry went exactly as I'd planned and just short of the Benbecula causeway I pulled into a passing place and started on the lunch Jane Stewart had made for me. I'd been there no more than three minutes when I heard the distant sound of a motorbike. The road behind me stretched out for a mile or so and then rose to a small ridge, which the bike had just crested. Thirty seconds later the bike stopped.

Luke Taylor and his lady friend were not only following me, they were doing so with great care. They had spotted me and pulled over to wait.

For once, time was on my side, but sadly the island of Benbecula does not inspire the romantic in its visitors as others in the chain do. The Ministry of Defence has built a firing range to shatter the dead calm of the place. On the beach, Hamish had told me, is a chillingly simple notice, every 200 yards, which says, "Do not pick up anything you find on this beach. It might explode and kill you."

The landscape has been uglified by a derangement of houses thrown up in typical army fashion, on the cheap, all out of proportion and right in your face. I drove through Balivanich, passing the NAAFI stores of Jane Stewart's upturned nose and from there as quickly as possible I crossed over into South Uist.

Three miles later I reached the junction where I'd planned to double back on the A road. At a sharp corner just before it, I pulled onto the verge, I got out and laid the tyre-burster across the tarmac behind me, then turned onto the main road that would take me back to Bayhead. I parked up behind a boulder the size of my house and hurried to a point from where I could look down, 200 feet below me, on Luke Taylor's impending problem. I heard, then saw the Goldwing approaching and, just as I'd been doing, they were taking it gently. They slowed a little at the bend but not enough to be able to stop when they saw the tyreburster. Taylor tried to swerve, but I heard the pressured hiss, hiss as the webbing clouts punctured both tyres and my crude device leaped into the air behind him. He pulled onto the soft verge, settled the bike and they dismounted. There was no panic, no anger, no surprise. They removed their helmets, hung them on the bike and walked back to where the blow-outs had occurred.

"What was it, Luke?" the woman asked.

He didn't know yet. "Some bloody thing in the road… flew up in the air." He spotted it, lying in the bracken a couple of yards from the verge, and went over to it. "Nails and stuff, taped down…"

He began to realise the implications and glanced all around, then up and down the road.

"This must be Hawk, or he'd have gone over it himself. Bastard's screwed us."

"Where we going to get repairs in this dump?" asked his lady friend.

"Well that's the bloody point. Army base, I reckon, but that's five miles back."

He took out his phone and tried to get a signal, looking round again, but not up. I suppose he did that when I fired the Land Rover but I wasn't there to see it. I was on my way to the ferry.

-24-

On the crossing to Leverburgh from Berneray I was joined by the six bikers, the easyriders who seemed to have become part of my life. To be fair, five of them were as indifferent to me as ever but Rodin's double was positively chatty, at least by his lights. The conversation covered the weather, past and present, the high price of petrol on the islands, the newness of the Cal-Mac ferry and then silence intervened. I downed my coffee and went up on deck.

Harris and Lewis pretend to be two islands and there's a tribal reason for it. A rift in the MacLeod family, way back, ended with them chopping the island in two and pretending there was sea between them. In truth the two places are joined at a tiny geographical neck, but are very different in character. You only see that difference once you set foot on the place: Harris is low, green and fertile at the edges, Lewis is tall with black and brown mountains reaching into the everlasting rain clouds.

I stocked up with some essentials in Leverburgh, itself the toy town of a soap magnate who bought the island in 1918 hoping to indulge his fishing fantasies, set off for Horgabost. Long before I reached it the name Gillies MacIntyre started poking itself in my face. According to hand-painted notices at the roadside, an exhibition of his work could be seen right now. All were welcome, even children. Just follow the signs to his gallery.

MacIntyre's house-cum-gallery was called Island View, a name that seemed both too English and too optimistic.

Today, however, the Isle of Tarasaigh was just about visible, the sea around it was calm and dark and such white feathering as ruffled the surface, came and went in a trice. Against some typically Hebridean cars, with small engines to beat the fuel prices, the Land Rover seemed positively extravagant. As I climbed out of it, I was met by the sound of voices and booze coming from behind the house. There, in the shelter of a few stunted trees, favoured guests were picking over the remains of a buffet. I wouldn't have minded joining in. I wouldn't have minded a glass of whatever was going…

A tall man in his fifties broke from the gathering and loped over to me, long arms, long legs, heading me off before I could reach the food and booze. He was stooped at the shoulders, giving the impression of an elegant gallows, and hanging from the face, once impressive features were beginning to show their owner's age. The eyes, however, were clear and sharp and would've seemed youthful in a man half his age.

"Hi," he said, stretching the word into two syllables. "Exhibition's in the house. Go in, make yourself at home, shout if you want us."

For such a Scottish name, Gillies MacIntyre had one hell of an English accent. Posh school, I assumed. Money floating in the background. Average painter with private income. Not the sort of bloke I would usually take to.

I was glancing over his shoulder at the company, a couple of men but seven or eight women, some of them looking pretty good for the time of year. Catriona Baxter was not among them.

"Do make yourself at home," Gillies said, nodding at the house. "Every room, upstairs included. If you use the toilet, make sure you give the chain two or three good pulls."

The paintings in the exhibition shared a common theme and were done with first-rate draughtsmanship and obvious enthusiasm. Little wonder, since most of MacIntyre's subjects were women who seemed to tackle everyday life with no clothes on. Here in the main room was the portrait of a dark-haired lady knitting without a stitch on. Making something to wear, maybe. Cheek by jowl with her, so to speak, another painting showed a woman arranging flowers, also in the buff. In the scullery the same woman was washing up with nothing between her and the fairy liquid. On the stairs, an oriental woman wearing only a skimpy apron was cooking in a wok. They all looked vaguely silly, they all looked ten years younger than MacIntyre.

He had told me to make myself at home and who was I to assume that he hadn't meant it? In a back room, used as a study, a bottle of Clan Campbell was cosying up to the laptop. In the main room I'd spotted a row of tumblers and in the kitchen there was bound to be a fridge. I turned to go and get the glass.

In what passed for a hallway a good-looking woman in her late thirties scuppered my plan. She had just entered from the lunch party and had been sent to keep an eye on me. The photo of her in Innse Gall had been a good likeness. It was Una Fulbright.

"See anything you like, Mr...?"

"Baxter," I said. "Alan Baxter."

She nodded, approvingly, as though if I'd said Bill Jones or Tom Smith she would've sent me packing. She turned to flick dust from a stone carving of a large egg-timer.

"Gillies is also a sculptor," she said. "He calls this piece Gneiss Woman after the local stone. Oldest stone in the world, they say. 3.6 billion years."

"And costing a mere £540. Seems cheap, considering."

She smiled. "I'm sure it's negotiable."

At that point I realised it wasn't just her photo in Innse Gall I recognised. She was hanging on most walls in the house, variously knitting, arranging flowers and playing solitaire in her birthday suit. She even bore an uncanny resemblance to the egg-timer.

"Baxter?" she went on. "We've a girl working here, just started. Would she be…?"

"Catriona, my brother's girl. I expected to see her here."

"No, no, Gillies sent her home an hour ago. She's worked like a Trojan today, started this morning at six."

I nodded with approval. "I'll pop in and see her. She gave me her new address… I knew I should have written it down."

"Luskentyre. Just up the coast. Gillies has just bought a blackhouse there, shocking price, but we can't let the Germans have them all, can we? Do you have a map? I'll show you."

***

As I rounded the final bend of the coast road to Luskentyre, there up ahead was the blackhouse, perched on a granite ledge as if it were about to leap off. A bunch of fir trees, curved and emaciated, stood trying to shield it, their backs to the prevailing wind. I parked on a bracken verge, half a mile shy of the house, and reached down under the seat for my shoulder holster and loaded six shells into the Smith and Wesson. I'm not sure why. She was just a girl, a kid in her twenties. What harm could she do me?

I was glad of the sheepskin jacket. The meagre warmth of the day was beginning to fade and an onshore wind was heralding a downward dip in the weather. Even the sheep knew it. An hour ago, they had been spread out like marble headstones on a hillside cemetery but now they began to huddle, backs to the Atlantic in preparation for the storm brewing. To be fair to the weather girl that morning, she had mentioned it but had given no times, no details. She just knew it was coming.

At the house a couple of seabirds, gulls of some kind, rose lazily from the turfed roof and headed towards a rocky headland being gnawed away by the sea. Below them a vast estuary of sand lay undisturbed, the surface cracked by a single stream running down from the hills. Walking beside it was a lone figure. I had left my binoculars in the car but could see that it was a woman. She held the collar of her jacket tightly under her chin, a woollen hat was pulled right down over her ears and the hair that wasn't contained by it flew wildly behind her as if trying to rein her in. The photo in Innse Gall hadn't shown Gillies MacIntyre's new assistant in much detail, but if this wasn't Catriona Baxter then who was it?

The blackhouse had that long untouched appearance, a stillness that said no one had lived in it for donkeys' years. I walked round to the back door, crooked on its hinges, standing half open and immovable. I entered and found myself in the animal shelter of this over-priced hovel and waited for my eyes to get accustomed to the darkness. The room reminded me of the old air-raid shelter at my grandfather's which, which I was forbidden to go in. I defied him of course and paid a price.

I went through a door to the main room, a part of the house in the process of being restored. The once earth floor had been laid with stone flags, the walls had been cleaned of ingrained peat tar. Furniture including a bed had been settled around the room. Through another arch, doorless, I could see the basics of a kitchen and if that had been installed, no doubt a bathroom backed onto it. But the main room held my attention. It was devoid of personality, save in the fundamentals, which, presumably, Gillies had supplied. Whoever lived here hadn't yet put their mark on the place. In fact they hadn't even unpacked their belongings. They didn't amount to much, half a dozen or so boxes of carryable size, each looking more than ready to move on at a minute's notice.

At a low table beside the neatly made bed, a small mirror had been propped up against the stone wall. It threw back the reflection of tubs, pots, bottles, tubes of lotion, packets of everyday personal stuff and, dead centre, a basket of cheap costume jewellery. Beneath the table was the box the stuff had been packed in. I pulled it out and folded back the flaps. Inside were clothes, meticulously folded, a couple of pairs of shoes in cotton bags and plain underwear still in its original packaging. As I went to replace it, so the merest glint beneath the bed caught my eye. It was a silver photo frame, placed there to be within easy reach of whoever slept here. I stooped and picked it up.

It must surely have been the photo Marion Korting had mentioned. It was rough and grainy and its subject was a small boy on the verge of tears. I knew him. Thousands, if not millions, knew him but right now I was the only one he was still talking to. He was telling me everything I needed to know about the murder of John Stillman's beloved daughter.

***

I sat on the bed and phoned Hamish. He answered almost immediately, as if he'd been waiting for the call and wanted to talk. There wasn't time.

"Has Richard Crane been to the shop?"

"Not yet, no. I heard he had a puncture down in Creagorry."

"Two punctures. Webbing clouts, carpet tape, cardboard box…?"

"I see," he whispered.

"Hamish, another job for you. When he does come to the shop, and asks if you've seen me, say you heard I'd gone to this gallery on Harris. Island View, Horgabost. You heard, right? Not from me, from… bush telegraph. Good man. Got to go."

I'd heard the snap of a door latch through in the kitchen. I sat motionless while whoever had entered switched on a strip light. From the shadow cast on the wall I could see that it was a girl as she took off her jacket and shook out her hair.

Then she removed her boots and dropped them onto the stone floor. A moment or so later she came through the arch between us and saw me immediately. She stood perfectly still and, as far as I could see in the less than perfect light, she gazed at me without a flicker.

"Hallo, Jessica."

She paused for a moment then said in a perfect Glaswegian accent, "You must have broken into the wrong house, Mr…"

"No, I've got the right place. And the right person. Though I won't say I'm not surprised by who you've turned out to be. Jessica Claydon."

She responded in a dry, practised fashion, "I'm sorry, you really are way off kilter. My name's Catriona Baxter."

"You can forget her. Too many people know she's an invention. Just like the name Teresa Stillman was. Nice accent, by the way. Dorothy Bowler said you were a good mimic."

She came a little farther into the room and stopped when she had a clearer view of me. "You didn't say who you are."

"Nathan Hawk."

She stepped closer and offered me her hand, formally, politely, the gesture making her seem older than she was, a refugee from another age. I ignored it.

"What can I do for you, Mr Hawk?"

"So you really don't know who I am?"

"No."

"Jack Daniels must have told you about me. Warned you…"

"Who?"

I smiled. "Jack Daniels. Your guardian, the man who keeps reinventing you to keep at bay all those people who want to kill you."

Even that didn't seem to ruffle her, but it did show how the inert facial features made her natural beauty seem as plain as paper. All the elements were there, the wide cheek bones, the nose perfectly sloped, the almond eyes, smooth forehead, the fine, silky hair – all of them lifeless. It was as if her entire face had been surgically lifted, along with her identity.

"As far as I'm aware, I've no enemies."

"You have millions. Are you a Jessica or a Jess, by the way, or have you forgotten?"

She shook her head in amusement. "If you want me to say that I answer to either, well… how can I? I'm Cat or Catriona."

I held up the photo frame I'd found beneath her bed. She bit down on her bottom lip then settled her face again.

"You know the little boy in this photo?"

"He's my nephew," she said and held out her hand. "Would you give it to me, please…"

She waited patiently until I handed it over. She turned to a chest of drawers, placed the photo in the top one and closed it. I stood up and made to leave the same way I'd entered.

"Right, then, if I've been given the wrong story I'd better go find the right one. I've told someone else they might find Jessica here, by the way. If he drops in, tell him what you've told me and I expect he'll go away again…"

I smiled at her, one hand on the doorknob.

"Who is he?" she asked.

"I didn't think he was anyone to bother with, until he started following me. He must have had a reason. Maybe he wanted to find the same person I was looking for, thought I'd make a better job of it than he would. His name's Luke Taylor."

A slight intake of breath gave her away. I stepped through to the animal shelter and, two strides into it, she called out to me.

"Wait! Are you sure it's Luke Taylor?"

I turned back to her. "Well, I didn't know who he was

until the other day and even then it didn't mean anything to me. In fact very little meant anything until I saw that photograph. Of your nephew. Who isn't your nephew at all. He's Luke Taylor's nephew. And you murdered him."

She looked at me and began to shake her head, not so much in denial as begging me not to go on.

"He was three years old, you were nine. You beat him to death with a doorstop, a stone from Porlock beach. You hit him so many times the pathologist couldn't count the blows. You beat him till he was unrecognisable and so were you, covered in his blood. He had to be identified by DNA and the shoes he was wearing…"

Her hands went up to her face, she stepped back into the main room and disappeared from sight. I followed her cautiously. She'd hurried through to the kitchen and slumped down at the table, face on her forearms.

"Don't say anymore," she asked quietly, in a perfect English accent. "Please, no more."

"So I'm right, you're Jessica Claydon, the child in the photo is Billy Cassidy? I remember him not just because his photo and yours were on the front page of every tabloid, I remember him because… well, far be it from me to give you any kudos but that's what you did to a whole generation. You ruined our faith in childhood."

"I've done my time," she whispered. "Twelve years. Why bring Luke Taylor here?"

"I need to catch him. I couldn't do it till I knew who you were. I didn't know why he'd killed your namesake Teresa Marie Stillman. To be honest I didn't know for certain that he had. I'm certain now. And he's going to pay for it."

"Not before he kills me!"

"Why should that bother me? I know people who would have had you hanged, young as you were. I reckon I'm… giving you a sporting chance." I heard myself saying that but somehow it didn't tally with my self-image. "Besides, he's not coming here, he's going to the gallery."

That didn't make her feel any safer. "How long will it take him to find this place? How long did it take you?"

I shrugged. "If I were you, then, I'd touch base with Jack Daniels. Oh, sorry, you don't know him."

She yelled at me. "Sergeant Daniels is in France."

"Well, that's not the other side of the world."

She hurried into the main room and reappeared a moment later with her phone, speed-dialling a number. When the other end rang she thrust it at me. The call had gone to message.

"This is Jack. Back in the office, Monday, August 10th. Leave a message."

And having wrenched the truth out of Jessica, including the fact that Daniels was her minder, I now found myself at a loss. Or, to be honest, in the very early stages of panic.

"What's he doing in France?"

"How do I know? I'm not his best friend."

"He must have warned you, left you with a contingency plan…"

"Well, he didn't! He wasn't expecting you to pay a visit!"

In other words he thought he'd warned me off. It had been presumptuous of him, but that didn't make it any easier to deal with. I sat down at the table and tried to think.

"Who else do you know in his team??"

"Nobody. He doesn't trust them. Most SOU officers are like you, they'd love to see Luke Taylor get his revenge."

The best thing to have done would have been to phone Hamish with a change of instructions, get him to tell Luke Taylor that I'd gone home, or gone… anywhere except Horgabost. But I didn't fancy the idea of a last minute cop out. After all, there I was, a spit away from the killer of John Stillman's daughter, weighing up whether to lose him on account of babysitting Billy Cassidy's murderer. I can't say I'm proud of the decision I made, but I made it all the same. I explained to Jessica that Luke Taylor was on his way to the island and there was nothing I could do about that.

"I think we should tell the local police," she offered, with strangely disarming innocence.

She reached out and passed me a tourist brochure. It didn't just give a phone number for the boys up in Stornoway, there was a photo of a clutch of them led by a Sergeant Malcolm Burns whose cheerful countenance told me that the worst crime he'd ever dealt with was poaching. Probably not even salmon but eggs. God only knew what he'd make of Luke Taylor. Or Jessica Claydon, come to that. All the same, I put his phone number into my mobile.

"When will Luke arrive?" Jessica asked.

"Two, maybe three days' time. But he will come. He's already killed someone by mistake, he has to kill you to justify that." I looked round. "I'd better stay here tonight. I'll go and get my car."

"You can have my room," she said, eagerly.

"No, I've got a sleeping bag. I'll bed down here in the kitchen."

As I went over to the door, she said, "I could make us something to eat if you like? There's salmon in the fridge…?"

Even a delicacy like salmon can pall in Scotland, there being so much of it. The trouble was, I was starving.

"Yeah, why don't you do that."

-25-

It was about ten o'clock when we turned in, Jessica to her bed in the main room, me to my sleeping bag on a pile of sofa cushions laid out next to the kitchen range. She'd given me a torch and I was reading the brochure by the light of it, avoiding the picture of Sergeant Burns who would need a great deal of explaining to when the time came. A belated text message came purring through as I tried to get comfortable. It was from Hamish who, using the shorthand of his generation, told me: 'Crane been to shop, asked about you, told him Horgabost.' He had then asked about ferry times to Harris, not simply when they were but the time of the earliest one. I reckoned he was planning on making the crossing tomorrow. A knock on the door distracted me.

"Can I come in?" Jessica asked.

"Yes, yes." Child murderesses notwithstanding, when a woman walks into wherever a man is sleeping, an odd sounding bell always rings. She opened the door carefully, as if I might have stripped down to my underwear, which I hadn't. It was a hangover from the days of dawn raids. No one ever went to bed before them, they just cat-napped fully dressed. I sat up and leaned back against the range.

"What can I do for you?"

"I want to tell you what happened," she said.

"I'm not sure I want to hear…"

"You'd rather carry on hating me?"

I wagged a warning finger at her. "Don't play the victim with me. You will lose."

She came fully into the room. "I'm not asking you to like me, I just want you to know what happened. Very few people want to hear it so in the end you stop trying to tell them."

"You had your day in court, Jessica. Christ, you had three months!"

"I was nine years old! What did I even know then, never mind being able to explain it."

"You think you can now?" I asked, sourly.

She pulled out a chair from the kitchen table and perched on the edge of it, leaning forward, hands woven together. For the most part she seemed to address the kitchen range rather than me, probably to avoid what she might read in my face.

"When Mark and Julie Cassidy moved in next door to us," she began, "I was just five years old. She was so beautiful, I can't tell you. And so gentle. I thought she was a kind of reward for my own mother being old and plain and crotchety. I remember the first time I went to tea there. It felt as if she'd invited me... because I was so important. The table was all laid out specially, she'd baked a cake, she'd rolled up the napkin and drawn place cards for us both.

"And from that day on things between us just got better and better. Mark was away at sea most of the time and Julie would take me places, to see friends, to shop, she even took me to where she worked, the telephone exchange, and on the weekends we would go into London, the river, the circus, train-rides, anything. I knew Mum and Dad were pleased, not just that someone was taking me off their hands but that an adult found me appealing enough to want to spend time with me.

"Then, one day Julie told me she was expecting a baby. I didn't really understand what had happened and much less how it might change things between us because this baby, she said, was for me. It would be someone for me to play with. Like the dolls I had, only more so.

"When Billy was born everyone was overjoyed, her house, my house, the whole street. And Julie was right, Billy was like a doll and I used go next door and help feed him, change him, play with him. It seemed as if what she'd said was true. Billy was born for me. And so it went on for a couple of years until, one day, I asked if I could take him out into the park on my own. I was eight, he was two. I had friends at school whose mothers made them take their kid brothers and sisters for walks. They hated it. And there was I offering. Julie said no, she'd rather I didn't. It was the first thing she'd ever denied me and I couldn't believe it. I guess you'd say that I had a tantrum and because of it Mum and Dad were called and I was taken home and put to bed. I was wretched with misery. My one true friend didn't trust me with our doll.

"Then Mark came home a week or so later and stayed. I went round to the house, a month or so after my tantrum, and he made an excuse not to let me in. He said Julie wasn't feeling well, Billy was sleeping. I knew it wasn't true. I'd heard them giggling through the wall, minutes beforehand."

She stood up, went to a cupboard and took out a bottle of water. She stood sipping it, eyeing her reflection in the window against the night. She put the bottle down and turned back to me.

"One afternoon, I arrived home after school, and there was Billy out in their front garden, just sitting in his pushchair, waiting. The front door was open. Julie and he were on their way out. She'd popped back to answer the phone. When he saw me he threw his arms wide, all smiles, like people who love you do. I leaned over the front wall, unfastened him, picked him up and carried him next door. The key to my house was in its usual place and in we went. As I closed the door behind me I could hear Julie, out on the front step, screaming to Mark. 'Jesus, he's gone! Billy! Billy, where are you?' It had taken me just thirty seconds to steal him."

She paused there, as she must have done a thousand times, to consider the ease and speed with which she'd devastated so many lives, not least her own.

"I took him to my room and on the way up he seemed to change. For the first time ever he didn't want to be in my company, didn't want to take my hand or look me in the face. When he did, he started crying, whining for Julie, making it seem as if he hated me. There were 33 steps up to my room. Don't ask me why I didn't stop on any one of them, turn round and take him back down again. I just didn't.

"People have asked what was going through my mind when I actually killed him, when I hit him with that holiday souvenir. I told them, after the first eight blows... nothing. I hit him once round the face but he kept on crying. I hit him again, he didn't stop. I hit him a third, fourth, fifth time as the crying got louder. The sixth time there was blood coming from his mouth. So I hit him again and he stopped crying. I sat him up but he toppled over. So I hit him again. And that's when my mind went blank...

"When the police came to our house and took me away I could hear Julie next door, weeping. I know now, of course, that he wasn't just a doll to play with, he was her life... and I destroyed that because, at the age of nine, I wanted to be the only thing in the world that mattered. Even to her." She shrugged. "That's it. I thought you should know the truth."

I wriggled fully out of the sleeping bag, stood up and kicked it to one side.

"That isn't a fraction of the truth," I said, quietly. "You've told me the bare facts and tried to soften them with being nine. You've greyed all the faces of those involved. You've stripped out the surrounding agony, the fact that Julie's husband died as a result of it, that Julie herself is as empty as a tin can. You told me the story, cold, remote and over-rehearsed."

She shrugged again, as if the terrible crime she'd committed had passed into history. "It was a long time ago... things fade."

"That isn't true either. You're as frightening now as you were then. Oh, sure some trick-cyclist has taught you how to cope with it all but you still scare us because we don't know how to feel about you. We don't know what to do with you. You've upended our sense of decency, Jessica, our peace of mind, our faith in the kids next door. That's a kind of power and don't tell me you never use it."

She turned away, picked up the bottle of water and drank from it.

"Did you ever try writing to Julie?"

"I asked if I could once. She didn't want to hear from me."

"Did you take up God or Zen or Tree-hugging or anything that made you stand back and look at yourself, or did you look inwards to your own survival?"

"You go into one of these young offender places, you have to…"

"Think of number one? Yes, well that's the attitude that stops you knowing what you really did. To Billy, his family, John Stillman, Teresa, your own parents… for Christ's sake, how on earth did they cope? To hell with dignity, the be all and end all of everything, eh? If my child had murdered a three-year-old, dignity wouldn't have got a look in. Devastation yes…"

"Not everyone reacts in such…"

"I don't want to talk about it anymore. Go back to bed and try sleep on this. Luke Taylor is travelling with a woman. I think it's his sister, Julie. They arrive here tomorrow."

-26-

The weather next morning was another reminder of why so many of my generation, who had sold up their dreary suburban lives and gone to live on this last frontier of Europe, the Scottish Islands, had regretted it within months. Yet another storm had arrived and was now thrashing down on the landscape, just as it had done for centuries. The rain whipped in from the sea and great shoals of water were driven across the machair, beaching against the back walls of blackhouses, all lit up by the occasional fork of lightning. It was the kind of storm Davey Laing would have loved for its power to keep the Boeings at bay.

I gave Jessica her instructions, repeating them until she was word perfect. I could see that she didn't like them, that however things turned out, she would have preferred to come with me, maybe to see Julie at long last, maybe to have Luke Taylor shoot her. Eventually I persuaded her to stay put until she heard from me. Meantime she was to phone Jack Daniels every half hour and leave messages, telling him exactly what had happened and laying on with a trowel the danger she was in.

I suppose it wasn't by chance that my memory dredged up a moment from Jessica's trial. It was just after the judge had passed sentence and Luke Taylor was being interviewed by a television channel and stated with chilling self-possession: "Believe me, when she gets out, we'll be waiting for her." There was something about the way he said it, with such purpose and determination, that I wasn't the only one whose blood ran cold on hearing it. Next day, he was quoted in papers, on news channels all over the world. He was even interviewed by police, to no purpose whatsoever.

So, what was I going to do with him? Challenge him, yes, to make doubly sure he was the man I'd spent all this time looking for, then arrest him with my right hand... in which would be held my old service Smith and Wesson. With my left I would dial Sergeant Burns. It didn't sound rock solid and if the best laid plans of men can go awry, then the worst almost certainly will. I thought they might be doing so when I arrived at the gallery to discover that Gillies MacIntyre wasn't there. His muse and good friend, Una Fulbright, was seated at the reception desk in the main room and told me that Gillies had gone to see a purchaser in Tarbert. His phone was switched off. She expected him back at 11 o'clock. And how had things gone with my niece Catriona...?

There seemed no point in being anything but blunt. Catriona wasn't her name, I said, anymore than Alan Baxter was mine. Mine was Nathan Hawk, Catriona's was Jessica Claydon. From the look on her face, the name meant nothing. I asked her to cast her mind back twelve years and see if the name Billy Cassidy rang a bell.

"A toddler. He was murdered. By a nine-year-old girl"

Her voice dropped in horrified disbelief. "You mean that Catriona...? Christ, I do remember."

"Catriona is Jessica Claydon." With her being suitably stunned, my next point was easier to make. "Billy's uncle has come to Harris to kill her. I've come to arrest him for murdering a friend of mine's daughter. He mistook her for Jessica. I hope you're getting all this, Una. If not, just trust me."

"Yes, yes, of course," she said, beginning to stroll the room. "When? When will he be here? I mean..."

"Some time this morning, first ferry."

"Right, right… How? I mean, just you on your own? Where are the police?"

"They'll come on afterwards. Listen, I have to get him inside, here in the gallery, to contain him."

"No! No, you can't do that!"

"Yes, I can."

I put my hand beneath my jacket and drew out the Smith and Wesson. It pre-empted further argument. "I need two other things. Land Rover out of sight, you in a safe place."

She considered it for a moment. "There's a room, right at the top of the house. Attic. Gillies uses it as a dark room."

And for much else besides, I thought. "Sounds good. When I tell you to go there, you go. Land Rover?"

She nodded. "There's an old cattle shelter round the back."

***

When I returned from the shelter, Una had calmed a little and was removing some of the choicer paintings out into the back room. I said I'd rather she left them where they were but she was determined.

"Better safe than sorry," she said.

I passed it off as displacement activity and began to manhandle the desk in order to give myself a straight view out of the door and up the road to Leverburgh.

"God knows what Gillies will say. He'll be furious, of course. You don't know him when he's had a rough day…"

I allowed her voice to fade as I sat back in the swivel chair and began the indeterminate wait. Outside the storm had almost blown itself out and left behind the gun metal sky that passes for a fine day in Harris. I'm not sure what eventually prompted me to do it – perhaps it was his photo on the tourist brochure in front of me, making him seem like the only sane person in my immediate future – but I called Sergeant Burns from the desk phone and a real voice, belonging to a real and present person, put me through to him. He was a gentle, decent creature, by the sound of him, and his innate courtesy allowed me to speak almost without interruption.

I took him right back to John Stillman asking me to find Teresa, my refusing to do so until my own daughter went missing and then my near conversion to the idea that I'd find Teresa alive. In the end I suggested that he got in contact with Detective Sergeant Jim Kelloway at Thame Police Station for proof of what I'd said.

"I'll do just that," he said. "Kelloway? Kilo Echo Lima Lima Oscar… do you have his phone number by any chance? Save me looking it up." I gave it to him from memory. "Thame? How are you spelling Thame?"

It felt like a test of my staying power but I sounded it out for him, NATO style.

""Sergeant, I'm hoping you'll be able to give me some backup when I call for it."

"Och, yes, I've understood that perfectly…"

"I'm expecting Luke Taylor to have taken the early ferry from Berneray and then to have made his way straight here…"

"Luke Taylor. A moment there. Luke Taylor is the uncle, Julie Cassidy is the mother? And Billy Cassidy the wee boy himself."

"That's right."

"And Teresa Stillman is…?"

Poetry wouldn't have helped any more than The Map. "Was," I said, sharply. "Teresa Stillman was the girl Luke Taylor shot, believing her to be Jessica Claydon."

There was a pause. "May I have a word with Gillies?"

"He's not here. Would you like a word with Una?"

"Perhaps I'd better…"

Sympathetic to my task, Una came to the phone. "Hallo, Malcolm, how are you?"

I could only hear her side of the conversation but I assumed he was asking her opinion of me, beginning with my sanity and moving on to my credibility. Her responses were encouraging. By the sound of it she'd been checking my history on the laptop.

"No, I think that's absolutely right… Google, Malcolm … Aye, there are photos and records … no, no, Gillies is in Tarbert. The Mitchells… No I haven't seen them for months… No, I do remember the case… wee boy, three years…"

I stopped eavesdropping. Through the open door and way, way in the distance, I had heard a familiar sound. In a bedroom, in the still of the night, it might have been the approach of a mosquito, but here in Harris, carried on a southerly breeze, I knew the sound was that of a motorbike.

"Get off the phone," I said as calmly as I could.

Una looked at me then finished the call to Burns with a short goodbye. I nodded to the stairs, she gave me one last glance as if it might be the last we ever exchanged, and left the room. Seconds later I heard her feet on the stairs and finally a slam of the attic door.

***

As the Goldwing pulled up outside the gallery, I flattened myself against the wall on the hinge side of the open door and drew the Smith and Wesson. I could hear Luke and Julie in disagreement about whether she should come into the house or not. She was determined to do so and Luke conceded. He warned her to stay out of harm's way, though. Julie said there wouldn't be any harm. My Land Rover wasn't here.

That must have lowered his guard, for even though I heard him load what I took to be a shotgun, I saw, when he entered the room, that it was a sawn-off. He'd broken it, stuck the barrel end through his belt, presumably to have both hands at the ready. Julie followed him in. Luke turned to her and saw me as I pushed the door closed with my foot. There was a moment of silence and absolute stillness and then he made half a movement to the sawn-off but changed his mind when I levelled the pistol at his head.

"Luke Taylor?"

He smiled. "What makes you say a thing like that?"

"Good manners." I glanced at his companion. "This must be your sister, Julie Cassidy. Now I look at you both up close, I see the family likeness. I can see Billy too."

"Who could forget such a face?"

I nodded. "Haunting, even after all this time. I wonder if John Stillman will feel the same about his daughter 12 years from now?"

He dipped his head and said quietly, "That was a dreadful mistake…"

"How did it happen?"

He looked up at me again. "Picture the scene, bunch of SOU dangermen just about to leave the office, head for the pub. One of them stays behind to phone me, number withheld, no name. 'The person you're looking for,' the voice whispers, 'is now called Teresa Marie Stillman'."

He shrugged and took a casual step towards me.

"Don't make any soppy moves, Luke. I will shoot you. I've done it before and, as you know, after the first time it gets a whole lot easier. So you found there was only one person in the UK with that name. Or only one who fitted the description."

"That's right. Even so, I went to meet her first…"

"And still got it wrong. You can't have asked her too many questions?"

"She didn't answer many."

"Her father was a criminal barrister, for Christ's sake! She'd been brought up to keep her trap shut."

"I know that now," he said, softly. "I didn't then."

I turned to Julie. "Where do you stand on all this, Julie? You happy to kill this girl?"

She looked at me with eyes deadened by unimaginable loss.

"It's been my decision, not hers," said Luke, before she could answer me. "I promised Mark that when Jessica Claydon came out…"

"You'd be waiting for her. I saw you say it. It was all over the telly, radio, papers next day."

"Just keeping my word," he said and took another step towards me.

"Do that again and I will blow your fucking legs from under you! Unfasten your belt, let the shotgun drop to the floor, then step away from it."

He smiled and shook his head. "You're forcing my hand?"

She uttered her first words since she'd arrived. "Luke, please do as he asks…"

He pushed her aside and started moving towards me again, kept advancing, and with a mixture of relief and reluctance I dipped the pistol and fired at his legs. Or at least I pulled the trigger. Nothing happened. I pulled it again and the resulting click was as dry and scratchy as the one before. So was the third.

There was another moment of silence and stillness, longer than the previous one on account of our collective amazement. Luke Taylor broke it when his face contorted before spluttering with laughter.

"Old coppers, eh?" he said, between intakes of breath. "Risk their lives for a drop of gun oil! Is that what it is, Mr Hawk? Not been used for centuries, dry as a bone and twice as bloody useless? Here…" He grabbed the stock of the sawn-off, pulled it from his trouser belt and snapped it together. "…use this."

He tried not to laugh again but couldn't help it. I hadn't found any of it particularly funny. In a matter of seconds the tables had turned and all for want of checking the Smith and Wesson after its hibernation in my safe, my own life was now in danger and so were those of Una Fulbright and Gillies MacIntyre, to say nothing of Jessica Claydon. I felt 90 years old, 360 degrees stupid and about as dangerous as a daisy.

Luke came to the other side of the desk. I tried to speed-dial Sergeant Burns's number but as I did so Luke smashed the phone with the stock of his gun, holding it like a club by the cut down barrel.

He looked at me and asked quietly, "Where is she?"

I heard Julie warn him again. "Go easy, Luke."

He repeated the question. "I said where is she?"

"Go fuck yourself."

He swung the sawn-off and it caught me on the side of the head. The next quarter of an hour of my life is a total blank.

***

I came to in the kitchen and for a second or so thought I heard my wife's voice, telling me that I'd been dropped off after a heavy night and the hangover I was about to experience was poetic justice without the poetry. I smiled and made to stand up. I couldn't. And the woman to one side of me obviously wasn't Maggie, it was Julie Cassidy and she'd been bathing a small cut just above my ear.

On the kitchen floor was a torn curtain, taken from the window over the sink, cut into strips. One of them was tied around my ankles and to the chair legs. My arms were behind my back and held with something a good deal more substantial than curtain material. It was Luke's belt, he told me, so I should forget the old cowboy trick of rubbing it up and down a strut in the chair to fray it.

He was holding the shotgun. The Smith and Wesson was on the kitchen table. The shells were beside it.

"Welcome back," he said. "Now it's my turn. Where is she?"

"My mind's gone blank," I said. "It happens after a blow to the head."

He turned to Julie. "He may be stupid enough to bring a useless gun with him but he won't have brought Jessica here. Go upstairs, see what you can find, you know what to look for…" She glanced at him, then down at the shotgun. "Don't worry, I won't do anything hasty."

Julie left the room and in time we heard her rummaging around upstairs, looking for clues as to Jessica's whereabouts.

"So… you're not going to help me. Fair enough, but shouldn't you consider your own position, as they say. You're tied to a chair in the presence of someone who doesn't have much to lose."

I shrugged as best I could. He perched on the table, facing me and laid the shotgun down beside him. His all too reasonable manner said more about his desperation than his self-control so I knew that I had to go carefully. I can't say I relished the idea of pleading with him for my life, but in Los Angeles, I gather, it's part of basic police training.

"Luke, this isn't as bad for you as it might seem…."

"It isn't bad for me at all!"

"You know what I mean."

He smiled. "Yeah, and I'm sure you'd do everything in your power to help me. You're forgetting something. Even the bloke from SOU who phoned me spoke of it. Duty. His duty to give me Teresa Stillman's name, my duty to avenge my nephew."

"That isn't duty, that's throwing your life to the dogs."

He growled with contempt. "Don't tell me you haven't got that same thing inside you, all ready to go, should anything happen to one of yours."

I felt a sudden draught round my ankles. Somewhere in the house someone had opened a door. Noiselessly. Was it Gillies returning from Tarbert? Was it Burns?

"I know what you mean," I said. "I can go over the edge, drop of a hat, and there's no one there to pull me back. No wife. There's a friend now but she's got her own life."

"The doctor?"

I nodded. "You got the address, Bayhead Post Office, from the parcel she and my daughter sent?"

"Yes. Thank you."

It was the front door, the door to the gallery, that had been opened. The light there dipped and rose again as whoever had entered passed in front of the window. Luke wasn't aware of it. He was still sitting on the kitchen table, his back to the main room, and until I knew who was out there that's where I wanted him to stay.

"So what about the twelve years she served?"

He chuckled. "You want me to call that quits and forgive her? I hear that all the time. People say I'd feel better if I did! They don't have to watch Julie drag herself through each day. They can't even tell me what forgiveness means…"

It wasn't Gillies out in the room. Nor was it Burns. It was Jessica and I was trying not to give her away with an involuntary glance, a minimal turn of the head, a shift in my position. Was she here to get what she really wanted? Luke to hear her, turn, pick up the sawn-off and kill her? End it for them both? If so, why was she being so mouse-like? Why, as I saw on the very edge of my vision, had she stopped at the side table and picked up Gneiss Woman?

"…but just like them, Mr Hawk, you want me to take what she did off her shoulders, say heh, let's all start again, minus two of the players. I can't do that. I can't make it right that she killed Billy. And since he can't speak for himself, I'll speak for him. She's going to pay."

Jessica had entered the kitchen but Luke still hadn't heard her. He slipped off the table and stood up. Beyond him, Jessica stopped.

"Okay, I'll tell you where she is," I said.

He stood absolutely still and tried to fathom my change of heart. "Where?"

Jessica had started moving forwards again. She was three yards away from him and took Gneiss Woman by the feet and felt her weight.

"I'll take you there. Leave you at the door."

"Just tell me."

"You'll never find it. Coast road, up in Lewis..." He must have wondered why I was getting excited, raising my voice. "I swear to God. I'll show you the house. Just go in, no guns, for Christ's sake, they'll hear you in Glasgow. Just one decent blow, back of the head and she's down..."

He screwed up his face. "What?"

And as he twigged that I was giving instructions to someone else in the room, he turned as Jessica brought Gneiss Woman down over the back of his neck. He dropped to the floor. And once there, he didn't move.

"Get me out of this fucking chair," I hissed. "Knife on the draining board. Quick!"

She did as I'd asked and cut me free. Twenty seconds later I was down on my knees tying another strip of curtain round Luke's ankles and wrapping his belt around his wrists. Jessica stood back, one hand to her face, the other still hold of Gneiss Woman. Had she killed again? She looked at me.

"Why did you come?" I asked.

"I don't know."

"I don't believe you. You came hoping he'd be here."

She nodded. "Then I saw you. What could I do?"

I laughed as much with relief as amusement. "You did just the right thing."

She turned to the door. Julie had heard Luke fall and had come running. She looked down at Luke in horror, then at me and finally at Jessica. Neither of them spoke. I found myself standing between them, just in case, and reaching out for Luke's shotgun. He broke the silence when he groaned. Julie went over and crouched down beside him, reached out and touched his face, said nothing. They both knew without voicing it that whatever journey they'd embarked upon was over. She stood up and looked at me.

"What now?" she asked in a whisper.

"If I were you, Julie, I'd get back on that big bike and head off home. The only crime you've committed so far is to break into my house and hang my daughter's jacket up. I'd leave it at that if I were you."

She shook her head and looked down at Luke.

"The keys are still in it," he said from the floor. "Go."

She was about to argue the point but Jessica drew her attention. "Before you do, Julie, I have something to say…"

We all knew what Jessica wanted to say. I turned and held up a forbidding hand but that wasn't going to stop her. She went over to Julie and said with quiet intensity… dignity, I suppose you'd call it if you had to give it a name.

"Julie, I am so, so sorry."

Julie looked at her for a moment and replied just as quietly. "I know."

There was no point in saying more. Neither was the person the other had known twelve years previously. Each would have been talking to a stranger. With a last glance at her brother, Julie turned and went. A minute later we heard the Goldwing being fired up and Julie Cassidy riding off into a freakish blue sky.

***

There isn't much more to tell, really. Burns turned up half an hour later with two others whose photos I recognised from the brochure. He had checked my story with Jim Kelloway at Thame and the whole business suddenly became a police matter rather than a story of my success.

The next day I began the long haul back to Winchendon. I made it in two leaps, overnight in Carlisle, rising early the next morning and reaching Mayfield House by four. I told

John Stillman everything he wanted to know and fixed up with him to have lunch in Oxford a week later. At Brown's. He said I should bring an invoice with me.

I drove back home only to find nobody there, not even Dogge. I showered and changed and walked round to Plum Tree Cottage at about seven o'clock. I could see Laura and Ellie through the window from the lane. They were giggling away at something one of them had just said and Ellie was doing her usual laughing thing, bending at the waist, slapping her knees. Dogge was leaning against the table leg watching Laura dice up some fish for a pie. I knocked on the front door and Dogge went berserk.

"Dad, mate," said Ellie, flinging her arms round me. "We were just talking about you."

"I heard the laughter."

"Ah yes, well…"

"Tell him," said Laura, kissing me on the cheek. "It's bad, but not that bad."

"The time you gave that bloke a bollocking in Tesco's," said Ellie. "You asked him if there were any prawns in the freezer out the back and he said he'd no idea?"

"What's funny about that?"

"You went on to say that he should have had an idea, that he should call you 'Sir', that he should stand up straight and look you in the eye when he spoke to you. Christ, that was bad enough! Then he told you he didn't work there."

I nodded. "Why does everyone remember the times you make a fool of yourself and forget the heroic bits in between? Is my name on that pie?"

"Not yet," said Laura. "Get another salmon fillet from the freezer, it'll remind you of Scotland."

It didn't. But the prawns kept reminding me of the poor devil I'd shouted at in Tesco's.

-27-

Heathrow's a nightmare to get to at the best of times but on the day Ellie left for Nepal we were seriously late. They were playing with the M40 again, digging it up all the way past High Wycombe and no one had forewarned me. Ellie sat in the back of Laura's car with a rucksack the size of a house beside her. I kept catching her eye in the rear view mirror. She was excited but terrified. It's a great combination of feelings.

We got there in time. We always do. And I busied myself getting a trolley and saying daft things to while away the anxiety. My youngest child was going to a country I knew nothing about, to be with a bloke I knew even less about, to work in some volunteer project that I'd barely had time to research. Laura said she'd looked into it. She said it was a blue chip enterprise with one or two names on the panel of advisors that she recognised. A worthy cause. Doing good for others. To hell with others, I'd said, she was only 19… and I'd no idea when I'd see her again.

When her flight was called we said goodbye at the departure gate. Ellie turned and walked through it without looking back. I stood waiting for a good two minutes after she'd gone, I guess in the vain hope that somewhere down that hidden concourse she would change her mind, turn round and come back. She didn't. Laura took me by the hand and pulled me gently away.

"Let's go home."

I shook my head. "When her plane's gone, yes. I want to be sure…"

"Breakfast, then," she said, and pointed up to Garfunkel's.

She ordered bacon and eggs for both of us and we sat at the edge of the restaurant looking down on the criss-crossing hordes of travellers. All I could home in on were men like me, seeing their kids off to faraway places they themselves had never been to. We ate in silence, with Laura accepting that there was no chance of lightening my mood until the reason for its heaviness had emailed us from Nepal to say that she'd arrived safely. Her plane hadn't even taken off yet.

And then, just as I was about to go and get some more coffee, a young woman who looked vaguely familiar spotted me from across the restaurant. She came over to the table and stood three or four feet away, waiting to be fully recognised. It took me a few seconds. The hair was black now, the eyes their natural brown, but the body had put on a few flattering pounds since leaving Harris.

"Hallo, Mr Hawk," she said.

The voice was different as well. A flawless North London accent. I smiled at her. "I'm sorry, I've forgotten your name."

She came right to the table and held out her hand. "Lucy Anne Forrester."

I looked at her hand luggage. It had a Qantas label on it. "Australia? Good idea."

"Thank you," she said.

"Would you like a coffee?" said Laura, gesturing to the empty chair at the table.

"No, no, thanks, don't want to miss the plane. Nice seeing you again, Mr Hawk."

"Likewise."

She smiled politely at Laura, turned and walked off. Unlike Ellie, she looked back just once as she went through the door. And then she disappeared forever.

End

Made in the USA
Coppell, TX
06 July 2024

34293203R00173